HAPPY AFTER ALL

OTHER TITLES BY MAISEY YATES

Other People's Weddings

Hero for the Holidays

The Hometown Legend

The Rival

The Lost and Found Girl

Sweet Home Cowboy

HAPPY AFTER ALL

A NOVEL

MAISEY YATES

Published by Montlake, Seattle

www.apub.com

ISBN-13: 9781662526374 (paperback)
ISBN-13: 9781662526367 (digital)

Cover design by Letitia Hasser
Cover image: © TopVectors, © Toltemara / Getty; © Callahan / Shutterstock

Printed in the United States of America

For Haven, my very own happy ending. I'm glad we ended up together.

Trope (noun)

a: a word or expression used in a figurative sense: figure of speech

b: a common or overused theme or device: cliché

the usual romance novel *tropes*

CHAPTER ONE

The Meet-Cute—an amusing or charming first encounter between two main characters that typically results in a romantic entanglement.

It's a truth universally acknowledged—at least, in a romance novel—that the moment the main character has her life in order, the exact person she doesn't want to meet will come along and knock all that careful order into disarray.

For example, when a respectable motel owner who has decided to focus on her career and her own personal happiness is beginning to feel satisfied with the way she's rebuilding her life, a disastrously gorgeous man will walk in and disrupt everything.

When Nathan Hart—room 32, staying for the whole summer, special requests: to be left alone—walks into the newly renovated lobby of the Pink Flamingo, I can't escape the feeling that that's exactly what's just happened to me.

I'm immobilized by the impact of him. I don't know where to look. I don't know how to breathe. I don't know how to talk to him.

I know how I would write him, though.

He was tall with dark-brown hair and green eyes that held mysteries she could only guess at. His hands were large and . . . capable. Capable? Well, they do look capable. *His forearms muscular, but not from work in a gym—oh no, he looked like a man who got his muscles from working the land or fighting a bear or . . .*

Then he makes eye contact with me. That's when I remember I've sworn off men until I pick up every last piece of my shattered self and glue her back together. That's when I remember I'm dedicated to the Pink Flamingo—my newly opened, newly refurbished motel in Rancho Encanto, California—and to my fledging career as a romance author.

Most importantly, I'm newly dedicated to myself.

To the refurbishment of Amelia Taylor, who lost herself in LA and had to move to the desert to begin to feel something like joy again.

If I were writing this, it would be a meet-cute. But I'm not writing it, so it's just me checking in a guest.

"Checking in. I have a reservation under—"

"Hart," I say, and then immediately want to go back in time.

He looks at me, and it's not friendly. It's not unfriendly per se, but I can see he wants to make conversation with me as much as he'd like to turn around, wander into the desert, and die of heatstroke. "Yes."

I came across as too eager.

I have nothing to be eager about except a guest. A guest—other than my long-term residents—which I've been told is a rarity in the summer when the heat hits 114 degrees.

This is my first summer.

My first summer since I answered a real estate listing that said: Midcentury Gem of a Motel on Route 66 on Sale for a Steal . . . If You're Able to Weather Record-Breaking Heat!

The record-breaking heat had seemed theoretical then. It does not seem theoretical now. It's . . . oppressive.

I've been questioning myself the whole time. As the renovations got more and more expensive, as the people in town treated me with abject skepticism. (And I get why—because they don't expect me to last. I'm not sure if I expect me to last either.)

It doesn't surprise me to feel like an outsider. I grew up barely feeling like part of my own family.

My mom is professionally bitter at my dad, and I look like him. Sometimes I think it would be easier if she'd found someone new and loved him more than she loved me. Had some new kids and loved them more than me, and lived *happily*.

Instead, it's just vitriol.

My dad remarried when I was eight and moved an hour north on I-5. I'm always welcome to come visit. But all my siblings are half siblings, and I'm like some odd mouse out, my hair brown and dull next to their shiny blond. I'm the kid from the Oops Wife. The accidental life. My dad loves me, I think. He also doesn't know where I fit. His real kids are half him and half Stacy, who is lovely and gracious, even to me. I'm half him and half the weird, bitter woman down the freeway who actually called Stacy while drunk once and told her she was a skank for stealing her husband.

I feel caught in the middle of this, or maybe I would if I'd stayed. My mom thinks my dad had an affair. I think he probably did too. He's been with Stacy for more than twenty years. He was with my mom for less than a decade. Who's the love story? In the end I believe it's him and Stacy, no matter how they got there.

Though, I think if I tried to sell that as a romance to my publisher, they'd say he was unsympathetic.

People are too complicated to be sympathetic, generally speaking.

I'm not naive enough to believe my life would have been perfect if he'd stayed with my mother. It would have been weird and bitter in a different way, that's all. Like I said, he tries.

Sometimes I just can't bear to be something he has to try quite so hard for.

Sometimes I wonder if I'm repeating the same dynamics here. Trying to fit in somewhere that doesn't really need me. Where I'm not really wanted.

Though, dealing with standoffish strangers isn't the same as a distant father.

From February to now has felt like a trial run for a new life. Like I'm working on a pitch for a book and not the book itself. Nothing has felt all that deep. Nothing but the weather has been scorching.

Until this man walked into my motel and I'm torn between the urge to sit in the wonder that desire might still exist inside my body, and the horror that I'm this easily pulled out of my Amelia as a Work in Progress Project by a (very) handsome face.

"I guessed," I say. "Not a lot of people checking in this time of year. The other reservation I have today is a family." I don't know why I feel the need to offer all this information. Even as I do that, I realize I wouldn't if he weren't so gorgeous.

Because he's handsome, I feel the need to try to make it clear I'm not responding to his looks (I'm really not)—I'm just a professional. So very professional.

I assume he's the kind of attractive that gets a lot of reactions all the time, not just from motel owners in small towns.

"Great," he says. I'm not sure why he says that. His tone doesn't make it sound like anything is *great*. He does *not* try to smile.

I've been so caught up in how handsome he is, I didn't notice that he looks . . .

Unhappy. Angry. Definitely not excited to be here in any way.

"The Hemingway Suite," I say.

"What?"

"Room thirty-two. That's what you reserved."

The corners of his mouth tense, then relax, and a crease appears between his brows and just as quickly goes away. Then he almost smiles. "Right. Of course. It has a desk."

"Yes," I say.

I hold up the keys, which are physical keys, and I feel like there's a certain charm to that. At least, I tell myself there is because my budget hit its limit four months ago.

In reality, I need to update. I've already had guests lose keys or take them, and it's just such a liability. I want a new, electronic system, maybe even a system that can allow guests to unlock doors through an app. But that's a dream for down the road when business picks up a little bit.

He looks at the keys as if they're more a nuisance than anything retro or charming. Then I pass them to him and our fingers brush.

I feel . . . something.

The heat from his skin, the roughness of it. It's like static electricity against my fingertips. I thought that part of me was dead, I really did, until right this minute.

I look at him, at his dark-green eyes. I don't think he feels anything, and I feel a rush of what I tell myself is relief.

What would I have done if he'd responded to the invitation my body is issuing without my permission?

The answer is nothing. Because the truth is, *he* specifically isn't the worst man to walk into my motel. *Any* attractive man would be. I'm not going there, I decide.

I can't go there.

I'm just six months *after*. There was a *before*. I was a different person before, and I had a different life. I had different dreams. I was planning for a different future.

I made a vow to myself that until I'd had as much time in the *after* as I'd had in the *before*, I needed to keep my focus squarely on myself, my new life, my friendships, my writing, the Pink Flamingo Motel. All the things I've dedicated myself to in the time since.

If I don't focus on that, I might run away. Back to LA. Or, God forbid, back to Bakersfield.

No. I'm not running. I chose this, even when it's hard to remember that. I'm committed to trying to last at least a year.

"I'll show you to your room," I say, because the reminder of why I'm standing there talking to him is one I desperately need.

"I think I can find it."

"I don't want you wandering around outside and dying. Plus, there are . . . armadillos."

"I don't think there are armadillos here."

I shrug. "I'm new. It feels like there should be." The truth is, I know there aren't armadillos. I looked it up as soon as I arrived.

But sometimes I just say things when I'm nervous. He makes me nervous.

He crosses his arms over his chest and looks at me. It's a very particular expression, and something about it scratches at the back of my brain. He looks familiar, even if I can't place him.

I lived in LA for years, so I've seen my share of unreasonably hot men, but I don't think he's an actor. Mind you, in LA there are unreasonably hot men who only ever wait tables. Toiling hotly in obscurity. It's a common story.

My ex Christopher was one of those men for a very long time.

Sadly, now he's a lot less obscure. At least to a niche group of people who love cheesy, romantic holiday movies. I did at one time. Another thing Christopher ruined.

Thinking about Christopher right now should help, though. His memory is a libido killer at this point, regardless of how good looking he might be. Nathan Hart transcends the tyranny of my Christopher memories.

I round the counter and find that the impact of Nathan is even stronger without it between us. He's not *Hollywood* handsome, I decide. He's too rugged for that.

So I still can't figure out why he's familiar.

"This way," I say cheerfully, leading us through the bright-pink lobby and out into the punishing heat.

I do my best not to react to it. I definitely don't have the fortitude of a local yet. I try not to let him see that.

The exterior of the motel is painted bright pink, and all the doors are turquoise. There's a gold sunburst on each one, around the peephole, and gold numbers on the left side. It's all arrayed in a horseshoe around the courtyard, our social area.

The courtyard is empty, which has become the norm during summer. My long-term residents spend their mornings and evenings there and retreat into the AC once it gets surface-of-the-sun-level hot. We have croquet, and tables set with checkers, backgammon, and cribbage—my older guests love that.

"We just revamped the courtyard area," I say, gesturing toward the gleaming pool surrounded by magenta loungers. "We do these things called dive-in movies where everyone sits on little floaties and watches films on a big projector screen. It's fun."

He doesn't react to that. He seems to be taking all this in with a level of skepticism.

"Every room has a different theme," I say. "But you probably saw that on the website. Malibu Dream House is pretty great, but I can see how it wouldn't be to your taste."

He says nothing, and I keep talking. "Yours is my favorite, actually. I mean, other than mine. I live here. So if you need anything, I'm around most of the time. I love your room because it's set up specifically for a writer and . . ."

I stop.

Suddenly I imagine him standing with his arms crossed and that expression on his face.

"Oh my God." It hits me then. "You're Jacob Coulter."

His eyebrows lift slightly. "I'm Nathan Hart."

"You . . . *write* as Jacob Coulter, though, don't you?"

He makes a deep noise in the back of his throat, and I can see that he's searching the doors for his number.

Jacob Coulter, who writes bestselling hardcover military thrillers. His real name is never on anything, and I think I read somewhere he protects it closely because he doesn't want backlash from the government for revealing details that border on classified.

When I was deciding whether I wanted to write under a pseudonym, I'd looked into all the reasons people did it. I'd also chosen one to protect my privacy, though more because I didn't want the people who knew me before to keep tabs on me in any meaningful way.

Though I'm writing category romances, and your picture doesn't go on the back of those. The author is secondary to the publisher and the category itself when you write them. If people want a small-town romance with no sex, they know exactly which line to choose. People who want glamorous settings, angsty conflict, and lots of sex choose the line I write for. The story is more important than the name on the cover.

Not true with Jacob Coulter, whose book series became a huge show on Amazon Prime. I've watched it, even though it's historically not my thing. The lead actor is extremely hot, though, and I'm only human.

I've never read one of his books, though I've seen them in so many bookstores, grocery stores, and airports that I've picked them up before and examined them.

"You looked just like the picture on the back of your book when you were glaring at me in the lobby," I say.

"I don't think I was glaring at you."

"You were. You're doing it now," I say. He continues to glare. "I'm sorry, I realize you probably came here to work and be left alone."

"I'm not used to being recognized," he says. "That's sort of a new thing."

Right. The TV show had most likely pushed that into a different sphere.

"Are you on deadline?" I ask, even though I've always found that to be an annoying question. When I was writing scripts, if I wasn't on deadline, I was out of work. I still feel that way now that I'm writing romance novels. It's one reason I chose the niche I did. It was the closest thing to steady work you could get in publishing.

Plus, I'd always read them, and I'd always gravitated toward stories with a romantic bent, even in my previous writer iteration.

Right before my life imploded in LA, I'd been working on a Christmas movie about a prince who marries a commoner, and I adapted it into a short romance novel instead—with way more graphic sex—and sold it.

After that book, I got offered a four-book contract, which I just started working on. I consider being on deadline a blessing, not a curse.

I work on writing while I man the front desk. It keeps me busy, and I like it that way. "Always," he says.

In that moment I like him just a little bit more.

Just then we arrive at the door of room 32. "This is it," I say.

I consider telling him I'm also a writer. I consider telling him my name.

"I would appreciate it if you . . . if you don't mention who I am." He looks pained at having to say that, which I think is funny. I've watched many minor celebrities posture and act as if being recognized is the last thing they want, when in fact they want it more than anything because it never happens. "I've never been recognized in public before. I'd rather continue not to be."

"Of course. You absolutely have my discretion."

"Thank you."

"There's an itinerary. I forgot to give it to you."

"I don't need an itinerary."

"We do a lot of really fun things."

"I'm just going to be working."

I nod, and he pushes the key in the lock and opens the door. Then he disappears inside and closes it behind him.

Over the rest of the summer, I barely see him. Every so often he leaves the motel property, though not regularly. Mostly, he gets food delivered to his room, and on the odd occasion I have to bring it from the lobby to him, we exchange few words.

I realize I should give thanks. Because the moment he walked into the motel, I felt like everything in my life had been turned on its head, but it wasn't. It was exactly the same as when he had first shown up.

Before he leaves in August, he makes a reservation for the whole of next summer. I start to wonder if I'm wrong.

If Nathan Hart is going to find a way to disrupt my life after all.

It makes me all the more resolved to stay until at least next summer.

CHAPTER TWO

One Year Later

> *Grumpy/Sunshine—a romance trope where one character exhibits a sunny, optimistic personality and the other has a more taciturn demeanor, resulting in friction between the two.*

I'm slightly surprised when Nathan Hart keeps his reservation. Almost as surprised as I am to discover I really am gritting out a second summer in Rancho Encanto.

Not that it's all gritty.

Maybe he's returning because I kept his secret. I didn't broadcast to all and sundry that A Very Famous *New York Times* Bestselling Author Who Happens to Also Be Sexy had stayed in my motel while writing a book, and honestly, I could have. It might have been good for the motel.

His newest book released in May, right before he was due to show up the second time, and I bought it to put in the motel lobby because *someday* I'll tell the world he wrote some of it here.

I read the back to see if it was set in Rancho Encanto, or a town that looked like it, but no. It's set in the Pacific Northwest.

When he walks into the lobby and our eyes meet, I have to come to terms with the fact that his return likely has nothing to do with me at all. He seems almost furious that I'm at the check-in desk, which is weird because I'm a goddamn delight actually, and his options are limited either way.

The only other person who ever works the desk is my friend and new tenant, Elise, who lives in the motel with her daughter.

Elise seems to have an endless well of energy. She's everything, everywhere, all at once. Always with a perfect manicure.

I'm supporting local businesses, she says whenever she shows up with a new sparkling set of nails.

Elise is the reason this summer started to feel possible. She moved in at the beginning of January, and I hired her to help me in February. She used to work full-time at Get Your Kicks Diner, but working at the motel gives her better hours and keeps her close to her daughter, and she's given me an emotional link I didn't know I was missing.

A reason to stay that isn't just . . . it was the place I ran away to.

I mark him as checked in, and I take out the key. This time I set it on the counter in front of him. He puts his hand over the top of it, and I can't help but notice how big his hand is.

I haven't felt anything like electricity since the last time I saw him. I've been working, and I've been happy—mostly.

I'm starting to feel more connected with people in town. I'm getting involved in different community organization efforts and small-business coalitions.

I don't need electricity. I've disavowed it, in fact.

But looking at his hand makes me miss it.

Before he can leave, I take out my printed handout and press it onto the counter with purpose. "This is general information about Rancho Encanto, including restaurants that offer delivery." He stares at me blankly. "And this"—I take out another paper and put it on top of the other—"is the itinerary for the week. A new one will be available in the office every Sunday and will offer information on events happening at the Pink Flamingo."

"Do I have to take those?" he asks.

I want to say yes. To see what he'll do. Unfortunately, I'm not that wedded to testing him, and also I'm supposed to be engaged in customer service, which means behaving in a manner that suggests the customer is always right, even when the customer is being silly.

Now, I'm also the owner of the motel, so I can do whatever I want. I can disenfranchise a customer if I feel like it, but I really shouldn't disenfranchise a famous customer whose stay last year was very helpful to me the whole following year and whose repeated business would be a big help into the next year.

So I don't say he has to. Instead, I smile and pull them back. "Of course not."

He turns and walks out of the lobby, leaving me there feeling . . .

Affected.

I don't indulge myself. I remember a conversation I had with Alice—one of my nonagenarian long-term residents—just the other day.

Alice was married for fifty-seven years. She's been widowed now for twenty. A couple of months ago I asked her if she'd ever marry again.

She'd smiled, serene, her chin-length white hair ruffling in the breeze. "No."

"Because you loved Marty so much?"

She'd laughed. "I did love him. But that isn't why. We married so young, we were flexible. Like saplings. Two young trees who bent around each other as they grew. Well, I'm a mighty oak now, Amelia. And I can't bend. Not again. Not for anyone else."

Alice is broad in all ways. Her smile is broad, her shoulders are broad, and so are her gestures. Age hasn't shrunk her or made her demure. I want to claim that energy for myself without waiting sixty years to do it.

I claim it now.

I get my word count for the day in the comfort of the lobby, fielding the occasional guest request, and once the sun starts to go down, I head into the courtyard, where most of my long-term residents have assembled for their evening social.

In addition to Elise and Alice, there's also ninety-one-year-old Ruth Moore, who told me that back in her cocktail waitress days she'd had to hide a knife in her girdle to keep handsy men in check. She's still petite and feline, her movements as precise and cutting as her dark gaze.

Then there's Albert Feynman, who is a playwright, or so he says. His hair is always slicked down, his glasses black framed and thick. He has a rotating collection of pastel button-up shirts, all with small embroidered palm trees on them. He's always a little indignant that I earn money writing *down-market smut*, while he can't sell his masterpieces.

I'm not entirely convinced he isn't on the run from the law and the whole frustrated playwright thing isn't a shtick.

Mostly because that's what Ruth told me one night while giving me a hard candy from her purse. I have no reason to doubt her. It gives me something interesting to think about while I clean out the pool, and I'm always looking for something interesting to think about when I clean out the pool.

Albert is nothing if not snide about genre romances, and while it annoys me, fighting with him about it gives me life.

I actually do like Albert, even if sometimes I'm not in the mood for disapproving eyebrows and snide asides.

I am *always* in the mood when he's being snide about others, of course.

All my long-term residents—except Elise and Emma—are over sixty. There's also Jonathan and Joseph Stevens-Fielding, and the cribbage ladies—Lydia, Wilma, and Gladys, who I think of as my personal Golden Girls.

I try not to let myself get roped into cribbage games because they destroy me every time without mercy, and sometimes they play for money, and frankly I haven't got any extra to lose.

The motel is my life, and it pays for itself almost entirely. My books pay for me, modestly. Somehow it all fits together, even if it's a bit rickety.

I *definitely* don't need to lose money to some canny old ladies who will only spend it on booze and cigarettes. I don't feel bad thinking this because I'll tell them to their darling faces.

"You'll only spend your winnings on booze and cigarettes," I say as I settle at the table, full from our barbecue dinner and a little sweaty from the lingering heat in the air. The sun is behind the mountains now, and it's finally starting to cool down.

"I am shocked, Amelia," says Wilma, her southern accent suddenly coming on much thicker than usual. "I am a lady."

I'm powerless against them. They're too cute. I love them too much.

I've spent the past year making a family here, and they're certainly better than any of the family I've left behind. I decide to join, resigned to losing my hair salon budget.

It's not a big budget. I've scaled back. I used to get my hair cut and dyed every six weeks. My natural hair color is a very dull brown (my mother calls it that), and Chris called it *mousy*. I didn't want to be a mouse in LA. I wanted to be glossy. I wanted to stand out. Even though I never had aspirations of being in front of the camera, I knew that my looks mattered.

The role of Amelia in LA was played by a fancier version of me.

But now my looks only matter to me, and I don't mind mousy, I decided.

The game immediately becomes hostile in the best way, with Gladys hurling insults at Wilma, and Lydia and I hooting with laughter.

Then I hear a door open. I look and see Nathan Hart walking out of room 32. He must be having an emergency, because if he leaves the motel, he certainly *has never done so* while we're sitting out here.

He doesn't seem bothered or seem to notice as he locks the door behind him.

"Oh, the handsome man is back!" Lydia says, her eyes going wide.

Lydia manages to look young and innocent despite being eighty-seven. I don't know how she does it.

"If I were younger . . . ," Gladys begins.

"I don't need to be younger," Wilma says, squaring up her shoulders in a way that emphasizes her assets. "I just need him to have mature taste."

It takes me a second to realize they're talking about Nathan. And his hotness. Which is apparently a universal thing, regardless of age.

"*Amelia* is just the right age," Lydia muses, that innocent tone not seeming so innocent to me now.

"Amelia runs the motel," I say, "and therefore can't fraternize with guests." Guests who are famous authors and who also *hate me.*

Hate might be a strong word. Maybe. But he certainly doesn't like me or want to be charmed by me in any way.

Wilma shuffles the cards in her hands. "What's *this*, then, sugar?"

"You know what I mean!" I hiss, looking back over at Nathan, who is now headed down the path that will take him through the courtyard and right past—

"Excuse me, darlin'," Wilma calls over to Nathan. "Could you help us with something?"

They all like to run their mouths, but Wilma will run it loudly and without shame. I should have known she'd cause me trouble one day.

Nathan looks . . . caught in a way I certainly haven't seen before. Apparently even surly hermits are powerless in the face of requests made by octogenarians. He starts to move in our direction, and I'm at once filled with horror and relief. Relief that he's a decent human being—as I do think there's a level of callousness you have to carry to ignore a woman like Wilma—and horror since I never know what to do around him, and I feel that particular brand of not knowing reads as exactly what it is: unwilling attraction.

I don't have experience with this, and I don't like it.

Mostly because there's no . . . *this*. I think he's attractive, but I'm never going to do anything about it, mainly because he has caution tape all around him, but also I'm not supposed to be thinking about men right now.

"We don't have a problem," I whisper as he begins to walk closer to us.

"I'll think of something," Wilma says out of the side of her mouth, then brightens. "We need your help fixing the string of lights!" She shouts this, as if suddenly hit with a stroke of brilliance.

She's lucky it wasn't an actual stroke. I'm not quite so lucky.

Nathan looks up, and so do the rest of us, and indeed, the string of lights above us is twisted and crossed with the one next to it.

He approaches, and I freeze like a meerkat sensing danger. He looks at me, and our eyes meet, and I think maybe it's time for me to introduce myself. Then I wonder if out here in the dim light he even recognizes me as the woman from the front desk. I'm mousy brown, after all. While I'm okay with this, I also accept that I don't stand out.

So I don't say anything even though he's looking right at me, and when he looks away, it's a relief. He reaches up over the table with ease and uncrosses the light string, and I can't help but notice the way his T-shirt separates from the waistband of his jeans and shows just a little bit of skin.

Then in a moment, he's done. He leans back, and the air rushes from my lungs in a gust. I'm still a little dizzy when he nods to Wilma. "Better?"

"Yes, very." She bats her eyes like the coquette she is. "Thank you."

He turns to walk away, and Lydia chuckles and says under her breath, "Hate to see you go, love to watch you leave."

I turn to her sharply. "Lydia!"

"What?" she asks, overpronouncing the *h* in the word. "It's true."

"At our age we don't get embarrassed if we're caught leering," Gladys says, her voice deep and no-nonsense. "First of all, no one thinks that's what we're doing. Old women couldn't possibly be sexual. Us sweet old dears."

"Second," says Wilma, "even if they did . . ."

"Who cares?" Lydia adds cheerfully.

"We're past the age of caring what anyone thinks," Gladys says.

"I want that," I say. "I want to bottle that and make it mine."

"Sorry, dear," says Gladys. "I think it's a thing that takes time, gray hair, wrinkles, heartbreaks, and all kinds of moments when you cared too much. Then one day you realize . . . it never got you anywhere you wanted to go. The people who only want you when you bend and twist to suit them don't stay anyway, and the ones who want you as you are settle in, and so do you."

I'm far too familiar with people who don't stay when you can't bend. I'm much more familiar with heartbreak than they know.

But I left it behind me on purpose. Speaking it out loud would bring it here, and I've never wanted that.

"Settle into what?" I ask.

"Yourself."

That is what I'm trying to do. It's why I've taken my vow of celibacy and all of that.

It hasn't bothered me once in all this time. It shouldn't be bothering me now.

It's just . . . him. And he's a problem I'm having trouble solving.

I pour the need for romance into my writing. I'm unfailingly cheerful in the face of Nathan's lack of friendliness.

I'm also nosy, though. I tell myself it's a side effect of being a writer. I always want to know about the inner workings of the people around me. I write intimate details for a living, and I'm curious—endlessly so—about the intimate details of people's lives.

What does he do for release when he comes here?

He has the face of a god and the body of . . . well, also a god, from what I can tell. Does he really spend the summers in total celibate monkhood?

It's a double standard, I guess, to think that he wouldn't. I've been celibate for two years, though I have circumstances.

I wonder about him more than I should. When I see the lights on in his room, glowing through his curtains, as I walk back to mine at night.

Even worse, I wonder about him when I get into the shower. When I get into bed.

My internal monologue isn't passing the Bechdel Test, and I'd love to blame my romance-writing brain—he's physically hero material, after all. I fear it's more to do with the fact he's hot, and I'm only human.

He's also a famous, interesting writer, which means I also fear I'm giving a lot of space to his eccentricities because they're potentially artistic, and I find that fascinating.

I've never been particularly susceptible to brooding artistic men. I was drawn to Chris because he was an extrovert. He could work a room, make people laugh and smile with ease. I live more in my head, and he always seemed to be in the present moment.

I never wanted to be with someone like me. I spend too much time thinking, too much time observing things around me rather than just living the things that are happening.

One thing that does bring me nicely into the moment is the giant shipment of decorations I get one afternoon. It's warm enough that I have to wait until evening to get out the parrot string lights, flamingo lawn ornaments, and magenta lounge chairs, but once the sun starts going down, I attack my new project with the kind of focus I've been giving to Nathan.

Wilma, Lydia, and Gladys arrive at the pool area in all their state. Wilma in glitter, wearing jewelry and with her hair wrapped up in a bathing cap; Lydia in a baby-pink suit with a skirt; and Gladys all in black. I watch as the three of them enter the pool, then go back to planting flamingos in the white rock borders around the Astroturf lawn. Landscaping is a losing battle in the desert, and water is too precious to waste.

Rocks, fake grass, and plastic flamingos are a great zero-moisture alternative.

I'm focusing on the task at hand when the door to the lobby opens into the courtyard and a delivery driver walks out, holding a paper bag.

"Room thirty-two?" he asks when he sees me standing there bent over a flamingo.

"Oh, yes, just . . . I'll get it." I walk over to him and take the bag, and I tell myself I'm being helpful and not angling to see Nathan. "Thank you."

I head toward Nathan's room and realize my heart is pounding a lot harder than it should be as I raise my hand and knock.

The door opens, and I see a momentary expression of surprise on his face—probably when he notices it's me and not the delivery driver—as he reaches toward the bag.

"Oh! Help!"

We both move toward the scream as soon as we hear it. I whirl around and look toward the pool, while Nathan is half out the door, both of our hands still on the take-out bag.

Wilma is screaming like she's in a horror movie, while Lydia is waving her arms. Gladys is looking at them with a hard stare, not engaging in hysterics of any kind.

Nathan lets go of the food and passes me up as he strides to the poolside, with me jogging behind.

"Oh, please help me, darlin'," Wilma says, looking forlornly down into the water. "The filter reached out and grabbed hold of my necklace, and it was a special piece that I got from my Lonny, bless his *dead, deceased heart.*"

Before I can fully take in what she's saying, Nathan strips his shirt off and jumps into the pool.

I know how I would write *that.*

His muscles literally ripple. Droplets of water follow the lines of each well-defined ridge. I've wondered what he does in his room at night, and the answer appears to be sit-ups.

He's glorious. A stereotypical representation of ideal masculinity.

Most importantly, he's being heroic.

Though I find his abs to be a point of importance as well.

He ducks under the water, and I watch, as do Wilma, Lydia, and Gladys, while he reaches into the filter. He surfaces a moment later with the necklace glittering in his hand.

"Oh, thank you, darlin'!" Wilma says. "Thank you. I don't know what I would have done if I'd lost it."

"Why did you wear it swimming?" As I ask the question, I realize just how little sense it makes that she would put on a precious piece of jewelry to swim.

"It makes me feel close to him." Wilma is looking at me out of the corner of her eye like I'm not understanding something.

"And . . . you value that closeness while in the pool?"

"We used to do calisthenics in the pool every morning. Until he died," she says, deadpan.

"I . . . Okay."

Wilma moves to Nathan and grips his arm. "Thank you, again. Darlin', make sure you thank him!"

"Thank you," I say.

He looks at me as he plants his hands on the side of the pool and hauls himself out. "No problem."

I'm too stunned to speak as I watch his muscles shift and bunch while he stands himself up, as I watch the water sluice down his chest and . . . well. Down.

He reaches out, and I realize I'm still holding his food, so I hand it to him and try very hard not to stare.

I fail.

"Enjoy . . . enjoy dinner," I say.

He nods and disappears back into his room.

"You're welcome for the show," Wilma says, laughing.

I turn toward her. "You're not saying that you . . ."

"I plead the Fifth," she says, giving me a smile that suggests butter wouldn't melt in her mouth—even in this heat.

"This is not a rom-com," I say to her.

"What's that supposed to mean?"

"You can't . . . scheme your way into an entanglement."

She laughs and laughs. "Oh, darlin', when an *entanglement* is meant to be, you can't fight your way out of it either."

CHAPTER THREE

As the summer shifts from June to July and from hot to hot as hell, there are fewer short-term guests and fewer planned activities.

As it climbs to near 118 during the heat of the day, there are no cribbage games outside. Not even after dark.

I'd love to say that here in my second California desert summer, I'm used to it.

The eighth time the words *it's so hot* come out of my mouth, Alice looks up from her romance novel—my romance novel, in that I wrote it—and says, "Why did you move to the desert, then?"

"A great question, Alice," I say as I move past where she's seated in the lobby with her feet propped up on a bright-pink ottoman. "Today, I don't have an answer."

But I don't feel like I might run away.

I'm preparing a barbecue for later. It's the only thing we do outdoors this time of year, because the alternative is cooking indoors, and no thank you. The long-term residents have rooms with kitchenettes, but no one wants to heat up their room when it's like this. It makes the most sense for us all to grill together.

"Because of the people," Alice says defiantly as she grabs a cookie off the plate beside her with crooked fingers. I made those cookies, and I'm warmed that she's eating them—in a good, emotional way, not a scorching-desert way—and in that moment, she's right.

The people are why I'm here.

Albert comes into the lobby holding a stack of plates that I asked him to get from the store earlier, his glasses fallen all the way to the end of his nose. "Alice," he says, looking over the thick black rims, "I would think a woman of your gravitas would be reading something more worthy."

"I like to read books with penises," Alice says, waving a hand, not bothering to look up. "Because I don't have them in my real life, and I don't want them. They're best in fiction."

I've never loved her more.

Albert is clearly appalled. He also clearly has no idea Alice is reading my book, which has my pen name, Belle Adams, right there on the cover, so chosen for my love of the animated *Beauty and the Beast.* I wouldn't be surprised if Albert doesn't remember my pen name. On purpose.

"It's a good fictional penis," I say.

"Damn straight," says Alice, taking another cookie.

"This is why I must go and fetch paper plates," he says, "because literary works are—"

"Boring," Alice and I both say together.

I wouldn't be so mean, but I *wrote the book* he's trashing without reading. I don't care if he loves literary works, and I think people should read whatever they want—though, I'm with Alice—but in this instance I'm going to be a little bit reverse snooty since he started it.

He gives us a dry look but doesn't storm out because the thing about Albert is he's opinionated. When you're opinionated back, he just deals with it. It's why I like him. He's not a hypocrite. He's free with his feelings, so if you want to, you can be free with yours right back.

"Does it bother you?" Alice asks, fixing Albert with a steely glare. "The claiming of female sexuality."

"Alice! You know it doesn't," he says.

"But you do agree that penises lack gravitas," I say.

"Well, that's not—"

"You're being toxic and elitist," I say, setting his plates down on the front desk. "Just because we want to read about big, throbbing peeeen—" I whirl around as that last syllable catches on my tongue and holds. Oh God oh God *oh God*, he's standing in the doorway. I let it die. I do not try to redirect, because that will only make it worse.

I'm in a slapstick comedy, and I don't even like slapstick. What's next? Am I a breath away from a pratfall? Is there a paint bucket I'm unaware of that I might step in? Is a pack of armadillos that *don't even live here* going to come through my office in a stampede?

The possibilities are endless, and all bad.

"We're debating gender politics," I say, fighting to keep my expression neutral.

Fighting to keep myself from imagining him as I saw him two weeks ago, with water dripping down his muscular chest.

"The outlet by the desk seems to be having a short," he says, his tone killing the manic joy in the room.

He does not acknowledge what he walked in on, nor my quip about gender politics. I notice he has a little gray by his temple. Not a lot. Why is that hot?

It shouldn't be. *He* shouldn't be. He's so committed to not being friendly, at all.

Also to being relentlessly handsome.

"I'll call an electrician," I say. "I assume it has to do with the sweltering, awful heat."

"How long do you think that will be?"

"I don't know," I say. "I'll get you a . . . a power strip. I just need to go to the storage shed."

"I can start the meat if you want," Albert offers.

Which is why I ultimately like him even though he can be . . . well. Himself.

"Thank you, Albert," I say, then switch my focus back to Nathan. "You can go back to your room or . . . or you can come if you want."

"I'll come with you; there's no need for you to deliver it."

"That's nice, thanks." I'm not sure it is nice because he's so visibly put out.

"Seriously," I say as he continues to follow me. "You saved Wilma's necklace. Let me just . . . get it for you."

"I'll come with you," he repeats, but his tone isn't friendly, and he doesn't acknowledge my reference to his recent heroism.

"It was very nice of you," I say as we walk out behind the lobby to a shed that stands separate from the walled courtyard of the motel.

"Do you think I'm genuinely so awful I wouldn't help an old woman screaming in a pool?"

"No, but she wasn't in danger, and I just think it was extra nice of you—" I give up and decide to try a different tactic. "I'm also a writer, which is just to say I get that it sucks to be interrupted when you're trying to work. Unless of course you wanted to procrastinate."

It isn't landscaped out here. It's scrubby and rocky and dusty, and I'm always afraid I'm going to see a rattlesnake. I'm hot as hell, and he makes me feel jumpy. I just want to get him his power strip and go back into the AC. Yelling at Albert about penises is infinitely preferable to being sticky and hot and feeling turned on in spite of Nathan, his rudeness, my vow of celibacy, and everything else.

"I don't procrastinate," he says.

I laugh. Then realize he's serious. "Oh," I say. "Well, that's . . . wild."

"I came here to work. Why would I procrastinate on the work?"

"I don't know. You spend three months locked away in a motel room and seem to do nothing but write, and you only put out one book a year."

His eyebrows lift. "Only?"

"I didn't mean it like that. It's just . . . you can do a fifty-thousand-word book in thirty days if you do sixteen hundred sixty-seven words a day."

"I'm familiar with the pitch for National Novel Writing Month. Thank you." He says it like that's amateur stuff. I can read it in his tone.

I guess I started it because I implied he was slow. But that wasn't really what I meant. I was just questioning the veracity of his statement that he never procrastinated.

"I write romance, by the way," I say as I muscle open the door of the shed after wrestling with the padlock.

"Mm," he says.

"That's actually what we were arguing about. Albert thinks romance is unrealistic."

Nathan's expression remains neutral. "It is."

I make a scoffing sound. "I . . . You . . ."

"I write military thrillers *based* on the military, and I wouldn't call them realistic. People aren't paying for realism. They want a narrative about heroism and blowing shit up. Within that there are some details that are real, but . . . nothing in real life is that simple."

This is the most he's ever spoken to me, and he's irritating me. "But you know when people say that about books you write, they aren't dismissing your whole genre. When they say it to me, that's what they're doing. People don't value emotion. They don't value hope, even if they should."

I chose romance because I needed to believe in happiness still. Even when my whole life fell apart, I needed to believe in it. Not just in happiness, but that happily ever after was possible, even if things had gone horribly, terribly wrong.

I never thought about it until I had my heart broken. After that I realized I had a choice to sit there in hopelessness. I did for a while, but then I decided I couldn't live that way. Hoping for happily ever after feels brave now.

More and more, I want to be brave.

"If I have a hill I'm willing to die on, that's the one," I say. "Falling in love when everything is terrible is as brave an act as blowing shit up. Except it's something regular, everyday people can choose to do. A radical act of real-life bravery."

I'm not sure I understand how deeply I believe that until the words come out of my mouth.

"I'm not saying there's anything wrong with it," he says. "But my experience is that when life gives you shit, there's really nothing much to continue to hope for."

I snort. "Says the millionaire *New York Times* bestseller with a TV series."

I don't know that he's a millionaire. I'm comfortable assuming, however.

"Right," he says. "Because *that's* the key to happiness."

Irritation and heat make me snap. "Then why do it? Why do *anything*?"

"I ask myself that a lot." He says that flat, not self-pitying, and yet I feel like he's being totally honest.

"I don't think you do. You obviously care very deeply about what you're working on or you wouldn't eschew all forms of procrastination and get pissed because your outlet quit working."

"I didn't ask for commentary. I want a power strip. The end."

My temper peaks.

"Then why the hell do you come here?" I ask, sweat dripping down my back now. "If you hate me and the faulty wiring in the motel and all the guests?"

He moves too close to me, his face maybe three inches from mine. "I just fucking *love* the heat," he says, his voice rough.

We stand like that for too long.

My breathing is labored, and I'm way too worked up about this and him.

I turn away from him and vanish into the shed, where I flick on the lights and give thanks to past me for taking the time to organize and label everything, because it would just be the worst if I had to prolong this moment.

I grab hold of a tub labeled *power strips* and peer inside—there could be spiders, but I don't see any, so I reach in and grab the needed item. When I turn, he's right behind me. He's tall. He's solid. He smells great. Clean, a hint of aftershave and soap.

If I were writing this moment, I could easily go florid with it.

Hints of spice and soap, of skin and *man*.

Something about that makes me snap.

"Here," I say, waving the power strip in the air. "Here is your power strip so you can go back to being a damned ostentatious hermit in the middle of this thriving community. If it were just the heat, you could go stay in an Airbnb in Palm Springs. What do you even get out of this? I have to know. You've spent two summers here without so much as a full conversation traded between yourself and the other residents." Or me. "*This* is clearly the kind of place where people hang out, and talk and laugh and do things, and why would you even come here once, let alone two times, if you hate that? You don't even know my name." *I'm Amelia,* I almost shout. "Do you get off on it? Being alone in your room and being dour about the place? You could go somewhere else—why here?"

I've gone too far and I know it.

Suddenly he's so close to me, and I can't take my eyes off him.

I'm caught in a web spun out of this thing arcing between us. I know what it is. I've wondered if I was the only one who felt it from the first moment I met him. Right now I think maybe I'm not.

Because his eyes are on me, and he isn't looking away. He's filling my space, my lungs, my sense of sanity.

He's close in a way no one ever is. In a way I never let them be.

I want to kiss him.

The realization is stark and intense. So clear and undeniable I can't turn it into a different thought.

My heart is thundering, my whole body on edge.

He says nothing.

He leans in closer.

I can't breathe.

He reaches out and takes the power strip from my hands.

All the air leaves my body, and I am left with the crushing sense that I was just the victim of my own overactive imagination.

He starts to walk away, but he stops for a moment and turns just halfway. “I didn’t choose it.”

I’m left to wonder what that means.

It’s the last thing he says to me all summer.

CHAPTER FOUR

One Year Later

> *Matchmaker, Matchmaker—when the community members in a romance band together to try to create a love match between the protagonists by meddling in their lives.*

It's 123 degrees. The kind of record-breaking heat where *dry* won't save you. Where the idea of your AC going out is terrifying because it could actually be fatal.

I didn't choose it.

I keep remembering what Nathan told me last summer. He didn't choose this. So why is he here? In the dead armpit of July.

I chose this. I chose this life and I like it. I like it, dammit, even while sweltering.

That's one reason I decide not to continue keeping his secret. Well, I tell Elise, which isn't really *not* keeping the secret. In the last eighteen months she has gone from a new friend to my *best* friend. It just doesn't feel right to not share with her that Nathan is in fact a famous bestselling author.

"No way," she says, staring at me from behind the reception desk.

I'm leaning over it, procrastinating, because I should be making use of the free afternoon to hide away in my place and do some real editing. I can peck away at a draft while I'm working. I need some actual uninterrupted time for revisions.

"Yes," I say. "Plus, he's a snob. I had a fight with him about romance. He said it wasn't *realistic*."

I feel a little bit guilty about that because the conversation did have more nuance than that. Though I found it annoying, and I'm still . . . A whole year later, I'm still off-kilter. With the whole *did-we-almost-kiss* thing.

He certainly didn't acknowledge it after it happened. He hasn't acknowledged *anything* since he came back.

"What a dick," she says.

"Yes. But I knew that. I don't know why I expected anything different from him."

"He's nice to me," she says.

I don't know whether to be annoyed or flattered by that. I must be projecting that conflicting feeling, because Elise gives me a strange look.

"I'm trying to figure out why he's mean to me," I say.

She shrugs. "I can't help you with that. Unless he's attracted to you."

That was kind of what I was hoping she would say. Though, also, it's not great.

"I don't have any space in my life for that kind of thing," I say.

"No," Elise says. "*I* don't have any space in my life for that kind of thing. I share a one-room unit with an eight-year-old."

I refuse to accept this from her. "You can't make it work? You, who always manages to have your nails done, have your daughter's homework finished, work your shifts, and make the best baked goods on earth? You could squeeze it in if you wanted. No pun intended. Or maybe pun intended."

Elise shakes her head, her gold hoop earrings chiming in time with the movements. "Ugh. Do you want to know a secret, Amelia?"

"You're always angry?" I ask, tongue in cheek.

"No, I'm always exhausted," Elise replies. I look at my friend and her perfectly done makeup, her hair in a neat ponytail. "I feel like I have to be everything. I don't ever want Emma to struggle, you know? Just because I chose to be an idiot who had unprotected sex with a loser, that's not her fault. It's not her fault her dad sucks."

"It's not yours either," I point out.

Elise pulls a face. "Thank you for saying that."

I don't want to be too pushy, but I sort of do. "You know, if you and Ben ever hooked up, it would be the perfect friends-to-lovers romance."

In my opinion, friends to lovers is much more realistic than enemies to lovers. Mostly, if a man is mean to you, odds are he's going to keep being mean to you. Mr. Darcy excluded. Not that I don't enjoy reading a good enemies to lovers. I just don't think . . .

It's realistic?

I hear that in Nathan's voice, and I find it irritating.

"No," she says, waving a hand. "I can't. He's too important to me."

Ben Martinez is the mechanic at the local garage, and I think he would be perfect for Elise. Honestly, he's a great surrogate father to Emma, and he treats Elise like the sun rises and sets on her.

"Why not?"

"Baggage," she says. "Which I thought you understood."

"Right." Elise knows about Christopher. Mostly. There were things about my life in LA that I just wasn't willing to share. The part where Christopher was a cheater? *That* I'd been more than willing to share.

"You seem to be a hopeless romantic for other people, just not for yourself."

I wrinkle my nose. "Do as I say and not as I do?"

"Really, really no offense, Amelia, but you don't know what it's like to try to navigate dating when you have a child. She's already been hurt by her dad."

I ignore the way that gouges me right underneath my ribs. She's right. I don't have to think about a child. That wounds me. Right in the most unhealed part of myself. But I know what she means, so I choose not to be hurt by it.

"I get it. It's complicated."

"You, on the other hand, could pursue whatever this thing is that you're obsessing about with Nathan."

"I'm not obsessing."

"Excuse me, miss," Elise says in her best Mom Voice. "Have the last four heroes you've written in the last year all had green eyes and slightly disheveled dark hair?"

I sputter, "So?"

"You write him. Over and over. As a billionaire. As a prince. As the boss your heroine calls Daddy . . ."

"I do not!"

I do. Dammit. She's right. I do.

"No one calls anyone Daddy," I mutter.

"Maybe that was just my overactive imagination," Elise says, grinning widely at me.

"I can't . . . I'm not a fling sort of person," I say. "I tried it once when I was in college. It didn't work. I ended up crying over a guy who didn't give me his number or an orgasm. There's no benefit there for me. Anyway, he works on his books here. Someday I'm going to have that put on a plaque in the Hemingway Suite. *Jacob Coulter wrote many novels here.*"

Elise reaches up to pat my head, and one of the jewels on her nails snags in my hair. It's so specific to her that I find it endearing. "I admire your aspirations. Maybe if that tourism boom Sylvia promised when she got elected mayor ever eventuates, it will really pay off."

Rancho Encanto is small, but it's charming. There are quite a lot of people who choose to stay here instead of in the thick of Palm Springs when they want a desert vacation. We offer something quaint, a little bit kitschy. Or, in the case of the Pink Flamingo Motel, a lot kitschy. But I like to think we know who we are and that we know who we cater to.

"Well, a boom would be nice," I say.

Our main tourist season is during the cooler months. That's why Rancho Encanto's main drawcard is A Very Desert Christmas, an event we have every year, with a parade, food trucks, craft booths, and

Christmas pageantry. Just last night I found out I'm going to be on the committee. I'm thrilled to be included in planning something that's so vital to the health of my new community.

Everyone is nice enough in town, but it's just the way with small towns. People are new for years and years. I'm lucky I'm being accepted into the fold this quickly.

Maybe they started believing I'd stay at around the time I started believing it.

The trouble with Nathan being in residence is that when he's here it seems like the entire motel sits up and takes notice. For all that the man keeps to himself, he can't reach out the door to grab his takeout without earning sly comments from my older ladies or wide-eyed looks of fascination from Emma and her friends.

Albert pretends not to notice the shenanigans, and yet I note that he does. I'm quite certain Jonathan and his husband are running a bet on something to do with Nathan, though I haven't figured out *what* yet.

I sit in my room and go over expense reports and tell myself I'll open my manuscript revisions at any moment.

At least, that's what's supposed to be happening, when I hear what might be an *actual ruckus* outside my door.

"Heavens above."

I open the door to see Wilma standing there with a hand dramatically pressed to her bosom. Today she's wearing a gold lamé top with angled shoulder pads and a large piece of costume jewelry around her neck that glints with every movement. I don't expect restraint from her, but this is more dramatic than a typical Tuesday.

"What's happening?" I ask.

"I'm having issues with the washing machine, but I expected you to be at the front desk." She clasps her fingers beneath her chin and stares at me too intently.

"I wasn't," I say. "Because Elise is working today."

"It's very difficult to get used to," Wilma says, shifting her body and looking at me out of the corner of her eye, and I really can't say why she cares so much.

"It's hard to get used to after a year?"

"Darlin'," she says, planting a hand on her hip. "I am eighty-four years old. One year is *nothing*."

"What exactly is happening?"

"I've caused a flood," she says. "It's just a big ol' mess."

As soon as the word *flood* exits her mouth, I'm halfway out the door, because I'm iffy on whether my insurance will cover water damage. That's one of those things I know gets contentious.

"How did you cause a flood?" I'm following her quickly to the laundry room.

"I don't know. I'm not a mechanic or a washer person."

"A *washer person*?"

"I'm being gender inclusive."

"Right."

Grandly, she opens the door to the laundry room, and it hits Nathan in his broad right shoulder.

"Sorry," I say.

He turns around, and his green eyes crash into mine.

I wasn't prepared for him. I like to tell myself I've gotten used to him. The impact of him. The perfect arrangement of his features.

That's a lie, and I know how much of a lie it is when my heart jumps up my throat and makes a play to escape through my mouth.

"He just happened to be walking by," Wilma says, "when the washing machine started to flood."

"Oh?" I ask, suddenly suspicious.

"Yes," Wilma says.

"She thought I could fix it," Nathan says. "Because I'm a man."

"What happened to gender inclusivity?" I direct the question to Wilma.

"I'm eighty-four," she says, waving her hand in the air. "It comes and goes."

I look up at Nathan. "Sorry about this. Obviously, you don't have to fix the washing machine."

"He said he might know how," Wilma says.

"Oh, did he?" I ask.

I definitely smell a rat. A rat in gold lamé.

"I'll get some towels, and I'll start to clean this up. But I'll call a repairman."

"I'm sure you don't need to do that," Wilma says.

"I'm not," I say. "No offense to Nathan's undoubtedly handy skills, but I'm going to need some evidence that he actually knows how to fix something."

"I'll just be right back," Wilma says, and then she leaves. Sweeps right out of the little laundry area, leaving me in this enclosed pink box with the man himself.

"No offense," I say. "But you're a writer, I'm a writer, and there's no evidence that either of us can fix this."

"Does this seem odd to you?" he asks.

Just then, Lydia comes in, with Wilma close behind. Lydia in her pastel-blue tank top, her hair all curled up, her blue eyes wide and innocent. "I thought perhaps you might need these," she says, dropping a handful of flat metal circles on top of the washing machine. "I must've accidentally taken them by mistake."

I stare at the pile of hardware. "You took bolts and washers by mistake."

Wilma looks between Nathan and me, and then the two of them melt out of the room again.

I shake my head.

"If she sabotaged the washing machine, putting it back together shouldn't be that difficult," he says.

"I don't know that she sabotaged the washing machine," I say.

"I think so. I think it's the same thing they were doing when they had me adjust the lights last summer. Oh, and when there was that minor disaster with the necklace in the pool drain. And just maybe they had something to do with the power strip."

"No," I say. "I can't believe it." I can believe it, but that many incidents . . . It feels over the top, even for them.

"You don't believe that they're . . ."

"I don't believe they're that committed to ogling you."

"I don't think they're ogling me. I think they're trying to throw the two of us together."

Him saying it like that, outright and too plain, makes me feel warm. He took the quiet thing and said it out loud. He's looking at me with those electric-green eyes, and I'm just standing here in a laundry room. Dressed in . . . I didn't even give my clothes a second thought.

I'm wearing a short pink sundress that exists to keep me as cool as possible in these hellish temperatures. It also covers very little of my body, though I can't claim that my body is an instrument of seduction. It has, for these past couple of years, been nothing more than an instrument to get me from one place to another. To fix up my motel. To make friends. To sit and write books, enjoy good food and conversation.

Not to *seduce*.

For good reason too. But I suddenly wonder what he thinks about my looks. About my body.

For one brief moment, his eyes get hotter. But then he looks away.

"They're harmless," I say.

"Why do you think that?"

"They're old ladies," I say.

"Why would you think a person would get less dangerous with time? It seems to me that their life experience and the willingness of others to underestimate them only makes them more dangerous."

I can't dispute that.

He picks up the washers and angles his head around behind the washing machine. "For God's sake."

"What?"

"She just popped the closest bolts and washers off and loosened a hose, which is where the water is coming from. But she didn't use her hands. She had to get tools."

My mouth drops open.

"What a fraud," I say. "She plays so innocent . . ."

"I'm telling you. It's the experience that makes them deadly."

"And I really do mean that you don't need to fix this."

"I've got it," he says.

"Do you need tools?"

"That would help."

I have a whole tool kit, in fact. I haven't used it, but I got it in case it might be useful. All I wanted when I bought this place was to be as self-sufficient as possible. Though I'm comfortable now with the fact that calling a repairman is its own kind of self-sufficiency. Just like hiring Elise was its own form of self-sufficiency. Freeing certain aspects of my life up so that I can do more than just live behind the desk at the motel.

That's when I realize what Nathan said is true. Elise working at the front desk sabotaged Wilma and Lydia because they were hoping it would make sense to get me over here at the same time Nathan was here, right as they made a disaster.

I'm going to have to have words with them.

I run to the motel office, where the tool kit is in the closet behind the desk. Elise sees me coming toward her, and I look right past her over to where Wilma and Lydia are huddled up in the corner. "You poor little dears," I say. "Don't know how to run a washing machine. So wise in your old age and can't figure out that you shouldn't go pulling hardware out of it."

They both tut and flutter and act as if I'm casting aspersions unfairly. Elise looks over at me, her ponytail swinging wildly with the motion. "What?"

"They are meddling in my life," I say.

"It's just *light* meddling," Lydia says.

"What does that mean?" I ask.

"It means," Wilma says, straightening her shoulders indignantly, "that nothing we're doing would have any effect if there wasn't a little bit of electricity between you and the handsome man."

"Oh, there's electricity all right," I say. "The kind that's liable to electrocute us both."

"The best kind," Wilma says, absolutely glowing in delight.

I move behind the counter and open the closet, starting my hunt for the toolbox.

"I'm going to need the whole story later," Elise says.

"I plan on giving it to you, but you might have to provide me with an alibi."

"As nefarious plots go," Elise says, "this one is fairly harmless."

"Unless I die of embarrassment," I say.

When I find the toolbox and march back into the laundry room, I realize that the real issue is there's some truth to what Wilma says. I'm attracted to him, and that makes me feel exposed by these machinations. I feel raw from the last time he was here.

From that encounter, and the near kiss.

"Just ignore them," I say, setting the toolbox down next to him.

He looks like he wants to say something. There's a heaviness to the set of his shoulders. The corner of his mouth tilts downward. Not a frown, but there's a hint of sadness there I can't quite read.

"I'm not worried about them."

Something about that feels a little bit insulting, but I decide not to interrogate it.

He looks at the toolbox and takes out a wrench, and then he crouches down, the hardware cupped in his large hand. There's a spot of sweat between his shoulder blades, darkening the fabric of his white T-shirt, and I realize I probably shouldn't find that sexy. I do, though.

I can see the muscles on his back through the fabric of that T-shirt. The way his biceps move as he maneuvers the hardware into position, as he tightens it with the wrench. Nothing is going to happen between us. I'm certain of that. I would have to be a totally different kind of woman. One who wanted to ride a man into wild oblivion for the sake of it.

As I have that thought, my internal muscles pulse slightly and beg the question: Are you *not* that kind of woman?

I ache right then. To feel pretty. To feel desired. To feel his hands working me as expertly as they are the nuts and bolts of the washing machine. How sad is that?

I catch myself bending over just slightly, trying to see what he's doing, and right then he looks up.

If there was no chemistry between us . . . then this wouldn't do anything.

I feel it, like a band tightening between us, growing tighter and tighter, making it harder and harder for me to breathe. I want to touch him. I want to reach out and smooth the lines on his forehead, run my thumb down past the creases next to those green eyes. I want him with a kind of visceral need that shocks me.

In my laundry room. In my motel.

I'm the one who pulls away this time. I take a step back, and only then do I start to breathe again.

"You didn't have to do that," I say.

"It was really not a big deal."

"Tell me if they rope you into anything else like this."

"I probably won't," he says. "Because I don't mind. And also . . . it was good to get out of my room for a minute."

"Tough scene?" I ask.

"Something like that," he says.

He has no reason to linger. I have no reason to keep staring at him.

"Well. I have to go. I have to . . . take my shift at the front desk."

I don't have to take my shift at the front desk. I'm a liar. But still, I grab the toolbox, forget the wrench, and sprint to the front office. I grip the neck of my dress and fan it a few times, trying to alleviate some of the heat coursing through my body.

To my chagrin, Wilma is still sitting there, and she laughs. "Hot flash, dear?"

"I'm thirty-one!"

"Hot flashes can be caused by more than just menopause. Though, usually there are hormones involved."

I look at Elise, who is determinedly examining her manicure and trying not to laugh.

"I should evict all of you," I say.

They care about me, though. That's the thing I can't ignore. That all of this, all the meddling and the antics, comes from a place of love.

Even on a 123-degree day, it's the kind of warming that actually makes me feel good.

CHAPTER FIVE

Save the Cat—when a main character does something early in the narrative to demonstrate that they are, in fact, a hero in the story.

The weather has been truly next-level terrible. We've congregated in a very small group in the lobby to listen to Alice play the keyboard while Ruth sings. Ruth is wearing a short sequined dress that I could believe she bought last week or wore back in her waitress days. She has a bright-red flower pinned into her curly black hair, and bright lipstick to match.

Alice is wearing her usual sedate style. Apparently she doesn't think a motel lobby performance rates sequins.

Even in her nineties, Ruth's voice is beautiful. Time and age give every note a haunting tremolo, and her rendition of "At Last" makes my heart swell.

She's reaching the crescendo of the song when the motel lobby door opens in from the courtyard, and Nathan comes in.

Right as they get to the part about love coming along.

No.

I reject that instantly as my eyes lock with his, as my heart crashes hard into my breastbone.

"There's smoke coming from somewhere," he says.

The last few notes of the song fade out, and I look at him. "Smoke?" I stand up. "Here?"

Elise, who was sitting on the couch with Emma on her lap, displaces her daughter gently and stands up.

"No. Toward town." He holds the door open, and I move past him, heading outside.

It's still hot as hell, and the wind, dry and thin, is blowing an acrid scent in the direction of the Pink Flamingo. When Nathan gets nearer to me, I realize he smells strongly of alcohol.

I look at him closely. His face is weathered, deep grooves bracketing his mouth, and there's a specific hollow look to his eyes. He's hungover. I don't know if he was out or in his room drinking alone, and I don't know what to do with either scenario. Right now, it's definitely not the most important thing.

The residents fill the courtyard, and all of us look off into the distance.

Sirens start to wail, filling the air.

My pocket buzzes, and I take my phone out. I notice Elise doing the same. There's a banner alert going across the screen with an exclamation point.

> Evacuation Level 3—GO NOW!—issued for parts of Riverside County.

I click the map and see that the alert encompasses the northern part of town. Residential buildings and all the big-box stores, schools, doctors' offices.

Another alert comes through immediately. Level 1—BE READY.

That's for the southern part of town. Old town, with its charming historic main street. The older houses, and my motel.

Shock makes my hands shake and my movements clumsy as I open the local Facebook page to try to get a sense of what's going on, while at the same time Elise opens a local news stream.

"The fire started at an apartment complex, and because it's so dry and the wind is so high today, it spread immediately to another complex next door," she reads out.

It's still seven miles away from us, but the high wind and the extreme heat makes my stomach feel hollow with terror.

My residents don't move quickly. Most of them don't drive. I start catastrophizing about what will happen if we lose this place. If we have to evacuate, I'm piling everybody into my car. I know Elise will take hers. We won't leave anyone behind.

"I'm going to go back to my unit," she says. "I just need to . . . We're going to have to pack things."

She runs back into the lobby, takes Emma's hand, and leads her outside and toward their unit. I can't quite parse the emotion I feel in that moment. Elise is being strong for Emma. The way she cares for her daughter makes me so conscious of an empty pit in my stomach. Of pain I try to forget.

I look away, and I think about my boxes of books in the closet. My clothes. It would be sad if I lost all the copies I have of my books. But mostly, everything I have is replaceable. Pictures are digital, and anyway . . .

This place. This place is what matters to me. The people in it. I don't need things. I need to make sure everyone here is ready to go and that they'll be safe if we have to evacuate.

This is my home.

Even if it's 123 degrees. Even if it's on fire.

I chose this place, and it's my home.

That echoes inside me as I start to go around the rooms, knocking on every door. By the time I make it halfway through, the courtyard is mostly filled with residents looking at their phones.

There's a level of anxiety in everyone. Though not Alice and Ruth, who are looking around with interest more than anxiety.

I can hear helicopter rotors overhead. There's a large one flying over the mountains, headed our way, with a bright-orange bucket being hauled beneath. Full of either retardant or water, I'm not sure.

If there's a lake around here with enough water in it for them to use, I would be surprised.

"Do you need help?" Nathan asks, observing the scene.

The temporary guests are particularly filled with anxiety, but I know they can just put their suitcases in their cars and drive off. It's not the same for them as it is for those of us who have made our homes here.

"Nothing is happening right now," I say. "Though I do have concerns if we have to leave. Because . . ."

"The older ladies," he says.

"*They* don't have any concerns," I say. "*I* do."

Smoke is starting to roll in our direction, and the blue sky is rapidly turning a yellowish gray.

"I need to get back in the air-conditioning," Alice says. "I don't have a smartphone, so I imagine you'll keep us from burning to a crisp?"

"Yes," I say. "I promise no one is getting burned to a crisp."

Elise returns from packing and sits at one of the bistro tables by the pool, keeping an eye on her phone, watching for evacuations, watching for more information. The smoke has turned into an oppressive cloud. It's too early for the sun to go down; the yellow, acrid smoke is simply blocking it out. The air is thick. It isn't only smoke, but ash. Like being surrounded by a campfire you can't escape. There is nowhere to move. Nowhere to go.

My eyes burn, and my lungs ache.

The fear I feel for my elderly residents intensifies.

Even if we don't have to evacuate, how can we withstand this? It's like being in hell.

"Everyone needs to get inside," I say.

I make a move toward where the residents are sitting in the courtyard. "Get inside. All of you. If we need to evacuate, we'll get a notice, but we can't sit out here breathing all this in."

"It's bad enough that it isn't like the motel ventilation is going to keep the air clean," Jonathan says.

"Maybe not, but it might minimize the amount of ash you're breathing in."

"No," says Gladys, planting herself firmly at the center of the courtyard. "I want to be able to see it. And I don't have a view out my window."

"We can't really see anything from here," I say. There's a glow over on the horizon, far too close in my opinion.

"If you really want to, you can sit in my room," Nathan says.

I'm surprised by the offer, but I feel like I shouldn't be.

Yes, he can be difficult with me sometimes, but he has consistently been good to the older ladies. He's consistently . . . decent.

It's like herding chickens, but I get Ruth to go to Alice's unit and sit with her. Lydia and Wilma are finally persuaded to at least get into the lobby. Albert didn't need to be told twice; he was off in the AC before I asked anyone to go.

Jonathan and Joseph leave begrudgingly.

But Gladys stands rooted to the spot, a strange light in her eye, and I recognize I'm contending with a lifetime of worries and fears that are manifesting in this moment. It isn't that she doesn't trust me, but something happened in her life to make her feel the need to be vigilant now.

"You can't stop a fire," I say to Gladys gently.

"I need to watch."

Her voice is trembling, and she's beginning to waver.

Then two things happen at once. She begins to fall, and Nathan moves into position, catching her in his arms and scooping her up off the ground.

It's effortless. I've observed his strength in an aesthetic way many times, but this is the first time I've really seen it employed. He sweeps Gladys into the lobby, and I follow.

"We need to call a paramedic," he says, laying her gently on the couch.

Elise races in after us, her phone pressed to her ear. "I'm already on with dispatch," she says.

Emergency services are slammed, but paramedics arrive within fifteen minutes, taking her vitals and giving her oxygen.

Everything is fine, and their best guess is that she essentially had a panic attack and fainted when her breathing became too shallow.

Elise is sitting on a stool behind the counter, tears silently falling down her cheeks. "Three of the apartment complexes are completely gone," she says, wiping at them. "My cousin Solis and her husband lost everything."

"They can come here," I say. "Her and her whole family."

"I'll tell them," she says.

Currently, I have five empty rooms, and I'm thinking of what we can do to house people who are displaced.

In addition to the rooms, we also have the courtyard, which is a safe place for people to camp out if need be.

I keep watching updates. The fire began in a residential space. Two apartment complexes and a housing development burned to the ground within hours. Then the elementary school.

It starts to get darker, cooler, but the wind doesn't stop. Off in the distance I can see an orange glow, and I know it represents so much loss.

On social media, people put out calls for places to shelter those who lost their homes. I respond, and within an hour, we have eleven families at the motel.

Nathan doesn't wait for me to delegate tasks to him. He's organizing people and supplies and giving orders to people who look on the verge of panic. He's keeping them busy, I realize, making them feel useful, while not overtaxing them.

"I'll make some food," Albert says, reminding me again why I like him.

Nathan joins in food prep but also gets some of the kids to help.

I make a list of supplies I think we might need and go into the closet where I keep toiletries. Nathan appears with a duffel bag. "Can I help carry supplies and distribute them?"

I nod. "Thank you."

I fill the bag with shampoo, washcloths, toothbrushes, toothpaste, floss, and other amenities, and Nathan carries it out for distribution.

Soon, the courtyard is filled with the smell of food and the sound of people talking, laughing, even though it's more because of trauma than anything being significantly funny.

We have showers, and between everybody there are enough clothes to go around. We're able to start laundering the dirty clothes people were wearing when they arrived. By the time we're done settling everyone in, it's one in the morning, and the fire is still burning.

We're still on alert.

"I'm going to stay up," I say to Elise. "You go be with Emma. I'm sure this is . . . terrifying for her."

"It's terrifying for everybody," Elise says. "I don't have to leave you alone."

"I'm fine."

Though I realize I'm not fine as soon as I find myself alone. It never occurred to me that this life could be threatened. The new life I made here. That I worked so hard for.

That means so much to me.

It's been my safety. My shelter. I wanted to leave all my darkness behind in LA, and this . . . It makes me realize there's darkness everywhere.

I wipe at a tear on my cheek, and I try to keep it together. I haven't lost anything yet. So many people here have. Everything. I have to keep perspective.

"You did good."

I turn and see Nathan standing there.

"Thanks," I say. "And thank you for helping."

"Yeah. Of course."

"You were actually in the military, right?" I ask.

Yes, I've read his bio.

He nods. "Yes. I was."

"I could tell. You were very calm. Very organized. Even though you were very hungover."

He makes a sound that might be a laugh and might be a groan. He sits down at the table next to mine. Not too close. "Yeah."

"You make a habit of drinking alone?"

I mean it to sound light and amusing, but it doesn't.

"Sometimes," he says.

"I just . . . I thought you didn't procrastinate."

"Procrastination, self-medication—what's the difference, really?"

"Good question."

It's so strange to me. That this man has now been in my life off and on for more than two years, that I know what he does, but nothing about the substance of him.

It feels like there's something connecting me to him, but also like there's a wall between us. I'm not sure which feeling is more real. I can still see the orange glow past the secure courtyard of the Pink Flamingo. The sky feels low. Heavy. There's grit on the bistro table from ash.

"I love this place," I say. "The people here have been amazing to me. This is just killing me."

"You can replace things," he says.

I look over at him. "Yes. Thanks for that. But it isn't easy. It's more than things; it's everyone's sense of security."

"I get that. I'm just saying, when everything is terrible, you can at least be grateful that it's something that can be rebuilt." Yet again, he isn't wrong, even if the way he says it is annoying.

I want to push him. I want to know more about him. I don't know if it would build the wall higher or tighten the tether.

"I imagine, having been in the military, this doesn't really faze you."

"Not really."

"I just mean because you are philosophical about it."

"Are you asking me if I saw terrible things? Because yes. Of course."

"Right. I just think that it either gives you perspective or . . ."

It makes me wonder if that's why he drinks. Maybe that's why he writes military thrillers. Sometimes I wonder if I write romance because I'm trying to go over the things that went wrong in my own. Though that's pretty well-worn ground at this point. I know for a fact I'm trying to reassure myself that happy endings can still exist.

"Or what?" he asks. "You didn't finish your sentence."

"I didn't really finish my *thought*," I say.

"I thought you were a wordsmith," he says.

"That is why they pay me the medium bucks, yes." Sometimes, though, something feels too heavy to put into words, and even if I don't know what it is right now, there is something heavy sitting between us.

"You were fantastic tonight," I say.

I can still hear helicopters flying overhead. The smoke is so thick, so intense, my throat is dry, and my eyes burn, but I can't bring myself to go inside. I feel like I have to hold a vigil here.

People are sharing rooms and sleeping in the lobby. People who have just lost their homes, and I feel like I want to keep watch for them.

"So were you," he says.

I don't have anything salty to say to that. I just want to take the affirmation that I did something right in a crisis.

I didn't fold in on myself. I didn't disappear.

"You should get some sleep," he says.

"Are you concerned about me?"

Our eyes meet and hold. I want to move closer to him, but I don't. I'm afraid of what would happen if I do more than I'm afraid of what will happen if I don't, so I stay there, rooted to the spot.

"You look exhausted," he says.

He doesn't say it in a way that offends me. There's concern underlying his words.

"You were the hero today," I say. "You should go get some rest."

He shakes his head. "I was in the military, remember? I'm happy to keep watch for a while. You go get sleep. Tomorrow . . . There's a lot of extra people in your motel. There's going to be work to do."

He isn't wrong, and I feel exhaustion roll over me in a wave.

"Right. Well. I guess I'll see you tomorrow."

"See you tomorrow."

As I go into my room and climb into bed, then check my phone one more time to make sure I haven't missed any new evacuation updates, I reflect on how aspects of today felt similar to the last emergency I survived.

The one that stole part of myself. The one that changed everything.

This is different. But it reminds me of those feelings all the same. It reminds me of loss and despair on a profound level, wreathed in smoke and flame this time.

But tomorrow I'm going to get up, and I'm going to be the hero in my own life. The one I need. That is the perk to being single.

I'm not going to wait for somebody to rescue me.

It was great to have Nathan here. Being the hero.

But I can be one too. For myself and for everyone I love.

I go to sleep determined about that.

CHAPTER SIX

~~Enemies to Lovers—a popular romance cliché where two characters destined to become lovers start out disliking one another.~~

Just enemies.

Over the next couple of weeks, the smoke that hung so thick in the air dissipates, but the aftereffects of the fire remain.

Many of my residents have lingering coughs, and a sense of fear and agitation underlies the community.

Elise's cousin Solis and her husband, Juan, plus their two children, Sofia and Angel, have moved into one of the family suites at the very end of the motel, and I've promised that they can stay until they have new housing.

There are motor homes being brought in by the government, filling empty fields on the outskirts of town. Temporary housing solutions for those who aren't simply moving to a different location in the aftermath of the destruction.

I drove through the burned end of town and I nearly choked on my grief. The hollow, black skeletons that were once houses and businesses are too awful to bear. I don't know how anyone who lost their possessions, their home, their safety, is managing it.

The resilience of children is one of the most amazing things to watch. Emma and her cousins fill the courtyard with laughter, and Elise worries about how awful they'll feel when they are supposed to go back to school in September, only to realize that school doesn't exist.

There is talk about temporary schooling happening in an old Walmart building on the edge of town.

That's the dominant conversation around the motel. The changes. The plans. The initial crisis is over. No lives were lost, no one was injured. The evacuation notice did its job. All that's left is grappling with the massive loss of property.

Which is no small feat at all. It's still too hot, and now the heat feels like an enemy. Not just a discomfort.

I've seen Nathan more since the fire than all the time he's stayed here in the previous summers combined.

He's helped manage donations and make deliveries. He's even helped manage barbecues. I've decided to continue feeding the community. My guests have donated money for us to make extra food so anyone displaced by the fire can come and have a good meal and a movie and swim in the pool.

Sometimes it's so crowded the place is overflowing, but it's healing something. Or at least it's trying to. I've done grief and isolation. Sadness by myself.

This feeling of wanting to rebuild the community is so much more powerful when we all come together.

I'm always surprised no one else seems to realize that Nathan Hart is Jacob Coulter. But then, they would have to be fans intense enough to stare at the author photo in the back of his book and watch all the extras for his show, the five-minute interviews he gave.

Also, they would have to stare at him as intently in person as I have.

I realize I recognized him because his looks captivated me even when they were just an author photo. Those green eyes. They're unmistakable to me.

They keep showing up in my books.

Despite my best efforts.

But the antipathy I felt toward him has faded. How can I have negative feelings about a man who has done so many wonderful things?

Yes, it's easy for me to get wounded by the almost kiss, and to be mortified by the ways my meddling residents have tried to push us together. But he . . . he's a good man. He just is.

The sky is blue again, and it feels like a miracle, even as the heat continues to be a menace.

Alice and Ruth are singing again, this time by the pool, for the benefit of all our guests and those who have come by for dinner tonight.

There is something beautiful about it. Having the same music that was going on when the fire started. It's defiant.

We won't be burned to the ground.

Nathan is on the edge of the festivities. He helped cook, and he helped serve food, but I can see he's considering leaving immediately.

Wilma seems to notice this too, and she stops him. "May I have this dance, darlin'?"

"I'm not much of a dancer," Nathan says.

"It's my dying wish," says Wilma.

"You're not dying, Wilma," I say.

"All of us are dying. Some of us are just closer to it than others. And I would like to dance."

Nathan looks like he can't find a suitable argument against that, and therefore takes her outstretched hand and begins to sway with her near the pool. There are other couples dancing. Juan and Solis are moving in time with the music, Jonathan and Joseph holding each other tight as they look into each other's eyes.

Wilma, for her part, looks delighted. I cross my arms and lean against the fence that surrounds the courtyard. Wilma twirls herself partly away from Nathan, while still holding his hand, then reaches out toward me. She extends her hand and pulls me close.

I find myself being brought toward Nathan. "Your turn, darlin'," she says.

And with that I find myself held against his hard body.

I don't know what I expected him to do. Push me away, maybe. Instead, he holds me, his palm on my lower back, the other hand clasping mine.

"Oh," I say.

"What did I tell you?" He says this quietly.

"You think she did that on purpose," I say.

"Yes."

"Well. There's no harm in giving her a show, then."

That's what I tell myself as I look into his eyes. As I let him hold me like this. I tell myself I'm doing it to make Wilma think her machinations are working. I tell myself it's not because I want him to hold me.

My own name is on the tip of my tongue, and I want to tell him.

Because despite everything we've been through, unless he's heard it shouted in the chaos, through the smoke, I've never told him my name.

It's so tempting. To close that gap. Yet it feels so risky, and I can't explain why.

We lived through a fire.

God knows I've lived through worse.

But there's something about him—from the moment I first saw him, the moment he walked into the motel—that feels so significant. And the idea of doing anything to disrupt it, to bring him closer, to push him farther away, seems like a very bad idea.

I can still smell smoke on all my clothes, so maybe it's just the wrong time to be risky at all.

The song ends, and he releases his hold on me. I still feel where he was touching me. I still feel *him*.

"There," I say. "That will give her something to talk about for days."

"Glad I could help."

"Always the hero," I say.

Something goes grave in his eyes. "No. Don't make that mistake."

I feel a tug on my skirt and look down to see Angel looking up at me with large dark eyes. "Miss Pink Flamingo," he says. "Can I have some more cake?"

"Of course, sweetheart." I move to the table to get him another slice of chocolate, and after I hand it to him, I turn and look for Nathan.

He's gone.

Once the courtyard clears out for the evening, I sit and take mental inventory of everything. Every moment of the day. Every beautiful thing that's still here. Everything that didn't burn. Every moment Nathan looked at me.

Every second he touched me.

Before I can second-guess myself, I stand up and make my way to his motel room.

Maybe I'm just going to tell him my name. Maybe that's all. Maybe I'm going to laugh and say it's funny how we've never actually been introduced.

Or maybe I want something more.

I don't interrogate myself. I just knock. And wait for him.

He opens the door, shirtless, and my heart freezes, my lungs going tight.

"Nathan," I say.

"Don't."

But he doesn't move away. Instead he takes one step out of the motel room, so close I feel him. The heat. The intense attraction.

He's vibrating with energy. I want to reach out and feel him under my hands like I did when we were dancing.

He moves his hand, like he's about to touch me. Instead, he lets it fall.

"I really don't need this," he says, his voice rough.

It's like I was in a trance, and his words snap me right back to reality.

"I didn't do anything," I say.

"You know exactly what you're doing," he says.

I'm at a loss for words. I have nothing to say. We just went through a fire. We're still going through it—the aftermath is going to linger for months. The trauma for years. He was so wonderful, helping organize things with military precision. He was a hero. Now he's acting like an outraged miss whose virtue has been compromised because I'm near him.

"What the hell kind of statement is that?"

The worst thing is, I know exactly what he's talking about. I feel it too. I won't let him blame it all on me. Or I'll deny anything happened at all. To my grave. One or the other.

"You run the motel I'm staying at. That's it. That's all it's going to be."

"You're full of shit," I say.

He says nothing to that.

I let him turn and walk away from me. I let him close the door on me. The really funny thing is it's a more definitive, *angry* thing than ever got said between me and Christopher in the end.

The fact that I'm still thinking about Christopher is a reminder that, yet again, as much as I hate it, Nathan is right.

I need to stay away from him. I'm closer and closer every day to being fully restored. But he's too broken for me to manage.

I don't have to know the details to know that.

Elise wanted an enemies-to-lovers scenario for me, and that's nice for her.

She might have to accept that sometimes you're enemies with someone for your own good.

CHAPTER SEVEN

Four Months Later

Reunion Romance—a romance plot that centers on past lovers reuniting.

Rebuilding is not a quick process. I know this emotionally. I'm learning how true it is in the context of an actual town as well.

FEMA helped initially. But there are still fields of motor homes, and no completed apartment complexes. Insurance payments have been slow, and most of the businesses haven't begun rebuilding at all. Funding for the school is even more complex, and for now the students are doing classes in the old Walmart, with cubicle dividers acting as insufficient classroom walls.

In the immediate aftermath, Sylvia had considered canceling A Very Desert Christmas.

Until we'd gotten the idea to make it a fundraiser.

The townspeople had come on board in a big way. Donating time and resources to making this the absolute best festival the town has ever seen.

I'm in charge of the Festival of Trees, which will be a display and an auction, where people in town decorate trees in different elaborate themes and then auction them off to the highest bidders.

There is a planned performance that Reigna, the longtime director of all the local community theater productions, has promised will be the greatest of all time.

The mid-November meeting is especially full, with more and more people in town coming up with ideas to make this event as big as possible.

I get out of my car, balancing several plates of cookies on top of each other. The best part of Christmas gatherings, in my opinion, is the endless variety of sweets that can be taken away from events on paper plates, so the holiday traditions mix and mingle and you get to try different recipes. I love it.

It might not be December yet, but the event is Christmas themed, and that means Christmassy sweets are happening.

It's the kind of thing I used to see in heartwarming movies. Which my life had never particularly resembled.

Now I've made it.

I take purposeful steps through the cracked parking lot and into the small sun-bleached building that also serves as a visitors' center. It has a rattlesnake painted boldly on the side of it.

I'm still upset there are no armadillos.

I'd prefer them over the snakes.

As long as our world isn't on fire anymore, I'll even take the snakes.

I open the door by leading with my knee, then turn sideways, pushing with my shoulder and granting myself entrance.

"Amelia!" Sylvia is there already, looking bright and chipper and wearing what everyone I know in LA would have called an ugly Christmas sweater as a title, not an insult. Sylvia just calls them sweaters.

She's the epitome of type-A efficiency. The sort of woman you'd expect to see in tailored suits, not in preschool-teacher chic. But she loves a chunky wooden necklace and a seasonal jumper.

"Hi, Sylvia," I say, setting my cookies down on the table next to the fanned-out array of holly-festooned napkins. There's a Crock-Pot filled with cider and some clear plastic cups next to it. Sylvia has brought fudge.

This year's planning meetings have felt deliberately, intensely warm. Like we're all determined to make magic wherever we can.

It's been such a tough few months. Every time I smell smoke, I break out in a cold sweat.

I know I'm not alone.

Doing this, doing something . . . at least that makes me feel active.

"Ticket sales are at a record high," Sylvia says, smiling brightly. "The Festival of Trees has never seen presales like this. The fundraiser getting picked up by the news in LA was such a huge thing for us. Thank you."

I try to hold back my smile. Let it go just half-mast, as I don't want to seem too pleased or too eager for her praise. But I am. Sylvia is like the supportive mom I never had, but I have the feeling if I told her that, she'd have to put four walls of reserve back up between us. She's lovely, kind, and warm, but only after you get to know her.

I've experienced the kind of sadness that drives people apart. I've never experienced something like what happened in Rancho Encanto after the fires. People came together. They supported each other. They're still doing it.

I hate contacting people back in LA, but I did it for Rancho Encanto. An old friend of mine is a producer on one of the local news channels, and I got her to feature the festival—and Sylvia—as a local interest piece, to try to draw people out of the city and into the desert for a little bit of fun . . . and to support a good cause.

So, I did do a good job, and I feel pleased with myself for it.

I'm feeling pleased in general.

Other people begin to arrive. Mary Thomas, who owns Get Your Kicks Diner and is wholly committed to her beehive hairdo and swing skirts. Bob Riker, owner of the local antique store—always with a pocket watch in his vest pocket. I can put a name to every face now, even if we've only spoken in passing, and I do as they all file in and take their seats.

I'm in the front row, like always, ready to bring my enthusiasm to the discussion, though all the planning is done.

"We're getting closer and closer to our special fundraising edition of A Very Desert Christmas!" That earns Sylvia a smattering of applause. "Big thanks to Amelia for organizing the news spot."

I didn't need the recognition for that, but I beam with pride all the same. I receive some applause, and my beaming intensifies.

"All assignments have now been allocated," Sylvia says. "If anyone is wanting to change their assigned position, they will have to take it up with their team leaders. If any teams need more volunteers, you can let me know. As for presentations . . . up first, we have Reigna giving an update on the carol concert and performance art piece."

Reigna Marsters gathers herself from her position in the row across from me. Gathering herself is a considerable job, as she's all flowing layers of fabric and wild box-dyed red hair. Every movement Reigna makes is an event, and it's not by accident.

She claims to have been deeply embedded in the entertainment industry some thirty years ago, though I never heard her name during my time in it, minimal though it was.

Maybe she was an essential and integral part of the industry thirty years ago and no one remembers her name now. Deeply on brand for Hollywood, if I'm honest.

Given her past life in entertainment, Reigna is the obvious choice for talent coordinator for the program, and she managed to get Macaulay Culkin to do the reading, which is a boon the likes of which Rancho Encanto has never seen. She claims it's because she was his acting coach when he was a child, but it's impossible to tell which of Reigna's stories have a grain of truth and which are lies made of glitter and enthusiasm. I like that about her, actually.

Because while her life might be embellished, she isn't boring. I appreciate that more than the unvarnished truth. I guess because I'm here making my own life out of pieces of truth and omission.

Reigna's posture as she approaches the front of the room is affected and dramatic, and it alarms me for some reason. Likely, I realize, because she's trying to alarm us.

"This is an announcement in two acts," Reigna says, her voice deep and theatrical as she holds up her finger. "First, a tragedy."

"Dear God," I hear Sylvia whisper as she pinches the bridge of her nose.

I can't tell if that's a response to the potential tragedy or just the overwrought drama of it all. I like a little drama. Sylvia does not.

"Macaulay is unable to make the event."

A ripple of noise moves through the room, and I make a sound of genuine disappointment. Getting him was a Christmas miracle that was unsurpassed. We'd gone through lists of possibilities based on Reigna's connections to people in the Christmas Movie Industrial Complex. Will Ferrell was too busy. Arnold was too political.

"What happened?" comes a distressed-sounding voice from behind me.

"He's involved in a franchise reboot," she says. "Very hush-hush, but it's now conflicting with the event, and apparently the studio's contract is more ironclad than ours. But he sends not only his regrets but a donation to our cause."

There's a smattering of disappointed applause.

"Well, what now?" Sylvia asks.

"Never fear!" says Reigna. "Act two." She holds two fingers up. "I have a replacement."

The response to that is a somewhat mollified rumble.

Reigna looks out at the crowd as if she's about to deliver a winning monologue. "Christopher Weaver."

My world tips over onto its side.

Chris.

Chris, who was struggling to land parts most of our time together, but who is now the undisputed king of Christmas rom-coms. He's had no less than three a year every year since our breakup. While that hasn't made him a household name by any stretch, he's wholly recognizable and will be a special draw to the kind of people who want to go to a holiday festival in the desert.

I have no idea what to do or say.

I'm lost in a memory from three years ago, and I can't get out of it.

Chris in our whitewashed house looking grim, me wondering why he's bothering to look grim when I know this is what he's wanted all along. He was just waiting for a chance to do it when it was far enough out that he didn't look callous.

"I'm so sorry, Amelia. You never should have found out like this."

I never saw it coming, and I can't speak. I had thought we might break up, but I never imagined that while I was coming apart inside, he was putting himself back together in the arms of another woman.

I'm back in the visitors' center, thankfully no longer beset by my memories, but sadly, my memories are more relevant to my present than I'd like.

Half the people in the room don't know him by name, and Reigna is explaining. The ladies are particularly excited, and I'm just unable to understand how I'm suddenly sitting in the impending doom of my past life.

He doesn't know where I moved to. Unless someone told him, and I'm pretty sure our split was neat enough that no one who knows where I am still speaks to him.

I don't do social media as myself.

I pretend it's because of the romance writing and motel, that maintaining an author presence under my pen name and a page for the Pink Flamingo is enough to keep me far too busy online as it is. That isn't why. I don't want handy Facebook memories reminding me where I was almost three years ago.

I don't want old friends to track me down with a *long time no see, girly, what are you up to?*

I don't want to feel obligated to friend my mother. Or anyone who knew me in high school.

I don't want people to know where I am, because Rancho Encanto is my sanctuary, and this is not the point of it.

So if I say something to Reigna, I'm breaking the spell. Worse, if I make it about my issues, it could impact the fundraising for the festival.

But then Chris will know I'm here.

He won't care.

That is the truth. Chris won't care.

I need to make him think I don't care either. I can let him come and be surprised by me, then act like it never occurred to me to reach out to him because our history is ancient and I don't care. I'm certainly not still hurt over the way he left me to isolate in my pain. Not hurt over having to split our lives in half and having to let go of all my dreams because that place—and him—became too painful to ever have to deal with.

This was . . . this was supposed to be amazing. Christmas is supposed to be a time for miracles, and this is what the universe gives me?

The universe can absolutely suck it.

I can feel Sylvia looking at me, and I'm sure I've done a terrible job hiding my reaction to the news, so I make sure to smile, but unlike my ex, I'm no actor.

I have no idea how believable it is.

We get through the rest of the meeting with no hiccups, and I even manage to say my piece about the Festival of Trees and give everyone instructions on how we'll be receiving their trees the day before the event, and I think I possibly even sparkle and look like I'm fine.

Afterward, everyone mingles and takes plates of cookies, and I'm angry because I can't enjoy my little Christmas fantasy come to life.

Sylvia heads to her car at the same time I do and surprises me by defying the conventions I've set for her in my head.

"Are you okay, Amelia? You seemed upset when Reigna made her announcement."

This is my moment. I can lean in and be honest. I can tell Sylvia I've been running away from my past for three years and I'm not ready for it to catch up with me. I can tell her that Chris is the last thing on earth I want to see, behind both Ted Bundy and the Microsoft Word paper clip.

But I don't. Instead, I shrug. "What nineties kid wouldn't be disappointed by the loss of the *Home Alone* guy? I was looking forward to it, and more practically, of course, I felt like it would be a huge draw when we unveiled it next week. I'm sure . . . I'm sure the alternative will be good, but it's not Macaulay Culkin good."

"I don't think you have anything to worry about. The ticket sales were great even without the announcement, so I'm sure that once . . . whatever-his-name-is gets announced, it will be a draw and no one will be disappointed because they won't have known."

I appreciate that she can't remember Chris's name, and I'm also very aware that she might be lying for my benefit because she might know *I'm* lying.

The thing about Rancho Encanto is very few people who live here are from here. Which means they left whole lives behind in places that don't get hot enough to scorch your soul from the inside out on a summer Tuesday. All have reasons for not necessarily wanting to drag that life out into the open for all and sundry to see.

We respect each other's baggage.

"As long as you think it's fine," I say.

"I do." She doesn't seem convinced of the whole thing, and I give the world's most half-hearted wave as I slip into my car, several plates of goodies piled high in the passenger seat, and head back toward the Pink Flamingo.

The neon sign greets me, along with the Christmas lights around the palm trees and Joshua trees in front of the place. It's pink and glorious and welcoming. I'm going to put the goodies in the lobby.

I know that Wilma, Gladys, and Lydia will be by for treats. They'll scent them like a small pack of dachshunds. I like that about them.

We'll chat, and I'll forget about Chris and fires for a while. About the real, shocking truth that no matter how nice a life I've made for myself here, it hasn't erased the one I left behind.

Even worse, it isn't staying behind me. It's coming right for my new life, and I'm not sure what to do about that.

It is the season of miracles.

And I got my ex.

If this were one of his Christmas movies, it would be a reunion romance.

That thought hits me when I'm alone in my unit.

It makes me laugh and laugh and laugh.

CHAPTER EIGHT

You (Again)—when two characters continually cross paths—seemingly at random—but it's an indication that their connection is "fated" or part of a bigger plan.

I've spent the last couple of weeks stewing about the situation with Chris. I come to the same conclusion every time. I'm not going to tell anyone that they've hired my ex-boyfriend, because it's too important. There are families counting on this. Our community is counting on this. I don't want to contribute to any issues. Now, I'm determined to find something that will raise even more money than Christopher Weaver's presence. Maybe?

It's still charitable, even if it's petty. I assume the charitable aspect overrides the pettiness.

I feel bad, but I haven't even told Elise. I just worry. I worry she will—out of the goodness of her heart—try to manage the whole Christopher situation, and I don't need that. I'm stronger than that.

Though, on December 1, I sit in my feelings. Because it's almost my birthday. My thirty-second birthday, as a matter of fact. While I feel like I've definitely changed my life since I moved here, there's something . . . melancholy about it. Or maybe I'm just filled with a sense of doom because five months ago my very safe life caught fire, and now a piece of my old life is getting set to invade. Maybe my feeling weird is normal, all things considered.

Maybe. Though I have to stop sitting in my feelings. I haven't been able to do any real work on my book since the Chris announcement, and this morning I finally emailed my editor saying change of plans, it's not a reunion romance anymore.

It only hurts a little bit. It's only ten thousand words to delete. Whatever.

This is my tenth book. I'm familiar with this game. At this point I'd rather burn it all to the ground than work on something I don't want to write.

There's no way I can write a reunion with . . . all that looming up ahead. Absolutely not. I don't write reunion romances ever for that reason, actually. I foolishly thought it's been three years and obviously the hero of the book won't have been a cheater, so it's fine and not at all the same.

But now, no.

Too real. Way too real.

I don't explain why. I assume my editor will think it has something to do with my muse.

Luckily she's fine with it and tells me so within ten minutes of my sent missive, and I respond with something about a different trope, but then I don't even remember what I told her five minutes later and have to check my sent folder to see what I said.

Enemies to lovers, I've now promised.

I can't avoid getting restarted.

I finally commit to making my manuscript full screen—always a harsh warning to myself to stop clicking around the internet—when the little cricket alert chime goes off on my computer. I have it set to crickets because I find it soothing. Or I did, two years ago, when I made the decision to make that alert a cricket sound.

Now it makes me grind my teeth.

Time to change it again.

I open my reservation software, and I see that a new request has come in.

I click the form, and my heart nearly explodes through the front of my chest.

Nathan didn't make a reservation after the fire, and I thought . . . I thought maybe the fire had chased him away. I thought maybe when he told me I needed to stay away from him, what he really meant was he was going to stay away from me. Because for whatever reason, that attraction passing so openly between us the night we danced had made him angry.

It wasn't just uncomfortable. It was like he was *mad* about it. I had, unavoidably, I feel, internalized that a little bit.

But there he is.

I scroll down and look at the dates, expecting to see summer.

December 2–26.

Tomorrow. He wants to come tomorrow. On my birthday. He was *just* here. He only ever comes in the summer, the exact same dates: June 15–August 25. Every time.

He doesn't randomly show up in December.

I had been convinced that he was . . . that he wasn't going to come again at all.

My hands are shaking as I respond to the request.

Yes, your room is available.

It takes effort not to sign my name. Because after all this, I've still never said it to him. He's still never used it. I have no reason to suspect he even knows it.

There's no real response. He just presses the confirmation button.

There is no calling it back. No stopping it. Nathan is coming tomorrow.

I go back to my manuscript, and I realize I've written another green-eyed hero. I don't want his eyes to be blue, because Christopher's eyes are blue. So now they're brown. I do not make every hero Nathan.

I almost text Elise to tell her that, but I'm sure it will make me seem guilty.

I'm *not*.

Nathan is checking in tomorrow, and I can't stop thinking about it.

He stayed after the fire. For the whole month of August, just like he always does. He was more aloof than he had been that first summer. The only time I really interacted with him again was when I had to bring him takeout that got left in the lobby.

I'd had to fight not to make a dramatic show of keeping my distance as I handed it to him.

For his part, he acted as if nothing had happened between us.

Then he hadn't made another reservation, and I had thought that was it.

Which was kind of great because it meant I could put my plaque up in the Hemingway Suite and he wouldn't be any the wiser. It would be better for me to exploit his fame than to actually have to deal with his grumpy ass.

But his grumpy ass is coming for Christmas.

I sit there, frozen for a moment. Thinking through the implications of Nathan and Christopher converging on my life.

I nearly laugh. Because Christopher doesn't know I'm here, and Nathan doesn't care that I am.

I would prefer I weren't, frankly.

I snort and type angrily for the rest of the afternoon. Thankfully, I have something to look forward to this evening.

The entire month of December is Christmas movies at the dive-in event, and tonight we're having another community barbecue and enjoying the entertainment.

We continued with our open barbecues after the fire.

So many people are still living in motor homes, and cooking is difficult. We have a general fund people contribute to as and when they can, and the courtyard is large enough to host extra people. Plus, the kids get to stay and watch movies on the big screen.

It gives them a distraction from the confined spaces they're living in.

I have decided I will be bringing out my pink floating lounger for the occasion.

The thing about having a December birthday and a mother who resents your existence is that the event tends to be minimized. Birthdays are very important to me.

When I lived in LA, I loved nothing more than celebrating my friends extravagantly and being celebrated extravagantly in return.

Chris was even good at that for a while. That's the problem with Christopher—I'm determined to try to think of him that way. Christopher Weaver, the public entity. Not Chris, my ex.

I have good memories of us being together. I have good memories of our little apartment, then of our home once we both achieved a little more success.

He felt like he might be my first real experience of a family.

Not like my parents.

We talked about marriage. We talked about a future.

If it hadn't been good for even most of the time, I wouldn't have been with him. Today is one of the few days I genuinely miss parts of my old life.

For the most part, I have drawn a pink curtain around myself. Around this place.

It isn't that I got a new identity and didn't tell anyone. My closest friends do know where I am.

Well. They were my closest friends.

They text less and less frequently. I'm pretty sure that's my fault.

We had this big shared friend group, and a breakup made that almost impossible. I could have won the breakup too. I think I did, actually.

He cheated. That was pretty straightforward; he didn't deny it. Everybody was mad at him, not me.

But I was the one who couldn't handle it. I was the one who couldn't spend one more minute in that whitewashed hell.

I was the one who had to run away to bright colors and romance novels and the unrelenting heat.

The problem with healing through metamorphosis is that bringing too much baggage with you makes it feel too difficult.

Maybe it's not healing.

Maybe it's just surviving.

The idea of radical acceptance and opening myself up to the universe helped me feel like I was thriving. One of the wonderful things about the desert is the preponderance of crystal shops and tarot readers. A feeling that you might be closer to something unknowable or supernatural. It's hard to access that when you're stuck in gridlock traffic.

But here, I feel it.

Vibrations from the earth, voices on the wind. Like I was fated to be here, as much as I don't want to believe the pain that brought me here was fate. I feel it.

Or maybe I just *want* to.

Like I want to celebrate my birthday floating in a pool watching Buddy the elf find his family. It's a distraction. From the loneliness that tried to crowd in.

From the anxiety I feel over the unresolved issue of Chris coming to Rancho Encanto.

I'm sure he has no idea I'm here. Our old friends who do know would have had to tell him, and I just don't think they would.

It's not like I changed my identity and started again, but I don't like to give my exact location to very many people. Least of all Chris.

It just felt like I had been dragging baggage with me everywhere I went. From Bakersfield to LA. I didn't want to bring it here.

I had forgotten I even had it. Sort of. Mostly, I forgot there was another life.

After three years in Rancho Encanto, it has become my life.

Normally I don't even get sad on my birthday.

It's the Chris factor.

The invasion of it all.

"I made you pie!"

I look up from the grill in total disbelief as Elise comes toward me with Emma, Sofia, and Angel trailing behind excitedly, holding the most beautiful lemon meringue pie I've ever seen.

"Pie! Pie! Pie!" The kids are singing what amounts to a hosanna chorus about the dessert, and I can't really blame them.

I want that pie, this weather, my best friend, the adorable kids to pull me out of my weird funk. I'm thinking too much about the past, which I really don't want to do. But the past is getting into my present, the *before* is getting into my *after*.

Then there's Nathan.

I'm still in a minor tizzy about his random booking.

Putting it mildly.

I got my feelings hurt, and I might have overreacted. Internally. It's not like I *yelled* at him or anything, but for heaven's sake. He warned me away from him like I'd accosted him.

The guy doesn't like me—he's made that very clear.

However, I think that's maybe part of why I'm drawn to him. Not in a playground way. Not in an I-want-to-pull-his-pigtails way. It's not that at all.

I've analyzed this possibly too deeply in the last five months, because I'm still thinking about him, in spite of being mad.

But I think I get it. Even better, I like the reason I've come up with.

He's safe.

He's never going to make a move on me. He's proven that. He's never going to look at me and see the fantasies I've had about him moving like a slideshow through my eyes and pull me into his arms. He's never going to ask me to make them real.

That's why I like him.

That's why he excites me.

I can't have him.

I'm not being martyrish, I'm really not.

He's safe like this. A safe space to have pleasant, warm feelings without ever having to worry about the consequences of those feelings, because there are none and won't be.

He's like the human man equivalent of Rancho Encanto itself. A place out of time and space, where my issues don't follow.

He isn't my reality.

But this pie is.

Elise and Emma are. Sofia and Angel are. Wilma, Gladys, and Lydia are. Even Albert is. Even though he's cornered Jonathan and Joseph off in the barbecue area and is saying something about the shortening attention spans of youths and the implications on real art. Then Jonathan says something about Marvel movies, and Albert is off to the races.

I know for a fact Jonathan has done this for the sole purpose of riling Albert up. I respect that about Jonathan. Also I'm tired of hearing screeds about the regurgitation of content and the soulless spectacle of green screen effects.

I shoot Jonathan a look, and he only smiles at me with innocence I know is fake as he takes a step closer to his husband, and the two of them tilt their heads to the side and feign interest in Albert's rant.

When Solis and Juan get back from work, they fix plates, and Elise starts to sing "Happy Birthday," and everyone—even Albert—pauses to sing too. The kids are screaming more than singing.

I think I might cry. I do a little. If my eyes being watery counts as crying. Because finding out my ex is coming to town knocked me on my butt, and the specter of Chris feels intense. I don't want to do anything to jeopardize the festival.

Christmas is supposed to be about miracles and stars aligning.

I can't even figure out what all this is. A cosmic joke?

"You're the best, Amelia," Elise says, setting the pie down on a table in front of me.

"Thank you," I say. "My birthday is *tomorrow*."

"I know," says Elise. "What's wrong with birthday week? Start treating yourself early."

"I love that for me, but it so happens I'm treating myself to a favorite at tomorrow's dive-in."

"Wish I could be there," Elise says, smiling. "My boss has me manning the front desk."

"You don't," I say. "It's *Die Hard*."

"How are you doing *Die Hard* in front of the kids? Is this Dive-In Way Way Way After Dark?"

"No," I say. "I found it at a yard sale. It's like one of those old CleanFlicks edits?"

"Good God, the movie is going to be five minutes long."

"I previewed it. Now he says, 'Yippee ki-yay, motherscratcher.'"

Elise cracks up and starts cutting the pie, which creates a small line of guests to sample her cooking. After she hands out the last piece, she looks over at me meaningfully.

"Room thirty-two is being cleaned," Elise says casually, pretending to examine her nails.

I take another large bite of pie. "Yes. It is."

"Random guest or . . . is he coming back?" She looks far too interested.

I narrow my eyes. "You know, other people do reserve that room."

"I guess so. But he has it blocked out often. Also, you're in a weird mood."

This is the drawback to having best friends. Best friends who actually care for you and notice your moods and want to offer support. I really should have thought that through. I sigh. "Yes. He is coming back. Tomorrow."

Elise is way too amused by this, her laughter making her bracelets and earrings jingle in time with her movements. "No way. For how long?"

"Until the day after Christmas."

"That's . . . Wow."

"I know. Especially since our last interaction—our last major interaction—was hostile."

"Because he thinks you're hot," she says.

"Maybe. Though why should I care about that if he's just going to be a jerk?"

"Good question." Elise sits there drumming her nails on the table, thoughtful for a moment. "I know he's very protective of his anonymity," she says slowly. "What if he would do an event?"

I blink. "What?"

"A fundraiser."

I realize that I have missed the actual kismet here. That I've been so distracted by my personal feelings about Nathan and what passed between us that I have missed the actual reason for him walking into my life in the first place.

Of course. It was never about me. What a main character point of view. It was about the town all along.

He's not my fate. He's Rancho Encanto's.

"You're right," I say. "He should. At A Very Desert Christmas. We can advertise that Jacob Coulter is going to be there. That he's going to sign books." I'm getting more and more excited as I start talking. "He could maybe give a talk. People love author talks. They love them way more than they love book signings. Everybody wants you to tell them how they can get published."

"Well, he could do that. Then you could sell tickets to the event, and it could all go to benefit the community!"

This is it. The thing I'm looking for. Something that will help me earn more money for the festival and will even keep me extra busy, and maybe farther away from Christopher.

I'm suddenly very grateful for my best friend, for her knowing me, and for her being able to look at a situation and see something I didn't because I was so focused on my own drama.

"You're a genius," I say, because I'm not going to gatekeep my level of admiration for her.

"Thank you," she says.

"Of course, convincing him of that could be . . . difficult." But I think of the way he was the night of the fire. He genuinely cared about everybody. "He is for sure a giant curmudgeon," I say, "but I must reluctantly confess I think there is good deep down in his heart."

Elise laughs. "How inconvenient."

"No kidding."

But now I have a mission. When Nathan shows up, I'm going to be the most pleasant version of myself possible. Bygones are going to be bygones.

Because now I have a ringer for A Very Desert Christmas. It fills me with hope, joy, and glad tidings. This is the cliché Christmas miracle I've been waiting for. It's not my ex coming in from the big city.

It's this *very convenient* circumstance.

I've been given my own version of a cheesy Christmas romance. *Sans* romance.

And I'm going to embrace the hell out of it.

CHAPTER NINE

I let Elise work the counter on my birthday, as planned, even though that means I won't see Nathan when he checks in. I tell myself that's a good thing.

First of all because I don't want to accost him with the book event idea immediately, and I'm excited enough about it that I don't fully trust myself. But second of all because after the way we parted in the summer, I'm not sure what to do or say when I see him next.

It feels like something happened when it didn't, and that is the story of everything with him.

I'm supposed to be taking the day off, so in service to that I'm wearing my pink bikini and lying on a lounger, reading a romance novel, because what could be better?

Of course, my mind is wandering. Nathan. Christopher. A Very Desert Christmas. Fundraising.

It's a loop I can't get out of.

Nathan. Christopher. A Very Desert—

Nathan.

My heart slams against my breastbone as he walks out of the lobby and through the courtyard. He has his usual travel bag slung over his shoulder, the usual wheeled bag trailing along behind him.

I'm lying out like a starfish, mostly naked, which has never crossed my mind when wearing a swimsuit until this moment.

I hope he doesn't see me. Which of course means he takes two more steps, then does. Our eyes meet and he stops, like he isn't quite sure what he wants to do next.

Then he moves nearer to me. Which is also on the way to his room, but he sort of purposefully arcs toward me instead of walking around the covered corridor.

I'm trying to decide what to say, but he speaks first.

"Glad you had the room free." But he doesn't sound especially glad or anything close to it.

I don't tell him I often have rooms free.

I wait for him to tell me why he's here.

Before I ever worked in a writers' room, I was always interested in telling everyone I met I was a writer and what screenplay I was working on. Before I ever sold a book, I enjoyed talking about the progress I was making on my novel. Now that it's my job and I do things like scrap a book because I can't deal with glorifying any fantasies involving an ex, I have much less interest in having a conversation about it.

Maybe it's the same for him, and that's why he never gives me any information about what keeps him locked up in my motel for days, weeks, months at a time.

Or maybe that's part of my problem. I'm always assuming things about him. What he feels about me or doesn't. That we might have a common bond because we're both writers. Or because he stays in my motel and likes how I decorated the room.

Maybe he doesn't. Maybe it's another thing he didn't choose. Maybe it's another maddening riddle.

I wonder if there's a chance I could answer one of them right and he might let me trot across the philosophical bridge that leads to his feelings. But I doubt it.

More to the point, I shouldn't care.

Just because he's hot. And tall.

"So am I," I say.

"I doubt it matters to you one way or the other who's staying in the room."

He's not fishing for a compliment or a sign he matters or anything half so charming. His tone is caustic. Enough that it surprises me.

Not that it's the first time he's been openly hostile to me, but still. The fact that he stopped to talk to me made me think . . .

It's really not fair. I'm making an attempt at cheer here, mainly because I have to. Yes, I've slipped up and I've been testy with him a couple of times, but he's just checking in, and each time he's checked in, I've tried. Tried so hard to start over with a clean slate. Here I am with my generic customer service cheer, and not *I have pictured you naked* cheer, and he's being like this.

His hostility, therefore, feels a bit like *I have pictured you naked* hostility.

That revelation makes my heart beat too hard. I know I'm staring. Still splayed on the lounger, a romance novel in my hand.

"I'm glad it worked out for you, because you're such a loyal customer," I say, and I'm not sure where I got that from because I'm not an actress and have never even had the slightest aspiration toward being one.

He is not succeeding in acting. His green eyes are far too intense.

Hard and glinting and suggesting I'm not alone in my attraction.

My breath gets shallow, my heart speeding up.

I'm not in a romance novel. I know that. I know that sometimes a guy is not your Mr. Darcy—he's just being mean.

I don't know his life. He could be married. Could have a live-in girlfriend, a long-term relationship. I'm assuming he's attracted to women, but the assumption is based on observations I've made over the past several years, and also the eye contact just now.

I really *don't* think I'm making it up.

"How have things been?" He pauses for a moment. "Since the fire."

It's not a question about me personally, and that's fair. Of course he wants to know how things are in the community because he's decent, and he was here during all that.

"It's . . . still a work in progress. The Aguilars are still living here full-time, until their complex gets rebuilt."

"That's . . . good."

"Yeah. Tonight's dive-in movie is *Die Hard*," I say.

"Not very Christmassy."

"Um. Disagree," I say. "It is in fact my favorite Christmas movie. Also, it's my birthday."

I don't need to say that either. I expect a half-hearted *Happy birthday* from him, which feels like the social contract.

I don't get one.

"I haven't been to one of the dive-in movies yet," he says.

"Oh, haven't you?" I say, as if I've never noticed his steadfast commitment to being antisocial.

"No."

"Tonight might be a good night to check it out. There are going to be a lot of events over the course of the month," I say brightly. "You can find the information—"

"On the itinerary in the office, thank you."

"Yeah. I know how much you love my itineraries." I smile, and he doesn't smile back.

He starts to move, and I hastily lie back in my chair, making it clear that if he's done with the interaction, I can be done with it too. I really am trying to be nice. I need his help, and that means I have to stop obsessing about attraction I wouldn't act on even if he offered.

I put my book back up in front of my face.

"Amelia."

I lower the book slowly, and I'm unable to keep the shock off my face.

He knows my name.

"Happy birthday," he finishes.

My heart squeezes, then expands. "Thank you, Nathan."

He walks away, and I hear his key jingling in the lock, hear the door open and then close firmly behind him.

If this were a romance novel, it would be a critical turning point.

But it's just my life, and I'm still sitting on a lounger by the pool wondering why my heart won't stop beating so fast.

CHAPTER TEN

I'm doing my best not to spin out over earlier. His use of my name is not evidence that he thinks about me the way I think about him.

That he's tortured himself over perceived near kisses or the hot-and-cold behavior he exhibits.

The truth is, I'm not even sure how I think about him. Beyond finding him attractive, that is.

He knows my name. What else does he know about me?

I have a brief bio on the website. Nothing about my writing, because I've always worried it might invite creepy men with creepy commentary and ill intent. I talk about it freely with the people who are here. But that seems different. Different from somebody perhaps coming because they have an idea of what a romance writer might be.

In one of the author loops I'm a part of online, I've heard terrible stories about prison mail.

There *is* a picture of me, and I include my name and the fact that I'm from Bakersfield. I don't have my last name on there. If my last name were on there, it really would defeat the purpose of me not being on social media.

I walk out of the walled courtyard of the motel and head down the sidewalk. The weather is glorious, a balmy seventy-two, which is just fantastic, and I am determined to enjoy the day.

I need to get a few last-minute things before the barbecue tonight, even though everyone pooled their money to buy most of the ingredients, which was wholly unnecessary.

But they're insistent on treating me for my birthday, despite the fact that Elise made me a pie last night. I *do* think it's lovely.

I get lost in that loveliness. It's a choice. One I made when I moved here, one I made often. When I was moving out to Rancho Encanto, I was behind the slowest moving Volvo I've ever seen, and it had a bumper sticker that said: DON'T POSTPONE JOY.

I was in pain, and I had every reason to wait until I healed to start enjoying sunsets and pie and new friends.

I took it as a sign from the universe. To try to let the joy exist alongside grief.

If I can do that, I can definitely choose to just enjoy the day.

Because it's much easier than pondering Nathan.

Nathan is easier than accepting that Christopher is going to come here, to my bubble. So this explains the perseverating.

I choose to focus on the scenery.

The sky is glorious blue, the mountains on the horizon purple. The spiky grass ripples in the breeze, and the naughty arms of the Joshua trees bend and sway as the wind picks my hair up off my shoulders.

I take in each feeling, each sound. I choose *joy*. Dammit.

Just then, the sound of a footstep breaks my tranquility, followed by a whole man, who steps out in front of me from a path to the right.

I stop, and so does he.

Of course it's Nathan.

Everything in me reacts predictably. My body does not choose joy. It chooses an adrenaline rush that makes my knees shake.

"Oh," I say, perhaps dimly, but this is the first time I've seen him out of context.

I've only ever seen him at the Pink Flamingo. Never anywhere beyond those hallowed walls, and here he is, seeming somehow taller and broader out in the wild.

"Going for a walk?" he asks.

This is near record-breaking friendliness for him, at least without the influence of alcohol.

"Yes. Though, not aimlessly. I'm just going to the grocery store for a couple of things." I lift my arm, which has a few canvas bags draped over it. As if he needs evidence.

"That's where I'm headed," he says.

I don't know if I should suggest we walk together or if that was the implication of him saying he was headed there himself.

I want to ask him that. I want to ask him a hundred things.

What I should want to ask him about is the fundraiser, and if he would be willing to help. Instead, I'm looking at the cut of his jaw.

"So," I say. "This is an unusual time of year for you to come to the motel."

I sneak a glance at him, and he's looking at me with a completely unreadable expression. So far, so predictable.

"I'm finishing something," he says.

"Oh."

Still maddeningly opaque, even if I *do* get it. I don't want to talk about my works in progress either.

I want to know. I don't talk to other writers in person that much. It's funny to me that of all the people I interact with regularly, I have a very big thing in common with him.

A new book? An unexpected deadline? Maybe an unexpected rewrite, which I've definitely had before. But it's not like he couldn't work on that somewhere else. Yet again, I'm perplexed by the mystery of him being here.

Honestly, he is to Rancho Encanto and the Pink Flamingo as he is to me in general. He's here talking to me; he doesn't have to be talking to me. He doesn't have to be here at all. He acts resentful about it, but there's clearly a reason.

I want to crack him open. I want to look inside his head.

I want to treat him like one of my fictional characters. I'm not sure I know enough about him to even do that.

I need his inciting incident. The thing that made him the way he is.

I have an author bio. That's it.

"Well, I'm glad that you . . ." I trail off. He's told me he didn't choose the motel. So maybe it's not the best thing to thank him for coming again.

I know, because it's in his bio, that he lives in Washington. On Bainbridge Island, actually. It's one of the things about him that has always struck me as extra strange. He comes to a place that is practically on fire during the summer, from the very rainy Pacific Northwest, and I would imagine someone like him doesn't especially care for the heat. That it would make more sense to come this time of year routinely. Getting a reprieve from dreary wet.

I can't imagine living in weather like that all the time. I don't mind a rainstorm, but without the sun, I think I would perish.

"How is . . . I don't know the older lady's name. The one who fainted during the fire."

"Oh," I say. "Gladys. She's doing great. She . . . she's good."

"Glad to hear it."

I decide maybe the weather and the Pacific Northwest might pass for neutral subjects. "So how is Washington?" I ask.

I can feel him looking at me and not looking ahead at where he's going.

"Beautiful," he says. "Particularly if you like rain, and the color green."

"I assume that you do?"

"Yes," he says slowly. "Generally."

"I'm from Bakersfield," I say. "I'm not sure if you're familiar."

"I pass through Bakersfield on my way here. It's where I cut over."

I map it out in my head. I've never been as far north as Washington. I've been to Portland, but only a couple of times, and it's been years. Still, I'm familiar with the long, desolate drive up I-5. So I know exactly what he's talking about. He takes the straight route on the interstate and goes east once he arrives in Bakersfield.

"You don't stay there, do you?" I ask.

"I have," he says.

"Well, my deep apologies. You know what they say about Bakersfield, right?"

He shakes his head. "I can't say that I do."

"The only time I want to see it is in my rearview mirror." He doesn't laugh. I clear my throat. "Anyway. There's a reason I left."

I'm okay talking about Bakersfield. I don't want to think about LA. Bakersfield is fine. Those are old wounds; they don't really hurt anymore.

"You weren't a fan?"

I'm surprised he's continuing this conversation. Maybe it's because it would be awkward otherwise. He can't exactly go sprinting up the sidewalk to get away from me. We're headed to the same location.

"It's really hard to say if I dislike Bakersfield or if I needed to get away from my mother."

He smiles ruefully at that, and it surprises me. "Difficult family," he says. "I'm familiar."

Excitement spikes in my veins. How ridiculous. I feel like I won a prize because he's continuing a conversation with me. Because he's given me a little piece of information about himself.

Difficult family.

Of course, given his whole aura, that feels like a foregone conclusion.

"Yeah. Kind of award-winningly difficult," I say. "But it's fine. It doesn't worry me at this point. It was much harder when I actually had to live with her. Now I have to call her on her birthday, and occasionally Mother's Day, and otherwise I think she forgets I exist. It works for both of us."

"Yeah. That's how things are best left with my dad," he says. I'm not sure what to think about him making that statement, but I realize it doesn't seem to cost too much. Like me, he's clearly made peace with the dysfunction there.

That surprises me, partly because I didn't take him for the sort of man who had made peace with anything.

"You don't live near your parents," I say.

He shakes his head. "No."

I'm not telling him where I was directly before I came here. There's missing connective tissue to both of our narratives.

We tell stories professionally, so I think we're both aware of it.

It's not drip feeding—that glorious authorial tool where you slowly weave your character's backstory into the front story instead of dumping it all on the reader in a two-page barrage of word vomit.

It's just withholding.

I don't know where he's from originally, or what brought him to the Pacific Northwest. I don't know what brought him here.

He's curating the things he tells me, and I can only respect it, because I do the same. Not just with him. With everyone.

There are great gaps in my own personal story I have no real desire to fill in for anyone. And haven't. Not here. I've learned that you can forge very meaningful friendships with people by focusing on the present.

I show up for the people here. For the people I care about. That makes my past immaterial, both to them and to me.

I look down, and then turn my head to look at him. I feel lost in what happened two summers ago. With the power outlet. When I had been mostly certain that he was going to kiss me.

That moment when I had admitted to myself that I wished he would.

"What's it like to be here in the summer when you are used to such rainy . . . cold weather?" I ask this because I don't know what else to ask without digging. Without making him shut down. I don't know how I know he will; I just do.

We're talking about the weather. If I were editing this story, I'd cut all this out since it's so clearly a stand-in for us discussing anything meaningful, but I feel locked up because I don't want him to get hostile and push me away again. I'm not sure he wants to have a deeper conversation with me *ever*.

"To me it's all the same," he says. "I don't go outside."

He's not being totally honest. He's outside right now. I can't decide if he's being deliberately difficult to end the conversation or what.

We arrive at the grocery store, a small sun-bleached building with automatic doors that groan when they open.

"I have . . ." I gesture toward the aisle that has wine in it. I make my way away from him, conscious of the fact that we aren't shopping together. For all I know, we may not even walk back together.

I want to push him, but I also don't want to make him be outright unkind to me. It's such a strange feeling, and I can't explain it. It's like I'm tiptoeing around land mines when I talk to him.

It's difficult.

I grab a couple of bottles of wine that come from vineyards within a hundred-mile radius. I also grab some fun drinks for kids. I want tonight to have a party atmosphere.

I happen to intersect with Nathan at checkout. He has a pile of frozen meals.

"You know we're having a barbecue tonight," I say.

"You mentioned," he says.

"I mentioned the movie," I say. "But there will be food. Of course you're invited. We kept on doing these barbecues after the fire and . . . it's been good for the community. You really helped that night, Nathan."

He doesn't say anything for a moment.

"I'll think about it," he says as the first of his meals begins to go across the belt. I can hear the *no* buried in the *I'll think about it.*

"I'm turning thirty-two," I say. "The same as your room number. I just . . . I thought it was funny."

It's been so long since I've gone on a date, or really had to work at getting to know somebody, that I feel like I might be out of practice. Because that was a very silly thing to say.

He lifts an eyebrow. "You're young."

I know how old he is because I've seen his driver's license. His birthday is in April, and he's closer to forty than thirty.

I'm not entirely sure if I should act like I know that or not.

"I'm trying to decide how weird it would be if I told you I know when your birthday is," I say finally as he pays.

He looks at me like I'm an alien. Which forces me to conclude I've made the wrong move.

He takes his receipt, and I'm ready for him to bolt out the door, but he lingers as my groceries start to go across the belt.

"I've seen your driver's license," I say.

"I'm aware of that," he says.

"I have a good memory."

Which is true, but it's also a little bit of a lie. Because I do specifically remember his, when it isn't like I know everybody's.

"I could have pretended," I say. "I could have pretended that I didn't remember."

The cashier, who I know, is looking at me and telling me desperately with her eyes to stop talking. But I'm in too deep.

"You *could* have," he says.

"Sorry I didn't hide my eye for detail."

He laughs, and I'm struck dumb by the sound because I've never heard it before. Then he takes my bags from my arms and begins to carry my groceries and his out of the store. I'm immobilized. Then I remember how to move, and I race after him.

He begins to head back to the motel, and I follow at a quick pace.

"If it were April," I say, "I would go to your barbecue."

Granted, I'm having a week of celebration dedicated to me, as I like to prolong such things, but he doesn't need to know that.

"Would that be customer service?"

"No," I say.

He looks at me like he has no idea what to do with me. It takes me a moment to realize that he's stopped walking. Like maybe *I've* immobilized *him*. I take an extreme amount of pleasure in that.

"So, what are you working on?" I ask. "New series, same series?"

"A never-ending project," he says. "But it's got to be done. I can't . . . It has to be done."

He really is being deliberately evasive. Which I guess is fair. He's a big deal. Maybe he can't talk about it. Maybe it's a secretive TV thing.

"I've watched your show," I say.

"Oh?" He looks surprised by that.

"Yeah, it's really good. The lead actor is hot."

He laughs. "I probably owe that guy a good portion of my earnings."

"Have you been on set?"

He shakes his head. "No."

"Did they invite you?" I ask.

"Yes, I've been invited. So I can really earn that honorary executive producer credit."

I laugh. I'm familiar with the vanity credit sometimes given to a big-name author. I worked on a lot of adaptations before I quit LA. I decide not to mention that.

"You haven't gone?" I ask.

"It might shock you to hear this," he says, "but I'm not very social."

I feign shock. "What? That is very unexpected information, Nathan. *Very.* Even with your lack of sociability, I'm surprised, because usually . . . I don't know. Having your books adapted is exciting. Or I think it would be for me."

"I appreciate it. I like the show. They do a great job. I guess I like what it's done for book sales but . . . I don't know. I don't need to go to Vancouver and stand around and watch other people work. I do my work shut in a room by myself. I'm not a team player. That's why I'm a writer and not in the military anymore."

I think he might be being intentionally funny. Which is unexpected.

"I like a group project," I say.

"You're a monster."

"I also like a solitary project. I enjoy writing my books on my own."

"Well, since you were so disdainful of my one a year, how many books a year do you write?"

I offer him what I hope passes as a conciliatory smile. "I didn't really mean that how it came out."

"I think you did," he says.

I sigh. "Four. Though they're only fifty thousand words."

"But you still come up with that many characters, that many plots, every year?"

I don't get into how fast paced we used to work in writers' rooms. How I got used to accepting different ideas, or feeling like things weren't perfect because I knew the important thing was getting it done, or compromising when compromises needed to occur. All of that had been really good training for writing the way I do.

"Yes," I say. "Though I always say ideas are the easy part. It's actually doing it that's hard."

"Agreed. So you write while you run the motel?" he asks.

"Yes," I say. "Between fielding requests from guests. I prefer to be busy. I'm also working on a Christmas tree for our Very Desert Christmas, plus organizing the whole auction." It's a good time for me to get that in there. Introduce the existence of it all. "It's a fundraiser this year, because of the fires."

"When do you spend time alone?"

This is a genuine question. He seems honestly concerned.

"Not often," I say. "I write in the front office between interruptions, or in the evening before bed. Generally, I'm alone then."

Always I'm alone then. But I don't want to say that, because that reveals I'm not sleeping with anyone, and it feels a little sad.

Especially to admit to him.

"And that works for you?"

"It's preferable," I say.

I like to have my characters' thoughts in my head. Or to have conversation happening around me. My own thoughts often feel hostile.

"Not my experience," he says.

"Yes. I have noticed that you prefer time alone."

I'm about to ask him if he wants to do an event. If he'll help me with the fundraiser. If he'll help me defeat my evil ex-boyfriend.

But right then, we arrive at the Pink Flamingo, and I can't bring myself to ask something of him for some reason. He's tired, and I can feel it. Not physically. There's something more, and I can't put my finger on it. He hands me my bags, and the beer.

"As amazing as your frozen meals look . . . Barbecue. In the courtyard."

"I'll think about it," he says.

Yet again, I already know he's lying.

I think he *did* think about it and he decided not to do it. I don't know how I know that. Like so many things about him, I just do.

"Great," I say. "Hopefully I'll see you then."

I say that like I don't know he's blowing me off.

Because I hope it will make him feel bad. A little bit.

As he turns to go, I notice a hardness to his expression that I can't untangle. Which is when I remember he's the same man who made me think he was going to kiss me when in fact he was just taking a power strip out of my hand. A man I thought I was . . . getting closer to, when after that near kiss, he didn't speak to me for the last month he was in residence.

I persist in trying to make Nathan someone I'm getting to know.

While he persists in making sure I can't.

CHAPTER ELEVEN

He doesn't come to the barbecue, and I can't say I'm terribly surprised. He's made it very clear he's antisocial and perfectly happy with that. Except he doesn't seem happy, not to me. Maybe I'm just nitpicking him because I'm in a state of anticipatory dread over tonight's meeting about A Very Desert Christmas and all I can think about is . . . if there will be more details about Christopher and his impending invasion on the town.

I'm fizzing with adrenaline by the time I pull into the little community meeting hall parking lot.

I take my seat next to Sylvia and smile. I'm still trying to look completely unaffected, even if I'm only marginally unaffected.

Right. You're definitely completely fine and not spiraling.

I feel this should not be deemed a spiral, since I'm at the meeting, I got my word count today, and I saw to my duties at the motel.

I'm functioning. So how can I be spiraling?

The truth is, I was fine before I got here. Really. I've been distracted.

The first portion of the meeting is dedicated to schematics. The schematics of everything being laid out in our venue. I planned this, so I'm more than familiar, and everything looks great, with every stall spoken for, and presales of tickets are still going at a brisk pace.

"The children's choir is doing a *fantastical* job," Reigna says when she gets up and it's her time to speak. "But that's not my surprise for you tonight."

She spreads her arms wide, the caftan she's wearing billowing around her like wings.

As if by the magic of her theatrics, a screen begins to lower from the ceiling behind her. There's a presentation, clearly.

Her theatrics really are wasted on a town this size.

They are a spectacle far too large to be contained in this room.

"We have a Zoom call scheduled," she says.

My heart scurries into my throat.

"With Christopher Weaver." There's a smattering of applause in the room, and I'm frozen. I haven't seen Chris in any capacity where he could also see me for three years. Yes, I have seen him on national commercials, and in promos for Christmas movies. But his twinkling blue eyes can't see me in those situations.

As Reigna begins to open her computer, as she clicks the link, my heart goes into a free fall.

What if he thinks I'm the reason he got the job?

I am undone by this.

I don't know what to do. I want to run; I want to hide.

I'm hoping Chris's vision is based on movement and if I freeze, he won't see me. If I run, I'll only create a bigger commotion, that I'm sure about. I barely breathe.

He won't see me.

He spent months looking through me when we lived in the same house.

I *hope* he'll look through me now.

Reigna clicks the link, and I curl my hands underneath my chair.

Sylvia looks at me. "Amelia. Are you okay?"

"Starstruck," I say, the word getting stuck halfway up my throat.

In this instance, the lie feels a little bit more painful than the truth. At least to my pride.

"I don't blame you," she says. "He's very handsome."

"Just . . . so handsome," I say.

I wish I were anywhere else. I wish a hole in the floor would open up and swallow me. This is an extremely dramatic reaction considering I was thinking I was somehow just going to get to the end of the month without dealing with this. Without talking to anyone about it, without admitting what the situation was.

But this is unexpected. I had no time to prepare for it. I was prepared for the fact his name might be brought up tonight, but I was not prepared to see him.

Even with hundreds of miles between us.

The camera flashes on the screen, and there he is, sitting at his desk, thankfully in a house that isn't familiar.

I'm so grateful we decided to sell.

If I had to see him sitting back in our place, it might have tossed me into an uncanny valley I couldn't scrape myself out of.

"Hi, everybody," he says, his smile wide, a Seacrest grin that's nearly painful to look at directly.

Everyone says hi, and I don't know how to react in a way that isn't self-conscious. I feel like a small burrowing animal that's been wrenched mercilessly out of its hole. I don't know what to do. Pull the fire alarm. Play dead. Try to blend in.

I opt for trying to blend in.

"Thank you so much, Christopher," Reigna says in her booming theatrical voice. "We are so appreciative that you have agreed to do a reading of the Christmas story for our event. Ever since we put your face and name up on the website, our ticket sales have skyrocketed."

I would love to see the demographic information on that. I'm quite certain that there are a lot of women from the ages of twenty to eighty-five who love clean, romantic Christmas movies and who are very excited to see him. I can't blame them. Looking at him now, I'm reminded of his appeal.

Honestly, seeing him in movies doesn't do him justice.

He's not a great actor. He's charismatic.

When he gets into casting rooms, he puts people under a spell. He's better in rooms than he is on sets, and in all the time since I've seen him, I'd forgotten.

"I'm really excited to get to come out and help," he says, sounding down to earth and accessible.

"Maybe you should tell us a little bit about yourself," Reigna says.

"Well," he says. "I live part-time in LA and part-time in Vancouver. Most of the movies I make are shot in Canada. I have two dogs."

He hates dogs. Or he did when we were together. This makes me angrier than it should.

"And I live with my fiancée, Natalie."

Natalie is not the woman he cheated on me with. For some reason, I thought his life had only gone on in terms of his career. I saw him taking off in Christmas films, and I actually haven't thought about his personal life even a little. I don't want to be with Christopher. At all.

But that doesn't mean that I'm prepared to sit here and hear about Natalie.

"We're expecting a baby in a couple of months."

Something inside me breaks and drifts away. Like a piece of iceberg falling into the sea. Emotional climate change brought on by his presence that I can't fight.

I knew he was out there living. I didn't think about it. I was focused on myself and my new life. It never occurred to me he might get married. It never occurred to me he would be having a baby. He's been building a career. He's so much more successful than he was when we were together—why isn't that all of it?

Why is there this too?

I can't breathe past it.

Like magnets drawn to the pain he causes me, right in that moment, his eyes connect with mine.

Absurdly, I *feel* it, I know that he sees me. Even though I know we are just a small bubble to him on this outward-facing laptop, I know he sees me.

I willed him to look at me with the force of my reaction, even though it was entirely nonverbal, even though I was motionless.

We were together for so many years, and right now those years are larger than all the years since.

He clears his throat, and his eyes get a faraway look, and I can tell he's focusing on the bigger picture now and pretending he didn't see me.

"Wonderful!" Reigna says.

They continue to have light banter, and maybe I'm on another planet.

Maybe I'm dead.

I'm not certain.

I just know that my hands are sweaty, and my lips feel cold. As soon as the Zoom call ends, the meeting adjourns, and I stand up quickly, ready to leave. Needing to leave.

"Do you need to go now?" Sylvia asks. "I wanted to ask you about—"

"I have to go check on something back at the motel. There was a . . . an electrical problem. In one of the rooms. Room thirty-two," I say, because all I can think of right now is Nathan and the power strip. And that he almost kissed me. While Christopher has a whole baby on the way. I have nearly kissed Nathan once. At least in my mind.

I'm not sure what hurts about this. I just know that it does. It isn't regret. I don't want Christopher. I don't want his life.

But it's something. The feeling that I missed a step somewhere and I'm not sure if I'm going to be able to find it.

"Oh. Did you have the electrical redone when you did your remodel?"

"No," I say. "I don't really have the money for that. Anyway. I need to go back."

I walk out to the parking lot quickly, and I block greetings like a champion, waving but not inviting further conversation. I'm shaking when I start the engine. By the time I'm halfway to the Pink Flamingo I realize I have no music on. I didn't plug my phone in. I'm just driving in the silence, letting the sound of my tires on the road and the wind whipping past the vehicle fill the car with a monotonous hum and rattle through my body.

I pull into my parking spot and get out. I'm walking into the courtyard when my phone rings. I look down at the screen.

Chris.

It still says his name just like that. Not Christopher Weaver. Or That Asshole You Used to Date, or Don't Answer, which would have been helpful.

Chris.

Like he calls me all the time. Like he's the only Chris it could possibly be.

"*Fuck.* Fucking. *Fuck.*"

"Are you okay?"

I whirl around, and there's Nathan. Standing there in front of the pool gate, looking genuinely concerned, but I realize I just screamed obscenities right in the open in my own motel, which is a family establishment.

I can't even be cool. I can't keep up my mystique. I can't lie.

"My ex is calling me," I say.

"Are you going to answer it?" he asks, crossing his arms over his broad chest.

"No," I say. "I don't want to talk to him. I don't want to talk to him so much that I moved to the desert. So there you go."

"Why is he calling you?"

"You know, I'm not even sure you would believe the story if I told you."

"Try me."

"Why?"

"Are you going to tell anybody else?"

It kills me that he knows I won't. "No," I say. "I don't want to tell anyone else. I'm not even really sure I want to tell you."

He stands there, looking at me, knowing, clearly, that I'm going to give in. I'm going to tell him.

"You know we're doing this Christmas thing."

"You mentioned that."

"He is going to be a featured speaker."

"Why?"

The logical question. Nathan is very good with logical questions.

"Because," I say. "He is the prince of cheesy Christmas movies. In fact, quite literally. He played a prince in one."

I've succeeded in shocking him. His face, normally either a scowl or carefully blank, actually shifts.

"Oh no," he says.

"Yes."

"He's an actor," Nathan says. I can't tell if that's an accusation or a statement of understanding.

"Yes," I say. "He's an actor. That's . . . how I know him. I used to . . . I was a writer. I mean, for TV. Sometimes I did adaptations. Mostly romance novels into movies."

Now he knows not just my name but all these other things about me.

I feel like I've lost whatever game we've been playing. If it was a game. Though, I can't really be upset about it, because I was about to lose my mind, and I really needed to tell someone.

I don't need to tell someone everything. In fact, I actively do not want people to know everything. But I needed to tell someone this, because clearly, I'm *not* handling it.

"Okay," he says.

"It was a very bad breakup. He was cheating, and I caught him. In our house. You know, it's so much more common for people to catch their partner cheating because of technology. Sloppy texting. Tracking someone's phone. Dick pics, even," I say. "It felt so analog to actually walk into my own bedroom and find him with another woman."

"Holy shit," he says. I'm gratified by his response. "Why would he do something that stupid?"

"In total fairness, he thought I was on a plane. My flight got canceled. Like right before I was supposed to get on it. I didn't text him. I just went home. Because I thought . . . I don't know, I actually thought he was going to an audition. I wasn't trying to catch him. I wasn't suspicious. At all."

In truth, I wasn't even thinking about it at the time. I wasn't thinking about him. That was another problem with the relationship, but it didn't justify his cheating.

"And you didn't tell anybody here that he was your ex-boyfriend."

"No. Because when I decided to be done with it, I really wanted to leave it behind. Really, really badly. I didn't want it to follow me. I didn't want him to follow me, you know? Only now he is. He was on a Zoom call tonight in the meeting. *He saw me.*"

"Oh."

"Yeah. Which is why he's now calling me. Likely because he wants to know if I'm responsible for him coming here. Do you know what—that is actually the most embarrassing thing. The most embarrassing thing is that he's going to think I wanted him to come here. It's too big of a coincidence to *just* be a coincidence."

"Why don't you call him back? Tell him you didn't have anything to do with this."

"That's even more embarrassing."

"How?"

"That lets him know I'm obsessing about it."

"You *are* obsessing about it," he points out.

"What would you do in this situation?" I realize this is an absurd question. I doubt this man has ever had his heart broken. I bet he has broken hearts multiple times, but I bet he isn't the one sitting around feeling sad. Or, even if he were, I bet the people he's been with wouldn't assume he was sitting around alone. He doesn't look like the kind of man who would ever be alone at night unless he wanted to be.

Granted, I have a front-row view to the fact he does seem to want to be. Often enough.

"I don't know," he says. "I don't have any relationships that ended like that."

"Lucky you," I say.

He huffs a laugh. A reluctant smile pulls at the corner of his mouth. "I know a little bit about pride, though."

"Okay then. Understand it from that perspective. This is possibly fatally damaging to my pride."

"Who is he? I want to look him up."

"No," I say.

"He isn't going to know," he says.

"But *I'll* know. I'll know that we stood here and googled him." I have kept myself from doing that for all these years because it's just too sad. He might never know, but I'd know.

"And you haven't done that?"

"No." I flash back to the things Chris revealed during the Zoom meeting.

Had I googled him, maybe I would've known all of that.

I keep myself on restriction with things like that. It's respectful. Or maybe it's just protective.

"Come on, I can figure it out by looking at the website for the event."

"I didn't know that you are evil," I tell him. He's already got his phone out of his pocket, and he's looking up the A Very Desert Christmas event. I don't even know what's happening right now. He is willingly engaging in conversation, and he is pushing for information.

"I'm appalled," I say.

"Are you?"

"Yes. I believe in digital boundaries."

"Is that right?" He looks up at me. "Amelia."

He says my name, and it hits me like an arrow.

“That is true,” I say, suddenly feeling warm. I clear my throat and look away. “I have . . . I have an idea.”

“Oh?”

I decide I have to stop standing in the courtyard talking to him where he can just leave. I have to stop doing this here. Here, we talk, he retreats. Here, we have a well-worn thing. I need to change the script slightly.

“I want to tell you more about this. I want to . . . Let’s go out.”

“What?”

“Desierto Encanto is less than a quarter mile down the road, and it’s a good bar. We can walk there. We can . . . have a conversation. I need a drink.”

“Okay.”

I didn’t really expect him to agree. Now he has, and I realize I have myself a date.

Kind of.

CHAPTER TWELVE

Fake Dating—a trope found primarily in romance stories, where the main protagonists pretend to be in a relationship (for business, for the purposes of impressing nosy family members, to incite jealousy). The fake relationship eventually becomes real.

Desierto Encanto is the best bar in town. There are neon cacti placed all around the room, and the walls are painted in a modern desert motif, with howling coyotes and sunset landscapes. The bar is a large slab of pink quartz, and the stools look like geodes that have been cut in half, all in blue, purple, and pink. I move up to the bar and take a seat on the stool and order two margaritas.

I look around the room, realizing that for as small as the town is, I don't know anyone in the bar all that well. Maybe because my best friend is a single mom who never gets to go out and my other friends are in their eighties and nineties.

This is the dating scene, which I've never been part of in Rancho Encanto.

"I'm sure you're wondering why I've called this meeting," I say, pushing the margarita toward him.

"I'm riveted," he says.

I tap the side of my glass. "You know, my ex-boyfriend . . ."

"The one I just learned about?"

"That would be him."

"Fucking fuck," he says, picking his margarita up and taking a sip.

"The very same."

"What about him?"

"He's going to help raise a lot of money for the town. By being here. By existing. He doesn't love this place, he doesn't care about it, he's just famous. Ish. And handsome."

"Okay," he says, fixing me with a gimlet eye, obviously suspicious about what I'm going to say next.

Rightfully so, in fairness to him. He should be suspicious of me.

I have ulterior motives.

"It occurs to me," I say, "I also know someone handsome and famous."

His gaze narrows. "Surely you don't mean me."

"I do," I say.

"What exactly do you think me being famous and . . . handsome is going to accomplish?"

For a full second all I can think is . . . *You'd make him so jealous.*

That's the stupidest thought. I don't want to make Chris jealous. But the truth is . . .

I feel like I landed myself in the middle of a weird Christmas movie with all the possible clichés. Except Nathan doesn't own a Christmas tree farm, and Chris would never ask me to go back to the city.

I wouldn't want him to.

I wouldn't want to move to Nathan's Christmas tree farm if he had one.

It's been established that the man doesn't want me, and also that he'd be too big of a project for me even if he did.

"I want you to consider doing a book event. At A Very Desert Christmas. If we can advertise that you're going to be there giving a literary talk . . . I think you would be a real draw."

"Right," he says.

"I know you don't love to do things like that. You're very private, you protect your identity. I get that."

"Yes, and you realize that everyone at the motel knows my actual name."

"Well, maybe half of them know your first name. Almost none of them use the internet. I'm pretty sure Albert is on the run from the law."

"Albert?" he asks.

For a moment, I'm about to explain who Albert is when I realize he's not actually asking, he's questioning the logistics of what I just said.

"Yes. Ruth told me."

"What did he do?"

"I don't know. Maybe he was a contract killer."

He shakes his head. "No. I've met contract killers. Albert is no contract killer."

"Point is," I say, "you don't have to worry about them going in broadcasting your identity. Probably anyone psychotic enough to look hard could connect the two."

"True enough." He shrugs. "I find that I give enough information that no one seems interested. They don't seem to realize that author me isn't . . . the rest of me."

"I don't do author events, so I don't know what that's like. Honestly, no one is interested in me. So I'm actually not trying to step on your privacy. I care about that."

"I really can't think of a good reason to say no to you, Amelia," he says.

I'm never going to get tired of hearing him say my name.

"That must devastate you," I say.

"You have no idea." He takes another sip of the margarita. "You really don't."

"I appreciate this."

"Don't be grateful to me," he says. "Please. I can't stand it. I'm not actually that great, and I certainly haven't been that great to you, so don't go thanking me for doing something that's really just my job."

The acknowledgment that he hasn't been very nice surprises me. He hasn't been, but he's been steadfastly acting like there's nothing weird happening, so having him just say that is kind of a shock.

"I'm going to be grateful to you," I say. "You don't get to tell me what to do. If you're going to own up to being difficult, don't be a new kind of difficult on top of it."

"I'll try, but difficult is about the only thing I know how to do these days."

Silence lapses between us for a moment.

"Apparently you also know how to write," I say.

"Some would say."

"What's your favorite kind of scene to write?" I ask.

He gives me long-suffering side-eye. "Fight scene."

I frown. "Least favorite scene to write."

"Sex scene," he says.

"Wow. I would be the opposite. Except I don't really write physical fight scenes. Also, your books have sex in them?"

"Have you never read one of my books?" He looks genuinely baffled by this.

"No. I don't tend to read male authors."

"That's sexist."

"It's not. Men don't read women. I've always felt like if I don't run out of women authors to read, I don't need to worry about getting to the men. Plus, men write sad books."

"It's not only men who write sad books. Women write very sad books sometimes. Also, I read women."

"Have you read me?"

"No," he says. "I don't read romance."

"I don't read dude books."

He stares at me. "Dude books?"

"Yeah. You know. What did you say about it a couple of years ago . . . acts of heroism, blowing shit up?"

"Don't underestimate the entertainment value of a good explosion."

I laugh and drain the rest of my margarita. "Since you're doing this for me, I promise I will read whatever book you're going to have sent to the event."

"Well, I await your review with bated breath."

"I'm sure you do."

He pays the bar tab before I can stop him, and I leave a tip. Then we walk out into the parking lot slowly, out of step, and I'm not sure which one of us is trying to break the connection. Or keep it.

We start heading back in the direction of the motel, in that same out-of-step fashion, like maybe it's a coincidence we're headed the same way. I don't know why he's doing it, I just know I don't want it to feel like I'm keeping him tethered to me.

Then I realize, I do need to tell him about the next meeting.

"There's a meeting tomorrow," I say. "Of the committee. I'd like for you to come and show your face and . . . I know I'm asking a lot of you."

He sighs heavily. "I was there the day of the fire, Amelia. I feel something about what happened here. You don't have to browbeat me every step of the way."

"I didn't mean to imply you didn't care. I just am aware that I'm taking liberties."

He laughs, short and hard. "Is this what you call taking liberties?"

I scrunch up my face. "Well. Not really."

My heart flutters, and anxiety rolls down my spine in a wave that makes me shiver.

I'm about to take liberties. I take a deep breath and decide it's time. "What if . . . what if Chris thought we were dating."

"What?"

"I'm going to look so unhinged to him. He's going to think I lured him here. I'm sure he already thinks that. But if you and I look even casually together at the event, and I'm sort of organizing your event and . . . It's going to be weird no matter what, but I won't have to do all kinds of explaining and he'll . . . He won't think I did it to try to get him back."

"You didn't, though," he points out. "You didn't even know he was coming."

"No!" I say. "I didn't, but be honest. Would you believe that? Like genuinely, would you believe that at all if you showed up at an event you got invited to and it turned out your ex-girlfriend was on the committee?"

His expression turns reluctant, and he lets out a long breath. "Okay, yeah, it would be hard to believe."

"See? We weren't casually dating. We owned a house together. I caught him in the act of screwing another woman. It's . . . it's a lot. Please."

"What would this entail?"

"Really almost nothing. We don't need to convince anyone here we're dating. It's just . . . you know, maybe some casual . . . touching, at the event." Just saying it makes my breathing ragged.

He stops walking. "You know . . . I'm probably the person least likely to ever involve myself in shenanigans. Yet here you are. Involving me."

I am, he's correct. There's no earthly reason for him to say yes to me. He pities me, and I get that. Though, right now I'm not above taking pity. I'm just surprised that he feels it for me. I can't get the way he talked to me that night out of my head.

"I know this means we'll be a little close." I clear my throat. "You did say you wanted distance."

"Jesus," he says.

"You *did* say that."

"Yes. I did. And you aren't letting me win that, are you?"

"You could say no," I point out. "You could continue to be the most antisocial man who ever lived, and you could say, *Fuck your fundraiser and fuck your feelings; your ex is going to just have to think you want to skin him alive.*"

He looks at me with no small amount of something that might be wonder in his eyes. "You're right. I could. Two years ago, I would have."

"But not now," I say.

"No," he says, and he starts walking again. "Not now."

CHAPTER THIRTEEN

As I drive Nathan to the meeting, I feel his discomfort amping up. He doesn't want to do this, and he is anyway. I've never met a man so grudgingly good. I've met plenty of assholes pretending to be nice, and plenty of assholes who don't pretend to be anything but what they are.

I've never met someone so grumpy, withdrawn, and generally cranky who seems like he's exploding with integrity he didn't ask for.

We have a little bit of time before the meeting, so I decide to drive to the other end of town first. "I want you to see what it looks like," I say.

He shifts in his seat as we drive through the ravaged part of town. On either side of the road there are hollowed-out apartments and restaurants. Some places are only ashen rubble. In the middle of one of the most severely burned-out spots, a fast-food restaurant still stands. Abandoned, but unharmed.

"This is awful," he says.

"Yeah," I concur. "I wanted you to see it because you've already agreed to help, so I know I'm not emotionally blackmailing you. But I want you to see how important it is. It's not just about me beating Christopher. Or about him not thinking I'm sad. This is what's left of this part of town, and unless we do something to help, it's not going to get better for a long time. I'll be honest, Nathan: I wanted a Christmas miracle. I think you could be it."

He rubs a hand over his face. "I want to help. But I'm not miraculous."

"You showed up at the right time," I say.

He's silent for a moment. "I can accept that."

We drive slowly back to the right side of town and into the parking lot of the meeting venue.

"This is it," I say as we pull up.

"This is . . . Well, there's a snake on the side of the building."

"You haven't gotten out in town that much, have you?"

"Not really, no."

"Well, welcome. I think it's charming."

"Yes," he says, regarding me closely. "I can see that you do."

We get out of the car, and I realize I may not have adequately warned him about how . . . quirky everyone could be.

But it's too late because we have entered the building and it is already filled with my fellow Rancho Encanto citizens.

I gesture to the front row, where there are still three empty seats, and try to fend people off as we cross the room. "He's part of my announcement," I say. "Just wait."

So we sit and wait for Sylvia to convene the meeting.

Once she does, I raise my hand. "I have business," I say. "I know we had everything settled for the event, but there's been a development."

"I hope it's not another Culkingate," Sylvia says.

"No. It's the opposite. Kind of." I stand up and make my way to the front. "It just so happens I have a guest staying in my motel who has agreed to put on an event. I believe it could attract a lot more people. We can sell tickets."

"Who is it?" Reigna asks, looking very concerned that I'm about to upstage her.

"Jacob Coulter," I say.

Nathan stands, and something in his bearing changes. It's like that moment when I recognized him from his author photo. There is a subtle difference in how he carries himself when he's being his author self. He might avoid things like the set of his own TV show, but he certainly knows how to behave when necessary. I wonder if that's why it's so important to him to have such a stark divide between his personal and professional life. Nathan doesn't perform for anyone. Jacob Coulter, on the other hand, really looks like he knows what he's doing.

"I've spoken with Amelia, and if it's something you think the venue can accommodate, we can sell a package that includes a signed copy of my newest book and a talk that includes a Q and A."

"That's amazing," says Sylvia. "Mr. Coulter, I am such a huge fan of your work."

Sylvia not only looks starstruck, she looks dumbstruck, because Nathan is gloriously attractive.

Then Reigna stands up, her hands clasped up by her throat like an indignant rodent, and I realize she thinks I'm stepping on her toes. She brought the celebrity, and I'm now competing with her celebrity.

I feel bad because I am. But only a little bad. Because if Reigna only knew . . .

"It's a wonderful idea," she says. "Though . . . what if he was *in conversation* with Christopher?"

I nearly die right there on the spot. "I . . . I don't know about that. As far as I know, Christopher Weaver isn't really associated with writing."

"He's in the entertainment industry," she says.

"Amelia is a writer," Nathan says. "I'd be happy to do an in conversation with her, but it makes the most sense for me to be talking to another author."

All eyes in the room turn to me. I can't even be irritated that he's outed me—it's not like it's a huge secret, and it would be churlish of me when I dragged him here.

"It's true. I am."

"Published?" Reigna asks, looking intrigued.

"Yes," I say.

"What do you write?" This comes from Bob.

"Romance novels," I say.

That gets a mixed bag of reactions from the crowd.

"Not under your name," Linda Calhoun says from the back. "Or I'd have seen it."

"I'm Belle Adams," I say.

"I've read you!" Linda says, much to my shock, though she seems to be the only person in the room who has.

"I think that's fantastic," says Sylvia. "It's a different kind of event and offers even broader appeal. We just need to rent another canopy and some more chairs, and there will be space right near the enchanted tree forest."

"I don't know," Reigna says. "It seems like Christopher should at least moderate."

I can think of nothing more horrendous. This is for Rancho Encanto and not me, though. Plus, it seems like no matter what I try, I'm getting myself more and more tangled up in the Christopher of it all.

"If he agrees to it," says Sylvia, "then he can moderate. But Mr. Coulter is right. It makes the most sense to have him in conversation with another author."

"All right," says Reigna. "I'll contact him immediately. Then we can update the website."

I haven't agreed to that at all, but I can't think of any reason that isn't the truth that I could possibly have for not wanting Christopher to moderate, so I say nothing.

"Excellent," says Sylvia. "We have two more weeks of ticket sales before the event, and we'll still sell tickets at the door. This is shaping up fantastically."

The rest of the meeting goes as scheduled, but afterward, I have to practically untangle Nathan's adoring fans from him. I'm very careful to not use his real name. By the time we get out of there and start heading back to the motel, I'm overwhelmed, and in awe of him.

"Thank you," I say.

He looks at me from the passenger seat. "Yeah. No problem."

Except I get the sense that it kind of is a problem, and he did it anyway. It *does* something to me. I just don't know how to process all these emotions. Because . . .

"I cannot believe that Christopher might moderate. That's like my actual nightmare."

"That does suck."

I laugh, because for some reason it seems like an uncharacteristic thing for him to say. I'm not sure that I should have an opinion on what's characteristic and not for him.

"I can have my agent call and say I don't want him to."

"Your agent would do that?"

"Sure. We've been together forever. He helps mitigate how much of an asshole I come across as."

"I don't have an agent. I submitted directly to the publisher. So I have no one to mitigate . . . me."

"Well. You don't need it."

I take that as the extraordinarily deep compliment that it is.

I park my car in the back lot, and we get out. We begin to walk toward the gate that takes us into the courtyard, and Nathan stops.

"So, your ex. He's the kind of guy that's egotistical enough to cheat on you, and most definitely then egotistical enough to believe you got him hired for this so that you could . . . what? Try to get him back?"

I study the ground. "I wouldn't necessarily say that he's an egotist."

"Why would you defend him at all?"

"I don't know that that's a defense of him. I was with him for years. He wasn't all bad. It was . . . There were circumstances. Anyway, a lot of my friends have been with men who cheated, and they chose to forgive them. I didn't. It didn't work for me. I think more people cheat than I realized."

He stares at me, those green eyes uncompromising. "He's a dick."

I'm taken aback by the vehemence with which he says that. I'm reminded again that I don't know anything about him. Not really.

I'm also reminded that I thought the same thing about him, more than once.

"I'm not happy with him," I say. "But I feel like I have to preserve some kind thoughts for him because he was somebody I devoted a significant part of my life to."

"Not in any way that counts," he says. "Or he never would have done that."

"Why does that matter to you?" I ask.

I want to know. I maybe even *need* to know why he's standing out here talking to me. He has come to stay at my motel for all these summers. And now, this Christmas. He has been here without actually being here all this time, with the exception of his heroism during the fire. I'm mystified by it. Baffled, even. Why does it matter to him what I feel about anything?

A couple of days ago I wasn't even sure he knew my name.

But he does.

He *does* know my name.

He walked with me to the grocery store. He's standing here now.

Casting aspersions on a man who isn't here to defend himself, not that I need him to be here defending himself. Not that I need him to get a fair chance. What I want to know is *why* this man thinks he has the right to criticize Christopher.

When it isn't like he's ever displayed an interest in me.

Or even the slightest bit of human warmth.

"Because," he says, "if I were in the position . . . I would treat you better."

"You don't really treat me that nicely."

Suddenly, the air shifts. It's like there was something between us, a veil dividing two worlds, and it's torn now. I can see him. Without any barrier.

What I see leaves me speechless.

His eyes are glittering with arcane fire. His whole body draws up tight.

I can see now the effort he is exhibiting in order to keep himself from moving toward me.

I can see that it isn't a lack of interest but an extreme amount of restraint that keeps him planted to the spot he's in.

I can see the truth.

It terrifies me.

I haven't touched a man in years. I've been protecting myself.

Sure, I stare at Nathan Hart from across the courtyard. I think about him when he isn't around.

I do not make decisive moves toward him because I know I will end up getting burned by the heat between us.

I was able to keep myself safe by only acknowledging that he felt the same in moments. Small spaces of time between one breath and the next.

But now I see it.

I see it, and I am undone. Stripped bare. Rendered speechless. Absolutely terrified.

"That's the problem," he says. "If I treated you nicely, it would only lead to one place."

My mouth goes dry. "Where . . . where is that?"

"I think you know."

I close my eyes. "I need to hear it."

I open my eyes just in time to see his gaze burning right through me. "It would lead straight to your bedroom."

CHAPTER FOURTEEN

Slow Burn—a term used in discourse, generally around romance novels, to describe a relationship that takes a very, very long time to go from spark to ignition.

I'm stunned by this admission, and yet I'm not.

I *knew* it.

I feel the same way.

But hearing him actually say it has me feeling overheated.

I don't know how I'd write this, and I hate that. Because I have nothing to distance me from it. I have no way to save myself by imagining some fictional blueprint.

"I don't treat you nicely because I don't have anything to give you that you could possibly want, Amelia," he says, his voice rough, using my name often and easy now, like he's proving to me how well he knows it. "I am a hollowed-out human being. I would never lie to you. But what I can offer you isn't something you'd want. I was doing you a favor."

I'm desperate for him to say more. Craving it now like cake or cocaine. I've never had cocaine, but I imagine wanting it feels like this. Yearning, desperately. Even knowing it won't end well.

He turns like he's going to walk away from me, like he's going to leave me standing there in the courtyard like he's done before. I'm not going to allow it.

"Don't," I say. "Don't say something like that and then turn away from me. Don't say something like that and then wander off. You have no idea who I am or what I want. Once upon a time I wanted marriage, but that's . . . over." My voice is hoarse, my whole body tortured from the pain of saying it, reliving it, admitting it. "That's who I was then. I came out here, and there hasn't been anyone since Christopher. No one. I've been by myself. All I've done is stare at you like some . . . horny teenager who doesn't know how to behave. You're right, a hookup, that wasn't what I wanted. Years ago. When I thought my life would look different by now. When I thought I would be different. We don't get to control everything, do we? What if that's the lesson of this place? I moved here to get away. I'm not sure that I did. My past is quite literally following me. But I'm different. For the last three years I have wanted something different. I have been happy with something different. I had nobody, not you, not anybody, protecting me these past three years." I take a deep breath, my lungs aching, my head pounding.

"Whatever you want, or whatever you don't want, own it. Just don't put it on me. Don't hold yourself back from me under the guise of protecting me, when you have no idea what I've protected myself from. I'm strong enough. The idea that you think you could break me with, what . . . your penis? That's hilarious. If you don't want to sleep with me, that's fine. Don't pretend it's an act of chivalry."

"I'm telling you that I think you deserve more," he says.

"Based on what? I didn't even think you knew my name."

"I have known your name from the first moment I saw you," he says, something in his expression shifting, getting leaner, hungrier. It awakens something inside me. "Just like I've known that if I ever let myself touch you, it would ruin us both."

"You have a lot of confidence in your prowess," I say, feeling brittle and more fragile than I would like to admit. Feeling hungrier than I would like to admit.

"Is it what you want?" His eyes are intent on mine, and I don't know how to respond to that. Do I want to be broken? No. But do I want him? Absolutely.

There is no question about that.

It's even more clear to me now that I've looked Chris in his eyes. Now that I looked back at my past and realized I don't want it anymore. It makes it even more clear that Nathan is what I want.

I've had plenty of opportunities to build fantasies around other men. There are a lot of men who travel by themselves and stay in my motel. There are a lot of men who are by themselves and have a drink at the tiki bar in town and who would definitely take the offer of a night of companionship.

Granted, many of those men are gay. However, the fact remains that if I wanted to, I could scratch a sexual itch with someone who isn't Nathan.

I want Nathan.

He is my Everest. A mountain I feel I need to climb. Like I have to do it to get to the view I'm actually supposed to see.

He is the summit.

I don't know why. I wish I did.

It would be easier if I wanted a man who isn't quite so . . . whatever he is. But I want him.

I'm tired of not having what I want.

"Break me," I say. It is a sensual demand. I'm not sure I know what it means. But I mean it. I feel it. Deep in the lowest part of me.

"Don't ask for that," he says, looking like he wants nothing more than to honor my unhinged request.

"Please," I whisper. "I want you. I want you to take me. I want you . . ."

I think about my room. With the bright-pink Christmas tree partly assembled, and I'm quite certain with my pajama pants lying on the floor.

I haven't been back since this morning.

I'm writing a sensual check my inexperienced ass probably can't cash.

He looks like he knows what to do. With his hands, with his mouth. I haven't even kissed him, and I'm sure of this.

I haven't even kissed him, and I am all but begging him to take me to bed. I realize the absurdity of this.

I also recognize that whatever he thinks about me, and it sounds like he has thought about me, I might not be what he's hoping for.

Maybe that's the real issue.

Maybe he doesn't want to spend the evening instructing a woman on how to properly handle him.

I nearly shiver at the thought. I really would like to learn.

Maybe this is some unhinged mixture of grief and rage.

Maybe I'm being fueled by only unhealthy things.

I don't care.

Right now, I *really* don't care.

"I don't want to hurt you," he says.

The joke's on him. I can't be hurt any more than I already have been. I'm not worried.

My heart has been shattered in just so many pieces that what I managed to do when I moved to Rancho Encanto was take those pieces and put them back together. Like a stained-glass suncatcher you might find in any of the gift shops around town. Beautiful, but not in its original condition.

It made me feel strong then. Even more confident. I wanted to shake my fist at the sky. The world could do its worst. The world already had. What did I have to be afraid of?

This is a turning point. In my healing, in my progress.

I have been here licking my wounds all this time. Suddenly it's like I'm okay with them. I don't need to protect them anymore.

I don't need to protect *me*.

"You could hurt me if you wanted," I say, taking a step toward him.

He makes a noise in the back of his throat that sounds pained. Like I'm the one doing the hurting.

He wants me. He could stand there making proclamations about how he's worried about me, how he's dangerous and bad for me and whatever else, but he wants me.

The man looks like he's in pain for wanting me.

I can't remember the last time that happened. I'm not sure it ever has.

I know for a fact that I've never wanted anyone like this before. It's not just sex. It's something more. Like now that I've found this well of sexual desire, of confidence, it's changed me. Turned me into the kind of sexual being I've never been.

Maybe this is who I was destined to be. A wild woman out in the desert.

Free and unfettered.

The kind of woman who might stand naked underneath the moon. Who would have one-night stands if it suited her.

I feel giddy at the thought.

But only if he doesn't reject me.

I don't think he will, though.

I don't think he's strong enough.

That makes me feel powerful.

"Kiss me," I say. "I've wanted to kiss you for nearly three years. I thought you were going to do it when you grabbed that stupid power strip from me. So kiss me now. You've already waited too long."

I don't expect him to move so quickly.

Fluid and without warning. He wraps his arm around my waist, and I can't breathe.

I'm held flush against the hard muscles of his body, and I never want him to let go of me. He hasn't even kissed me yet. But he's going to.

It's not in my head, and I don't think it ever was.

When he closes the distance between us, I'm undone. I curl my fingers around the fabric of his shirt, hoping that's enough to hold me up. It isn't. Thankfully, his arms are strong around me as his mouth makes contact with mine. As he kisses me, firm and sure, it's definitely the hottest thing I've ever experienced in my life.

His tongue sweeps over my bottom lip, and I gasp, opening for him. His tongue slides against mine, and I wonder if I'm going to set a record. Because suddenly, I feel everything, everywhere. My breasts are heavy, my nipples tight, I'm wet between my legs, and I feel close, so close to coming I can barely believe it.

I'm not fast. Historically.

Pleasure, for me, is a complex mechanism. I need time and space, and the chance to get my mind in the right place. He's in charge. Of everything. Of what I feel and how intensely I feel it. Of where my mind goes. It's him. Everything. My every thought, my every fantasy, right in this moment—everything is him.

He kisses me like there is nothing else he would rather do. Maybe like there's nothing else he even knows how to do.

He kisses me like it's his job. I kiss him back like I'll die if I don't.

Maybe I will.

Maybe I need this to live.

He cups my face, his hand large and rough, and he makes me feel small and fragile in a way that makes me feel special, not reduced, not like less. I'm somehow infinitely more. Free to melt against him, free to feel, more than I ever have been.

When we part, he's breathing hard, tortured, ragged breaths that assure me I'm not alone in this insanity.

"Your room," he says.

I feel that's best. It feels wrong to have sex with a guest in his room.

And we're going to have sex.

I have no doubt about that.

He takes my hand, and I lean against him as we skirt the edge of the courtyard, heading toward my room, which sits on the edge of the motel. We're in the shadows, and everyone seems to be away for the night anyway. Still, my heart is thundering, the thought of being caught . . .

It only fuels my excitement, actually. If I'm honest, everything about it excites me.

The little fizz of naughtiness I feel makes it all the better.

As if anything could make it less.

We walk, careful to avoid the light, and when we stop in front of my door, I reach into my purse and produce my keys.

We move inside, and I click on the lights a split second after I close the door, locking it firmly.

It is a mess. I didn't plan on having anyone come visit. I was right earlier when I wondered if I had left my pajama pants on the floor.

If he notices these things, he seems completely unbothered by them. He doesn't say anything about the room. He isn't looking around—he's hungrily taking in details about me. He claims my mouth with his.

He kisses deep, intense. He kisses like he doesn't care if it becomes more.

He kisses like the kiss is the destination. Slow and thorough. Perfect.

I begin to tremble as he moves his lips along the edge of my jaw, down my neck.

Then he stops. "Do you have condoms?"

I feel a flush of color work its way up my neck. "I do." I need to explain them, since I told him already that I've been celibate for a while. "I keep them behind the desk. You know, customer service. I have a few boxes in the closet in here. I keep some of my extra things here because it isn't like I have security."

He looks at me like I'm strange, but also wonderful, and I feel like that glance is one of the nicest compliments I've ever been given.

I move away from him, and I go to the closet. Open it. There are dryer sheets, some small boxes of detergent. There are travel packs of aspirin, small hand sanitizers, stacks and stacks of brochures.

And boxes of condoms.

I take out one of the large boxes. "Bulk protection," I say.

"Wow," he says. "People take these a lot?"

"Enough."

"They just come ask you for emergency late-night condoms?"

I nod. "Yes."

"You must see interesting things here."

"Oh yes," I say. "I get all the people-watching a person could possibly want."

I'm standing there holding a giant box of condoms, and I don't tell him that he has been my favorite people-watching for the past couple of years.

I set the box on the small round dining table in the room, and I don't even bother to try to tear it open delicately. Instead, I ravage it, then pull out a strip of condoms wrapped in blue and tear one off the strip.

Somehow, I don't die.

Of embarrassment or anything else. Because that's how much I want him. This positive conversation, the pause to hunt for protection, hasn't killed my excitement, hasn't dimmed the tension.

He's a stranger, but he's also a man I've seen, a man I've felt desire build for all these years. He is the perfect combination of things.

A mysterious lover, but someone I trust.

I didn't know such a thing could be possible.

He moves to me, cradling my face again as he leans down for a kiss. He's so much taller than me. He makes me feel so small and delicate.

I move my hands up his chest, around his broad shoulders, up the back of his neck. I push my fingers through his hair.

He kisses me deep. I'm still holding on to the condom, clinging to it for all I'm worth.

Clinging to him.

The kiss becomes feral, and he moves his hands down my waist, to my hips. He holds me hard and pulls me against the incontrovertible evidence of his arousal.

I nearly swoon.

He moves his hands down farther, along my thighs, and squeezes me tight, lifting me off the floor and urging my legs around his waist.

This is the kind of acrobatic sex I didn't think was actually real, but I can't say that, because he's still kissing me. He takes us both to the bed, exerting perfect control as he lays me down slowly onto the mattress, pressing me into the softness, trapping me against his hardness in the most delicious way.

With one hand, he grabs the back of his collar and strips his shirt off, revealing the body that has left me speechless on more than one occasion.

Perfectly defined muscles covered with just the right amount of hair. I breathe out, watching as I press my hand to his rock-solid pec and move my fingertips down his abs.

This is like a love scene I would write. I want to capture every detail, every moment. The way my skin looks against his. The way I'm soft, the way he's hard. The way I'm smooth, the way he's rough.

How his whiskers scrape across my skin when he kisses me. Leave the whisper of a burn behind.

The guttural sounds he makes as he tastes me, as he kisses down my neck, my collarbone.

The rustle of fabric as he takes my shirt off, the rush of relief as he unhooks my bra with one practiced hand, proving me right about his prowess with one easy motion.

He looks at me like he's a man who's been crawling through the desert outside our door and I'm an oasis. I have never felt so proud to be naked in front of a man before.

I had gotten to a place in my long-term relationship where I knew Chris appreciated my body and I didn't have to be self-conscious.

The way Nathan Hart looks at me makes me feel like I'm a gift.

I've never felt anything like that before.

I've made myself into nothing. I can't remember the last time I've felt sexy or like my body should feel good. But I feel it now.

I've never felt like this.

I have felt—in the deepest part of myself—like something broken for the past three years. A failure. Empty.

He looks at me like my body is precious. He looks at me like my body is perfect.

I can't look at my body that way.

I barely look at it. I don't look in the mirror when I get out of the shower. I don't examine my figure to see how my bathing suit fits. I ignore my body, if I'm honest.

It's probably why I've been celibate.

Because I pretend it isn't there.

I withhold joy from it. I withhold satisfaction.

And he looks at me like *this*.

I don't want to cry, because even though I'm not super experienced with passionate sex-only interludes, I know that men don't want women crying in the middle of them.

So I wrap my arms around his neck and kiss him. He growls, all wild, and I love it, and then he kisses a line down my neck, straight to my breast, sucking one nipple deep in his mouth. I arch up off the mattress, my pleasure too great to be contained. I cry out, and I'm not even embarrassed. I don't care if anyone can hear me through the walls. I don't think they can. If so, I probably would have heard my fair share of sexual encounters on the other side of that wall over the years, and I haven't.

But I don't care either way.

He blazes a trail down my body with expert kisses and pushes his hands into the waistband of my pants and underwear, drawing them down my thighs. I lift my ass off the bed and help him get it off—all of it—because I need to be naked with him. Against him.

Then he's pushing my legs apart and his mouth is on me. He feasts on me like he's starving, but I'm the one who's ravenous. Desperate for more. For everything. His mouth plays havoc with me, his fingers stroking me, taking me higher, further than I've ever been.

When I shatter, it isn't with a rush of completion. It's like a wave that crashes over me and doesn't stop. I am shaking, and it's relentless. It is both the most satisfied I have ever been and the most desperate for more I've ever felt in my life. As I'm riding out the last vestiges of my orgasm, he moves up my body and kisses me. Then he moves away, just for a moment, and is undoing his belt buckle, taking off his jeans and underwear faster than I've ever seen any man move. He is . . .

I give thanks.

He is the most beautiful naked man I have ever seen. Thick and long. Undoubtedly the most incredible specimen I've ever beheld.

I know a moment of trepidation because it has been a long time, but the little wicked part of myself that has risen up aggressively since he first kissed me in the courtyard is thrilled. She wants to feel it. She maybe even wants to hurt. So that she knows. That she's claimed. That it's real.

My breath catches as he tears the condom open and rolls it down his impressive length. Then he's back, kissing my mouth, sliding his hand around to cup my ass as he lifts me from the bed and presses the head of his cock to my slick entrance. He goes slow. I want to beg him to go faster.

He whispers things against my mouth, and I can't understand them. It's like he's praying, or saying a spell that keeps me held in thrall.

I take him, inch by glorious inch.

It's everything. So is he.

When he's inside me, all the way to the hilt, he presses his forehead to mine and rests just for a moment. I'm strung out.

Desire is building deep, and I'm desperate to come again.

He begins to move, withdrawing slightly before thrusting home.

Again and again.

I never want it to end. I want to live in this moment for as long as I possibly can.

His movements become more erratic. He becomes less careful.

I encourage him. I beg him for more. My fingernails turn into claws I scrape down his bare back, over the sculpted muscles and that gorgeous skin.

He fucks me into the mattress like I'm unbreakable and precious, and I want to be both. For him. For me.

I have never felt stronger. I have never felt more beautiful.

I bite his lip, and he growls. He grabs my wrists, holding them fast in one hand as he moves them roughly over my head, pinning me down as he continues to take me.

"Nathan," I say.

The tendons in his neck stand out, his teeth clenched tight. I can see that he is fighting to hang on to control.

Good. I want him to lose it.

"Yes," I say. "Fuck me just like that."

"Brat," he grits out.

"Please."

"Not yet," he says.

He rolls his hips forward, and I feel myself getting closer to the edge.

I didn't think I was going to be able to come again, but now . . . Now I don't think I'm going to be able to hold myself back from it.

He slides his hand between our bodies and moves his thumb over my clit, pinching lightly, and I'm done. I fly over the edge. This time when I shatter, it's complete, and he takes it as permission to let go.

He comes on a growl, his mouth against mine, and he trembles.

Just a bit.

I rejoice in the reality that I made this mountain of a man shake.

He moves away from me, and I'm dimly aware of him going into the bathroom. I fling my arm over my face.

Part of me can't believe we actually did that.

Another part of me can't believe it took so long.

As I lie there looking at the texture on the ceiling, I can admit to myself that this had a feeling of inevitability to it.

A necessary step in my development. Maybe in his. But I don't let myself wonder about that. I want to revel in what it means for me. At least, right now.

When he emerges from the bathroom a moment later, he stands there, naked and perfect, and maybe a little bit uncomfortable. Like he doesn't know if he's supposed to come back to the bed or get dressed and leave.

"If you're looking for guidance on the protocol for all of this, I'm afraid I'm not the person," I say. "It's not really my area of expertise. Hookups, I mean."

"Mine either," he says.

I have trouble believing that. He is an outrageously skilled lover, and I feel like maybe it's that thing decent men do when they downplay their prowess and body count because they don't have anything to prove.

"You really should write more sex scenes," I say. "Or enjoy writing them more because . . . goddamn."

I let out a ragged breath.

"I needed that," I say. "I want you to know, you don't need to feel bad for me or obligated to me in any way. I am not going to have a breakdown about it or go chasing you through the yard with a boiled bunny."

"Jackrabbits everywhere just breathed a sigh of relief," he says.

I didn't expect him to be amusing.

I find myself smiling. "I just mean it doesn't have to be weird. You don't have to avoid me. You don't have to . . . walk by me tomorrow and pretend it didn't happen."

He moves to the bed and sits down, though he leaves a bit of space between us. "I wouldn't do that."

"You've done it before, though," I say. "Like I said, I thought you were going to kiss me when you got the power strip from me."

"Yeah. I thought I might too," he says. "I didn't because I was trying to avoid this. I'm very aware of what I can't give you, and we've been through that already. You said not to worry about it. So I won't."

"Well. Maybe we can . . ."

"I promise I'm not going to act like I don't know you," he says. "But tonight I'm going to go back to my room."

"Oh," I say, feeling a little bit blindsided.

"I think it's best for tonight," he says.

"Okay."

"We don't need to decide what it is," he says.

I nod. I *agree*, because if we try right now, maybe he'll say it can only be once. If we try right now, maybe I'll beg for more.

I don't really want either of those things to happen.

I watch him get dressed, and I try to cling to all the good, empowering feelings I had just a few minutes ago.

"Good night," he says before he slips out the door. I flop back onto the bed, my heart thundering.

I slept with Nathan Hart. I gave myself that gift. Though as I lie here, I am acutely aware that I don't know any more about him now, other than how he looks naked, than I did before.

But I feel beautiful. I choose to focus on that.

At least when Chris comes to town I'll be able to walk around with this feeling inside me.

It might not have changed everything, but it definitely changed *some* things.

I have to figure out how to be happy with that.

CHAPTER FIFTEEN

Let's Get It Out of Our System—when the protagonists in a romance novel agree to keep having sex until their desire burns itself out.

When I wake up the next morning, I realize everything that happened the night before.

I am stunned. Completely motionless, lying naked in my bed.

I had sex with Nathan Hart.

I've spent years carving out a life for myself, a life that's just about me. Now suddenly there's this man.

Like he hasn't been a factor for years.

Right. Well. A fantasy object, yes, but nothing real.

I get up and wrap myself in one of the pink cotton robes that hang from a peg on the wall, and then I make my way over to the coffee maker and choose the brightest, pinkest mug I have to start my day. These things are normal, and I find I'm in desperate need of normal at the moment.

I pick up a coffee pod and pop it into the machine, and I'm stopped midmotion by a knock on the door.

I freeze.

Nobody knocks on my door. I don't advertise my room number to guests. They can call me at the number I provide, and I can be paged from the front desk.

My long-term inhabitants, of course, know where my room is, but I know who this is.

I know it immediately.

I go to the door, flexing my hands, trying to act like a normal human, trying to collect myself, trying to decide whether I think there is any hidden meaning to the fact he's here.

I scrunch my face and open the door.

Thank God it's *him* and not some rando, because I'm only wearing a robe.

He shaved. He's in fresh clothes. He looks new and glorious, and not like the last vestiges of the night are still clinging to his skin. I happen to know, without checking a mirror, that I look a wreck.

"Good morning," he says.

"Morning," I respond, moving away from the door, making it clear he's allowed inside.

He takes the hint and comes in.

I feel defenseless. In my robe, completely naked beneath. He's wearing armor, and not the kind he often does. He is enshrouded in taciturn distance. Rather, he looks like a normal—albeit an extraordinarily handsome—man I might meet anywhere. A man who could have done anything last night. A man who probably didn't have world-destroying sex.

I say nothing because he's the one who came here.

He's the one who has a plan.

If I say something, there's no telling what it will be. I feel I would have no control over the words that might tumble out of my mouth. I don't trust myself.

"I'm sorry about last night," he says.

I lift a brow. "About the sex or the abandonment?"

"The abandonment. I'm not sorry about the sex, even if I should be."

"Good. Because I'm definitely not sorry about the sex."

I haven't decided if I'm sorry about him leaving. I could cope with it at the time. I recognized the need for a little bit of distance then.

Right now, though, I feel a little bit *raw* about it.

"Is that diner in town any good?" he asks.

If he's using me as a brochure, I'll punch him. Especially since he's never shown any interest in my brochures before.

"Get Your Kicks?" I ask. "Yes. Though even if it weren't, it's the only diner."

"Do you want to have breakfast with me?"

I'm surprised by the overture, especially after the way he left last night. Hell, he has a pattern. Get close, pull away. Often aggressively, so this is . . . a pleasant-ish surprise.

"We don't need to go out."

He looks around the room, and his voice pitches lower. "We do."

I blink, and my stomach pitches sharply. "Oh. Oh. I need to get dressed," I say.

"I'll wait outside."

He's trying to avoid sexual situations. He's trying to put distance between us without being an asshole. I don't really want him to do that.

Something bold overtakes me then; I'm not sure what it is. I'm not sure if it's bravery or insanity. I'm not really sure I care. I put my hands on the belt of the robe and undo it. "It doesn't matter," I say. "It's nothing you haven't seen before."

I turn away from him, my heart pounding. I'm wondering who this woman is. I guess she's the woman who threw caution to the wind last night and kissed this man, took him to her room, even knowing it was going to be sex and sex only. Even knowing that I struggle with it.

This wasn't like anything else I can compare it to.

Not to the previous one-night stand I attempted to have, or to any past relationship. Not just because it was fantastic. Because I feel so different.

I drop the robe, and I feel his gaze burning into me as I make my way over to the closet and pull out a dress. I retrieve some underwear and a bra from the stacked drawers I have in the closet, and I retreat into the bathroom to put them on, because my boldness has reached its end.

When I emerge a few moments later, I'm dressed, with my hair arrayed into a more decent shape, a small amount of makeup on my face.

"Breakfast it is," I say.

"Really, that's what you're going to play now? Like you didn't just take your clothes off in front of me?"

"It wasn't a lot of clothes," I say. "I didn't know you were a prude, Nathan. Many places in the desert are clothing optional."

He moves toward me, intent in his green eyes, and lowers his head like he's about to kiss me, but then he stops. Maybe he's waiting for my permission. I decide not to give it to him. To see what will happen.

He moves away from me and then steps to the door. "I can drive us," he says.

I feel a little giddy rush because I've never ridden in his car, obviously. Even though I've seen it. A hunter-green classic car with a rounded shape that reminds me of a British spy movie.

It is deeply him, somehow. Not just because it matches his eyes.

I follow him out to the parking lot, and I get into the passenger side, brushing my hand over the cognac-colored leather as he makes his way around to the driver seat.

"Why breakfast?" I ask as he buckles his seat belt and pulls us out of the parking lot.

"Because I thought we should talk, not fuck," he says.

I didn't think real men talked this way. I just thought I wrote them saying hot, dirty things like that, but he's killing me.

"Fucking sounds like more fun," I say.

Why not be this person? Why not be brave and say exactly what I want?

Or at least, all the things I know I want.

"Agreed," he says. "But I think if it's going to happen again, there need to be some ground rules."

"Ground rules?" I ask, looking in his direction. He isn't looking at me, though, because he's driving. "That sounds more like a military school than a fling."

I'm the one who introduces the word first. *Fling.*

I'm the one who tries to name it. I'm not sure it fits. But it seems like the right label. Light, but not contained to one night. Something that's easy.

I've never had one of those before. Just a college boyfriend, a one-night stand who left me unsatisfied and sad, and a relationship that scooped me out like a melon and left me hollow and alone.

Maybe it's time for something I haven't done before. It seems like a step in my development, maybe.

"Games aren't fun if you don't know the rules," he says, but his voice is not light.

"Oh. Well."

"It's best to be clear, I think."

"Well, you'll have to forgive me—I don't know the protocol for . . . flings. It's a fling, right?"

"I think that's the discussion that needs to be had," he says.

I wrinkle my nose and rest my elbow against the window as we make our way into town. The diner is painted a bright aqua color, with a large neon sign that stands proudly beside it, pink and yellow and retro. GET YOUR KICKS!

"It's a tourist attraction," I say as we pull into the parking lot.

"Oh good. I was hoping to get some tourist action in."

I laugh. "You aren't. Which is one of the very strange things about you. You're here, but you're not a tourist."

"No," he says.

I feel those walls starting to go up again. Ridiculous, actually, because we had sex, and he's still acting like these basic comments are intrusive.

But I have to remember that he's the one who showed up at my door this morning. He's the one who felt like he needed to make the connection. He's the one who . . .

I just need to relax and let him take the lead here. I'm not good at that. I want to control things. I recognize that.

It's one reason I left the place I lived when I went through my dramatic breakup. When I decided I needed to heal. I needed to be in absolute and total control of all the things around me. I couldn't help it. It's who I am. So, I need to let him be the one to make the move here. I need to let him be the one to take charge. Because he's the one who knows what he's thinking; I don't. I don't want to change whatever he intends.

I want to let it play out. That, I think, might be growth. Or at least something like it.

We walk into the diner and are greeted by the waitress I don't know, which is sort of a relief because it will minimize speculation. We get seated at a small, shiny table for two nestled in the corner and are handed menus the size of small novels.

"I personally like the omelets," I say. "But the pancakes are also great if you like a sweet breakfast."

"I don't. I'll do an egg-white omelet, if they have it."

"They can do that," I say. "They just might laugh at you."

"Me and my cholesterol are okay with that," he says.

He doesn't look like he could possibly have cholesterol problems, but I'm not a doctor. I have, however, examined every square inch of his body.

Still, it is something of a relief to know he doesn't look that way on accident.

Based on the frozen meals he was buying, I wouldn't have necessarily guessed he was health conscious.

The waitress swings by our table again. She has two mugs and a pot of coffee in her hands.

"Coffee?" she asks.

We both say yes.

"Do you know what you want to order?" she asks.

"Veggie omelet," he says. "Egg whites."

She looks at me with a hint of judgment in her eyes, and I feel validated by this.

"The farmer's omelet," I say. "The whole egg. Extra cheese."

She takes our menus and leaves.

He looks at me, and I look back.

"Here's the thing," he says, as if he can't hold it in anymore. "I'm leaving after Christmas. I'm not coming back."

I'm shocked. After three summers, I was starting to think he'd always be my summer.

"You . . . You're not coming back this summer."

"No," he says. "I don't need to. I . . . This is the last time I'm coming. So anything after December . . . It's impossible."

"Right," I say.

Then I just wonder, because I have to, if this is why it finally happened at all. He knew he wasn't coming back. He knew he wouldn't have to deal with me again after this. Maybe I have no right to be mad about that. The truth is, we're a loose end. I definitely felt it. Like he was the summit I needed to climb. Really, in more ways than one. So maybe it's fair. It's okay that . . . the desire to finish with me was the inciting incident. It's okay that it was the reason. The final ingredient that created this alchemy.

"I'm more than willing to play the part of doting boyfriend to piss off Fucking Fuck, because it sounds to me like that guy deserves to die mad."

He does. Nathan really has no idea.

"I don't know that he's going to care that I'm dating someone three years later, when he's engaged to be married, but I just don't want him thinking that I'm angling to get him back. Because I'm not. I don't care if he's jealous or if he even really makes note of it, honestly, I just don't want it to look like I creepily orchestrated some weird small-town fantasy. Can you imagine? This man, the king of Christmas movies, shows up to my small town, and there I am, in my little Christmas tree grove, like I plan on trapping him in Hallmark Hell. No thank you."

"Okay, that's fair. I get where you're coming from."

"What I want is to keep my pride, and this will help me do that. While you help raise money for the town. Is it petty of me to want to have you raise more money for the fund than he does?"

He shakes his head. "Well. Yes. But there's really nothing wrong with being petty, especially if you're raising money for the town either way."

"Right!" I say. "That's also what I thought."

I want to ask him why he's not coming back. It must have something to do with whatever he needed to write here. Which he clearly doesn't want to go into.

I tap my finger against the ketchup bottle.

"So . . . somewhere in all this," I say, "we'll continue to have sex."

He looks at me across the table, and right then, the waitress returns and sets two plates down in front of us. He looks up at her, then back at me.

"Thank you," I say.

I continue to stare at him as the waitress walks away.

"Yeah," he says. "That was the subtext."

"Let's not do subtext," I say. "I feel like subtext is for long-term relationships and not for sex between relative strangers. Clarity. That would be good."

I can respect his boundaries. The ones he throws up every time I get too close. But I need him to be up-front. This isn't a book, and I can't read his thoughts. I wish I could. I wish I could get a nice monologue about what exactly he's thinking.

I can't even imagine what I'd write for him right now. Mostly because I'm afraid it would hurt my feelings.

She was looking at him with hope, the kind that made him pity her like she was a small, tragic creature. The sex had been fine, but he was longing to escape . . .

Yeah, no, she wasn't going to continue on with that.

"Yeah," he says. "I can do clear."

"Can you?" I ask.

"Yes," he says. "I can."

"Great. So this is like a holiday fling."

"Yes. Big fan of flings."

For some reason the way he says that is hilarious to me. Mainly because I can tell . . . This man has never done a casual thing in his life. I don't know why I'm so certain of this. I think it's the intensity. He's just way too intense for anything light, airy, or flippant.

Except I think he's maybe trying to do that with me, and I'm not sure how I feel about that.

"So does that mean you're going to involve yourself in the activities around the motel?"

"Doubtful. I have something to finish. It's . . . kind of personal. I . . . I'm actually not trying to be insufferable."

"It just comes honestly," I say.

"Yes," he says. "I am a naturally insufferable asshole. It is like breathing for me."

I laugh at that too, even though I get the sense there's more truth to it than humor.

"Will you come to the dive-in movie?"

"Tomorrow?"

"Yes, tomorrow."

I don't get into the subject of schedules. Like, are we going to have sex every night? Part of me hopes so. Another part of me has no idea what I would do with that much sexual activity after such a long dry spell. I fear it could leave me physically damaged. I also fear I might decide it's worth it.

That's just where I'm at, at the moment.

It's a strange thing. I'm emotionally compromised, but I'm also so physically exhausted that it's difficult for me to sort through the hierarchy of needs here.

Sex for me has generally been part of a relationship, and even then, the most important component to me has always been maintaining emotional closeness through the physical connection.

This is something else. Something I've never experienced before.

He rocked my world. What I really wish is that I could focus solely on that. That I could see him as nothing more than a gorgeous body that has been inside mine and made me feel pleasure like I've never known before.

I wish I didn't care so much about him.

That would be nice. It just isn't me. I can appreciate that he was kind to set boundaries. To set an intention, even if those intentions leave me feeling slightly wounded.

"I need to get some work done," he says.

"Yeah, same." I do my best to lighten my tone. "I kind of run the place where you're staying. I'm not sure if you know that."

"Do you have writing to do today?"

"I have a word count to get every day," I say. "What do you do?"

"I have scenes and I work on them, and when they're perfect, I move on, but I don't think of it in terms of word counts or page counts. It comes together that way."

"Gross, Nathan. That's so unstructured it offends me."

"I'm an artist, I guess."

I laugh. "Ohhh."

"And you always meet your deadlines?" he asks.

"Deadlines turn me on," I say.

"What else turns you on?"

My face gets hot. "Your omelet is getting cold."

I take a bite of my own fiercely.

There is a tone shift, and it's like he's a different man. Like he managed to pull himself out of whatever space he'd been in just a few moments before.

His emotions are so intense I can feel them like the changing of the tide. Even if I can't quite get a handle on what they are.

"Actually," he says, looking at me, his omelet half-gone now. "Part of what I was going to do today was go to Joshua Tree. Research. And I was wondering if you wanted to go."

"So you are writing something set here," I say, rather than answering his invitation.

"Kind of," he says.

"Why are you so vague?" I pound the table lightly.

"Because I can't . . . I can't talk about this one."

I scowl. "Are you afraid you'll scare your fragile boy muse away, or is it actually a contractual thing?"

"Neither. I just don't want to talk about this while it's a work in progress."

"But you're involving me."

"Not really."

"You invited me."

"You didn't accept."

"Okay, I accept. And I feel involved."

"Your feelings aren't facts, Amelia. I don't know if anyone has ever told you that before." He says that in a totally teasing way, but honestly, he has no idea how well I know that.

Enough that it dampens a little bit of my enthusiasm.

But he's asking me to go with him to Joshua Tree, of all places, and I'm more than happy to drop everything to make that happen.

"I just need to do a couple of things at the motel."

"What about your word count?"

I lift a brow and make direct eye contact with him. "I left my hero sweating, and shaking, with a hard-on. It would be very mean of me not to continue the scene today."

His eyes change, and he leans forward, a conspiratorial look on his face. "I can relate to him."

"You're the one who left me last night."

"I'm sorry about that," he says. "I had to . . ." He looks away from me, and I can tell he doesn't want to finish that sentence. "I had to think about some things."

"Oh." My response sounds flat. I feel flat. I don't know what he means by that. I don't understand why sex with me required great contemplation after, but worse, he doesn't want to share it with me.

"I don't know how to explain it," he says, his voice rough.

That does it. Things click into place for me.

Heartbreak. I get it.

I get it, because it echoes inside me. Not present heartbreak, but the past.

Trying to sort it out and figure out who you are in the present.

It's way too familiar to me.

I could push for his story.

I already know he's not coming back, is the thing. I already know that this will end. So what I also know is that now, I want things to be good between us.

I want us to be my new bubble. The bubble Rancho Encanto can't be because Chris is invading it.

I want to be his bubble.

I get the feeling he doesn't have one.

He's letting me in, a little at a time. It works, I assume, because he's not letting me into a place I need to live. I don't need to worry about how dark it is once I'm inside.

There's a time limit on this. The clock is ticking.

But today, we have this.

He's going to pretend to be my fake boyfriend, I'm going to pretend that everything is great and that looking at Christopher doesn't hurt me. And we are going to my favorite national park.

All is well.

For the moment.

I'll take that.

CHAPTER SIXTEEN

I'm lacing up some hiking boots when there's a knock on my door. It's not him, I know, because it's fifteen minutes before we are supposed to meet, and the tenor of the knock is different.

I open the door, and it's Elise.

"I hear that you came into the diner this morning with a tall and dangerously gorgeous man," she says. "Not my words."

"Who told you *that*?"

"Mary."

Mary, the owner of the diner and Elise's former boss. I didn't even see her there.

"Mary is a snitch," I say.

"Tell me," Elise says, her eyes glittering brightly.

I sniff. "I may or may not have had breakfast this morning with Nathan, and now we're going to Joshua Tree."

"Oh my God," she says, her eyes going wide. "You slept with him."

"I did," I say, unable to keep a somewhat smug smile off my face.

"Good for you," says Elise. "I thought you were a nun."

"The same can be said about you," I say.

"I have a reason," she says.

She means Emma.

I know she's not meaning to be hurtful. How could she? She doesn't know.

I haven't told her, and that's my choice. My way of coping. When I got to Rancho Encanto, I was floundering. Swimming against the tide of my life. I set up the motel, I got my life in order, and it's felt really nice to lie here in more still waters . . . floating.

I realize it's been a lot of floating. I've found a writing routine that works. I don't deviate from it. I love what I write, but I have other ideas. Still, writing something new, finding an agent, all of that sounds like paddling, and I'm resistant to it.

Telling anyone here my story sounds like paddling.

I turn my focus to her.

"Yeah. I know you have great reasons. But don't you ever miss it?"

"Yes. I do. A lot. That's why I have a vibrator. It doesn't give me any trouble."

I hard relate to that. I also know it's still lonely. Even when the vibrator is very good.

"You could—"

"Stay out of my personal life," she says, "or I will be all up in yours aggressively."

"Isn't that what you're doing right now?"

"Maybe," she says. "Or maybe . . . Yes. I am. I'm curious, and I want to live vicariously through you."

"He's hot, it was fantastic, he is proportional."

She presses her hand to her chest. "That is what I love to hear. We do not like hearing that a handsome man is very disappointing."

I lift my brows. "I heard about that a lot when I lived in LA."

She snorts. "Oh, please. Tell me which actors are disappointing."

I shake my head. "No. Because it's actually just really sad. Some guys have to wear modesty garments not to hide their junk but to hide their shame."

"That's hilarious."

"Well . . ."

She pauses for a moment. "You don't really ever talk about LA. I bet writing for TV was interesting."

"It was sometimes," I say.

Maybe it's because my past is encroaching that it doesn't feel sacrilegious to mention it at all. "There were some fun things about it. I met some interesting people. I got to write on some really great TV shows. But . . . everything has to end, right?"

"Not everything," says Elise. "At least I hope not, unless you're planning to leave."

I shake my head. "I'm not. I just mean . . . There are moments when you can definitely feel that a phase of your life is over. I don't even like talking about it because I prefer to be in the present."

"I get that. With Emma . . . It's so hard. I'm thinking about the future all the time, and I'm thinking about all the things I'm not giving her, and everything I'm not doing right. I need to tell you something. I need you to just . . . I love Ben," she says.

"I know," I say.

"No, I'm in love with him."

I nod and say again, "I know."

"How can I be a partner, a wife, a girlfriend, whatever, *and* a decent mom? I already feel like I'm stretched to my limit."

"That's because in your mind, all you can see is a relationship that's as toxic as the one you had before. Her dad didn't help you with anything. Being with him made everything harder. I'm given to believe that's not how love is supposed to be."

I think back on my relationship with Christopher. He hadn't made everything harder. For a long time he had made things good. I feel a swell of emotion. Maybe this is why I avoid thinking about it. Because it's easier to make him a villain. Instead of just someone who was walking on broken glass the same way I was.

"I really think that what you could have with him . . . It could be real. It could be functional. He *likes* you. Sometimes I think that is the wildest missing piece to relationships. Someone feels like they love you, or they want to sleep with you, but they don't like you. He likes you. I also think he might love you."

"This conversation wasn't supposed to be about me," she says.

"Yeah, but we're friends, so we're not keeping score."

I'm so grateful that I have her. She's been there all these years. I guess I've been there for her too. But she really doesn't know how much she means to me. I've stopped short of telling her.

I stop short of telling her a lot of things.

"I want to believe what you believe, Amelia," she says softly. "I want to believe in romance novels and friends to lovers and happily ever after."

My heart gets tight. I think of her life, which hasn't been easy—I know it hasn't. Emma's dad really sucks, and Elise's heartbreak was doubled because he didn't just hurt her, he hurt their daughter.

"Elise," I say. "Whatever happens with you and Ben, you already have a happily ever after." I try to force a smile, but it's hard. I feel pressure against the backs of my eyes, and I take a deep breath.

"Someday," I say, "we'll have a whole conversation about LA. About who's well endowed and who isn't. Today, though, I'm going to go on my hike. I want you to think about Ben, and everything you deserve."

"You're wonderful," she says. "I'm grateful I have you, because if . . . if I try something with Ben, and it goes bust, at least he's not my only friend."

I laugh, because what else can I do?

"Human hearts are absurd," I say. "I think if Ben likes you enough, no matter what happens, he'll still be there for you. Even if you give this a try and it doesn't work romantically. I think with the two of you, it wouldn't destroy your friendship."

"You make him sound like the perfect guy."

"Well, let's not get loopy, but he's pretty awesome."

"So the thing with Nathan . . ."

"Just sex and . . ." I wrinkle my nose. "He's helping me with something."

"What?"

"We really don't have time to get into that right now. I'll update you after the hike," I say.

Unless I'm having sex. But I don't say that part.

Elise and I walk out of the room together, and that's when I see Nathan, standing in the courtyard, surrounded by the cribbage ladies.

"Just move it slightly to the left," Lydia is saying, guiding his movements with the overhead string lights.

"No to the *right*," says Gladys.

"Please, give the man his due respect," I say.

"We do respect him," says Lydia. "And all the time he must spend working out."

"I'm so very sorry," I say, moving over to him and taking his arm reflexively. The gesture is not lost on the ladies. "They're incorrigible, and I feel like I have to warn you that they're just objectifying you."

Wilma huffs. "We are frail, darlin'; we need a man's help."

"Somehow I think you all do just fine on your own," Nathan says.

"I wouldn't know," says Wilma. "I always have a man when I need one."

I'm about to take Nathan by the arm and lead him away when Emma and Sofia come flailing across the path, with Angel close behind them.

Nathan looks down at the scene, and I'm surprised when he smiles at their antics. I can't quite parse the feeling it gives me to watch them play. It's like the peak of joy mingled with the pit of sadness. A valley with a beautiful view.

"He's a pirate!" Emma shrieks.

"I'm a monster!" Angel shouts back.

Emma stops and points at Nathan. "No, *he's* a pirate."

Then she and Sofia run away, giggling loudly while Angel stumps after them.

"A pirate?" he asks.

"I don't know," I say. "Maybe it's a vibe."

I sort of wish he were a pirate, in one of those old-school romance novels. Then he could take me off to his pirate ship and we could forget about practical things like reality.

"Plundering and ravishing is something I'm known for."

"I wouldn't be surprised," I say, my cheeks getting hot.

We walk out of the courtyard and into the lot.

"We can drive my car," I say. "If you want. It's a lot of dirt roads, and I have my little Jeep."

"Yeah," he says. "Sure."

We get into my car, and I pull out of the parking lot, taking the familiar road to Joshua Tree.

"I have a pass," I say. "I love to go up there. It's beautiful when it rains."

"I've been," he says. "It's just been a while."

"Really? You haven't visited in the summer when you come here?"

"No. I haven't been in about . . . nine years."

"Oh," I say. "That is a long time."

"Yeah," he agrees. "So, what is the deal with all the people who just live in your motel?"

"Oh, well, I think Jonathan and Joseph have always loved the desert. Albert, like I said, may be on the run from the law. The older ladies are all widows."

"Odd, living in a motel, isn't it?"

"I guess," I say. "But I do, so I can't really throw stones."

"I just mean . . ."

"I think it's a little less constricting than assisted living, and none of them need any medical help. They have a sense of community, and the rooms are small enough, and they get maid service. They're not alone. I think that's important. Alice is in her nineties. She was with her husband for a long time, and when she lost him, she lost the life she loved. She moved to the Pink Flamingo, and she made friends. I'm grateful, because those women are the first healthy maternal figures I've ever had."

"Right," he says, sounding distracted. "You mentioned that your mom . . ."

"Yeah," I say. "She's a whole thing." I'm silent for a moment. "What about your dad?"

"My dad's career military," he says. "So that's what he wanted for me."

"Military," I say.

I saw the military in him the night of the fire, and I see it now. Tall, broad shoulders, muscular. There is something hard and dangerous about him. But at the same time, he doesn't possess an ounce of military precision. He isn't the type to follow orders.

"Yeah, it's a family thing, not just a me thing. I'm a West Point grad. I did my four years. And that was it. When I tell you that is not good enough for Captain Richard Hart, I'm not exaggerating."

"Sorry. That must be difficult. My mom didn't even have any expectations of me—she just didn't seem to want me there. Especially after she and my dad split up. He had an affair. So, my experience of men and fidelity is . . . limited. But you know, my dad ended up with this great woman. She's really nice. My mom is a sour cow. Even though what he did was wrong, I . . . I don't blame him. It's a tough one."

"Family is complicated," he says. "My mom was . . . She was always great."

"Sorry," I say. I pick up on the past tense even though it goes by quickly.

"Yeah. Well. That's the natural order of things, right?"

"I suppose so," I say.

It hits me now, how long it's been since I've done this. Not just the sex. I was extremely conscious of how long it had been since I'd done that. Talking to a man while being naked with him is still so fresh.

Except I've never done it quite like this before. Aspects of it feel inside out.

I don't know him. That's the thing.

I turn the radio on, and it's country music. I don't touch the dial. He doesn't either. I wait to see if he makes a comment. About playlists or his favorite kind of music, but he doesn't. Normally, I would plug my phone in. Normally, I would select one of my carefully curated playlists. This is a test, though.

I forget that almost immediately because "Save a Horse (Ride a Cowboy)" comes on, and I'm too amused, singing loudly, and though he doesn't join, he does laugh, and I consider that a victory of sorts.

When we pull off the main highway and hit the dirt road that will take us to Joshua Tree, I feel a change in him. He doesn't say anything, and that doesn't really surprise me, because he seems wedded to saying nothing when possible, about anything.

I show my card and ID so that we can get in, and as we drive by the large boulders and beautiful Joshua trees, I'm consumed by the same sense of awe I always get when I come here.

The desert healed me in so many ways.

I look at him to see if he's having the same experience I am, but it's impossible to tell.

"Do you know where you want to go?" I ask.

"Just driving around is fine," he says. "Stop where you feel like it."

For some reason, I feel like he isn't telling the truth, but I also don't think he's going to actually tell me what he thinks. I pull off the road in front of one of my favorite spots. There are trails around some massive boulders that look like they were dropped there by a giant divine hand.

I suppose that's a testament to how I like to think about the world. But I don't think of the minerals and scientific process by which rocks are formed.

I prefer to think in terms of the fantastical. Because no matter what, I prefer to believe in a little bit of magic.

He takes out his phone and snaps some pictures as we walk through the dry brush. Uncharacteristic clouds gather overhead, and it adds to the moodiness, both of the landscape and the moment.

We get back to the car and begin to drive, and the rain starts to pour down, even as the sun shines. I look across the way and see a rainbow stretching over the tops of the Joshua trees.

"Wow," I say. "I've never seen that before."

He says nothing. He has grown more and more quiet over the course of the day.

I stop the car so I can take pictures of the rainbow. I realize he's doing the same, even though he doesn't add commentary.

The rain stops as we drive on ahead to one of the hiking trails. We get out, and I stretch my arms and legs, mostly because I have this reckless energy in my body and I need something to do with it or I'll throw myself at him. Kiss him, maybe, or worse, just hold him. "Do you want to do the hike?"

He looks at me, and there's something like wonder on his face. "Yeah. This . . . I did this hike."

"Oh?"

"Last time I was here."

"Oh," I say. "Well, are you interested in doing the hike again?"

"Yeah," he says. "Let's do it."

We fall into step as we make our way up the narrow, rocky path. "Watch for snakes," I say. "But not armadillos."

"There are no armadillos here," he says.

"Obviously, Nathan, that's why you don't have to watch for them."

I take a step, and my foot comes down on a rock. I slip forward, and he catches me by the arm. I look up at him. He's gazing down at me in a fury.

"Thank you," I say.

"Careful." He doesn't release his hold on me, and he doesn't sound angry. I don't feel like he's mad at me, but he's definitely mad. Maybe at the rock. I can handle that.

We continue the trail together, and he keeps holding on to me. His hold transitions from the hard grip that kept me from falling to a looser grasp on my hand. It doesn't feel quite like holding hands in the traditional, sweet sense.

It feels more like he doesn't want to lose track of me.

There's something I find sweet about that. Maybe I'm deluded because I'm so attracted to him. Maybe I want to spin a one-night stand into gold.

But he's so difficult I can't help but find the strangest things endearing. Taking me to breakfast. Bringing me here. Looking angry at the ground because it almost made me fall. The scenery is familiar. *He* isn't familiar in it.

Experiencing this with Nathan is new to me, and I can't help but look at him against the grand jewel of the sky, the strength of his body in contrast to the rocks, and the way he stands tall and straight next to the gnarled Joshua trees. This is my world. I'm captivated by the sight of him in it. The trail takes us to a flat plane through what might count as a grove of Joshua trees.

We stop when the trail ends, looking around at the vastness.

I don't know what drives me to do this, but I take his other hand in mine.

I haven't experienced romance since I started writing it. But I know how I would write the scene.

My heroine would be nervous and filled with trepidation. She can't see what the hero is thinking.

My heart is involved, which I didn't really want. I now have to resist thinking of him that way.

He's *not* the hero of my story. I have to remember that.

He's a secondary character walking through the pages, on his way to his own story, but for some reason it doesn't feel that way. I don't know whether I'm happy or a little bit sad that all these years and all these changes haven't done anything to make me cynical when it comes to romance. I have waited, maybe subconsciously, because part of me knew I could never be neutral about it. Part of me knew I could never take feelings out of sex entirely.

Until I know what I want, it seems like maybe I should. Instead, I decide to hold his hands. Instead, I look at him, and I let him see some of the feelings turning around inside me. Feelings I don't even have a name for. Feelings I maybe don't want to name. For one moment I expect him to turn away. There is a conflicted, dark look in his eyes that is so strong I'm sure it's going to win. Then he lowers his head and kisses me. There in the desert, with nothing but the Joshua trees and crickets to bear witness.

It's deep, intense. Harder and more passionate than I would ever expect from a kiss that can't lead to sex.

His lips are firm and certain, his tongue sweeps over mine, and I feel a wave of need rise inside me.

Then he steps away and drops my hands.

I wish I knew what he was thinking. But I don't ask. I recognize that the frustration I feel with the brick wall that is Nathan Hart is actually frustration with my own fear.

I'm walking carefully around the hallowed ground he stands on, because I know there are land mines.

I'm afraid of losing him before I have to.

I *am* going to lose him.

He's leaving at the end of the month, and he isn't coming back. He made that very clear. If I connect the dots in a logical way, then I have to come to grips with the fact that the only reason he actually kissed me this time, the only reason it went this far, is because he isn't coming back. It's not a coincidence.

It's him making sure I can't confuse this with something more than temporary.

And I'm *still* afraid to lose him any sooner than I have to.

I am, in fact, terrified of it.

Something happened just now, but I can't parse what it is, and I'm afraid that if I ask, he's going to turn and walk into the desert and I'll never see him again.

So I don't ask.

Instead, I allow the walk back to the car to be entirely silent, with no mention of armadillos, and no holding of hands.

I take us back to the motel after.

"Thank you," he says. "I need to go and get work done."

Let me in.

"Okay," I say instead. "Will you text me?" I ask.

"Yes," he says.

But he doesn't. He doesn't come to my room that night, and I text him a reminder about the dive-in movie and the barbecue tomorrow, but I already know he's going to try to avoid it.

Breakfast was a fluke.

Today was a fluke.

Whatever progress I thought I made with him, it wasn't real. There's really no such thing as progress to be made. He's going to leave here and never come back. It was research for books all along. It was never fate; it was never me.

He didn't choose it.

I can't write his story. I can only write my own.

CHAPTER SEVENTEEN

If I'm honest, December is a little bit too cold for a dive-in movie. With temperatures hovering dangerously close to the fifties, people don't really want to languish in the water for a couple of hours. In the summer, everyone is happy to grab a flotation device and a cold drink and watch mayhem on the big screen that I have mounted at the end of the pool. But in the cooler months, they tend to take seats at the tables and lounge chairs around the pool area.

Not me.

I love the pool and I don't care how cold it is. As I use my hand pump to blow up my pink flotation device, I deliberately choose not to think about Nathan standing me up last night and ignoring my texts today.

Flings don't need to keep in touch, I guess.

Or maybe the fling was flung and I'll just see him for fake dating and a book event. Sounds great.

The idea of that makes my stomach twist into a knot.

Elise crosses the courtyard to where I'm fighting with my floaty.

"Your enemy turned lover is a no-show?" she asks.

I try to hide my disappointment, though I'm not really sure why. "He's working."

"On what?"

I let out an exasperated breath. "I don't know, Elise. How is the Ben situation?"

"Rude, honestly," she says.

"Ben?"

"No, you. I haven't done anything about it. I'm not going to fling a cataclysmic wrench into my life on a whim."

"Gee, why not?" I ask, my tone dry. I feel I've done just that.

Though maybe the wrench was flung years ago, and it's bouncing around in all my inner workings still and always.

I squint against the fading light.

The sun is beginning to set, and my dear Albert is manning the grill, which is honestly the nicest thing. He can be such a pain but is essentially sweet. My cribbage ladies made Christmas cookies to share, and Solis made a chocolate cake that she garnished with fondant holly leaves and berries.

We have four extra families for dinner tonight, and the kids are running around the yard scream-singing Christmas carols that I'm sure they're rehearsing for the pageant.

In many ways, my heart is full.

I resent that Nathan has the power to make me feel . . . anything else.

"Who can say," Elise says. "I will. I . . . It's hard. I feel like right now I'm happy. Right now things are good. I wish they didn't need to change, but I also think they do."

That's a little too close to my own issues.

Yesterday morning I felt pretty good.

Right now I do not.

"Life just . . . keeps on going." I look around the courtyard at all the families, at all my residents. I pick up my pink flotation device. "We need to get the movie started."

The festivities get going, the movie beginning to play the familiar, cheerful intro. Families are seated together around the pool, and I feel a real sense of joy that even my Nathan sadness can't kill.

People make memories here.

Which is something I can be proud of.

They can have the happy childhood memories that I don't.

All due to something I created, that their parents chose to give to them.

If I can't have everything, at least I have that.

During the midway point of the movie, I get out of the pool and make my way over to the cake table. Solis is cutting and serving cake for everyone, putting the knife in a cup of water between slices. Something I learned from her when I first arrived. My family is so fractured that before I came here, I hadn't had the chance to spend time around a functional family.

It's been one of the greatest gifts I've gotten. The warm family dynamics I get to see with Emma and Elise, and Juan and Solis and their kids. The infinite wisdom I've been able to receive from women like Alice.

And along with it, an insight into how beautiful life is when your hair goes gray and your skin develops lines from all the years you've lived.

"Cake?" Solis asks me as she bats Angel's hand away from the frosting.

"Yes," I say.

Suddenly I can't leave Nathan's absence alone. He's ignoring my texts.

"Can I have another slice?" I ask. "Please. We have a missing guest, and I feel like I should deliver this to him."

"Of course," she says as she hands me another plate with a heavy slice on it.

I pause at one of the empty bistro tables and set the cake down, and then I put my swimsuit cover-up on. It's pink and flowy and covers pretty much everything, so I feel appropriately girded as I make my way to his room.

I don't know why he hasn't texted me, and I'm aware this might feel like too much to him. Like me pushing in when he set a clear boundary.

But I can't leave it alone anymore. I might have lost him anyway, and one thing I can't deal with is the reality that I might not be able to know him *ever*.

I want to.

I need to.

I knock on his door, and I wait.

I hear noise. The sounds of his footsteps, the movement of a chair, the leg scraping against the floor.

He opens the door, and a wave of alcohol so strong it smells like despair rolls out as he does.

He pushes his hand through his hair, and his eyes are stormy. Clear in spite of his obviously inebriated state.

"What?"

I'm not deterred by how unfriendly he sounds, not now. Not when I've kissed him and touched him, had breakfast with him and made out with him in a national park. Not now that I know he disappointed his dad, even though he's a bestselling author.

"You're ignoring my texts, you didn't come to the dive-in movie—"

"I didn't come to the movie because I didn't want to."

He didn't say he wanted to ignore me, though.

"Yes, I know. Because you're antisocial."

He snorted. "Yes, we covered that ground."

"Are you okay?" I ask.

He looks stunned for a moment. There is something in his eyes that looks like fear. As soon as I see it, it vanishes. "No," he says.

He does not elaborate, but this is honest, at least.

"Can I come in?"

Again, he looks afraid, like a drowning man who wants to reach his hand out but is scared to stop paddling. Terrified that it will sink him.

So I do something I would never normally do if he were just a guest. I push past him and into the room.

He's not just a guest. Whatever he might say.

"This is somewhat beyond full service," he says, and this time the words are slurred, and I am left in little doubt of how drunk he is. If I had doubts, they are erased by the near-empty bottle sitting on his desk.

"This isn't why we call it the Hemingway Suite," I say. "Anyway, we're beyond *full service*, aren't we?"

I've never been in his room during a stay here. He gets limited cleaning, and I'm never the one to do it. So I have never seen the evidence of him living in my motel. He does have a computer on the desk. Along with a notepad. Stacks and stacks of folders, papers. The wastebasket is full of crumpled lined papers with writing on them.

The bed is a mess.

He is a mess.

He's such a writer, honestly. Maybe that's the beginning and end of his mercurial nature. Maybe this is all muse bullshit.

We are a difficult bunch, I am well aware. Not just because of my own self, my own propensity for getting lost in my mind, in a story, and disconnecting from the people around me, but because of everyone I have ever socialized with who has the same profession.

Writers' rooms and the publishing industry writ large attract narcissists. People with delusions of grandeur. They attract weirdos who want fame and yet fear it in equal measure. They attract people who like the fictional world better than reality.

It is a melting pot of incompatible neuroses and psychoses and dysregulated emotional trauma.

Also alcoholism.

So really, this could be his whole story.

I still don't think it is, though.

"You should eat some cake," I say, shoving a plate into his hands. They are unsteady, but he takes hold of it. "Get something into your stomach."

"I ate," he says.

"How long ago?"

"I haven't managed to kill myself yet," he says. "Tonight isn't going to be the night."

"Sure. But I'm not just the motel manager anymore, and you aren't just a guest. I would like a little more assurance than you won't *die*."

"Why?"

"I've known you for three years," I say. Almost three years. Two and a half. Close enough. This is ridiculous. It's ridiculous for him to act like I haven't seen him every summer for three years, and now again just four months after he was here last. It is ridiculous for him to act like after we slept together, after we spent the day together yesterday, that I won't care about him.

"I'm just a guy you fucked," he says. "Once."

I know him in many ways. That's the thing.

And I'm tired of pretending that I don't.

I'm tired of pretending I feel *nothing* for him just because this is temporary and at the end of the month he's leaving and not coming back. He's the one being absurd, not me.

Not only could I write this, I would write it. The hero pushing someone away, holding them at a distance by reducing what they shared—this beautiful, revelatory experience—to *fucking once.*

He's trying to hurt me. I won't let him.

"No. You're not." I want to say more. I want to do something to bridge this yawning gap between us. I shouldn't. Because he is a customer. That should be all. It just isn't.

Maybe it's my own pain recognizing his.

Or maybe it's my overactive imagination. Or maybe it really is just that he's handsome.

I can't be sure. But what I do know is that I know a man in pain when I see him.

I know what it's like to feel like you're drowning and have nobody there to grab hold of. So even though he isn't reaching out, I can't leave him thrashing there.

I just can't.

I sit on the edge of his bed, and I set my cake off to the side. "Why do you come back here every year? You said you didn't choose it, but I have no idea what that means."

I recognize that he wouldn't answer this question if he weren't drunker than the armadillos we don't have here in the California desert.

But I don't care.

I want to know.

He looks away and sets the cake plate down on his desk. Then he sits heavily in the chair, his legs spread wide, large hands on his muscular thighs. He is frozen like that for a long moment.

And then he finally looks up at me.

"Because I didn't choose this place. My wife chose it."

CHAPTER EIGHTEEN

The Dark Secret—one or both protagonists commonly have a deep wound that may be hidden from those around them. The revelation of the dark secret can bring the protagonists closer or tear them further apart.

My entire world crumbles.

His *wife*.

That is the last thing I ever expected him to say. That is the last thing I expected to be . . . possible.

A wife.

Does he have children? I can't imagine it.

Or maybe I can. I think of the way his mouth softened into a smile when he watched Emma, Sofia, and Angel running around in the yard. When Emma called him a pirate.

Am I so stupid? Did I miss a thousand obvious signs?

I try to imagine him going to bed with the same woman every night and holding her close, but it makes me sick.

I try to imagine him whispering words of love to a woman, saying vows to her.

Then cheating on her.

This man who exhibited so much heroism the night of the fire. Just a bog-standard cheating husband. It's so not how I think of him that I feel like someone has taken a massive rock and thrown a hole through the fabric of my reality.

I feel torn.

It makes my bruised chest feel raw. No longer an old wound, but something new.

I look at his sculpted face, his green eyes. There is a woman who loves that face. There is a woman who has experienced those green eyes lighting up when they look at her.

My guilt is paralyzing for a moment. Then I feel horrendously jealous. Horrendously, horribly jealous.

"You're . . . you're . . ."

"My wife is dead."

The words are flat. Final.

Like death, I guess.

He had a wife. She loved him. He loved her. She's dead.

These are the new things about him that I know, and I hate them. I saw it on his face at the diner. This deep loss. The kind that leaves you blank, forces you to start over, but I didn't imagine a loss like this.

I feel hollow. I already know there's nothing insightful or deep to say to something like this. I already know that the void grief leaves is so vast and empty there are no incantations you can fling down into the pit that will begin to fill it.

"I'm sorry," I say, because there is nothing good enough, so I might as well say that.

There were so many times I wished people would say something that simple, that easy to me.

That instead of trying to make me feel better they could just say *sorry*.

That instead of telling me I could try again, that there was probably a reason it had happened, they would have just said sorry.

Because they don't have to be sorry, and it doesn't fix anything. But neither do platitudes.

Neither does silence.

When your own pain makes other people so uncomfortable they can't even look at you, it's unbearable. And I don't want to do that to him.

He nods. He doesn't say it's *okay.*

It isn't okay. Of course it's not.

He's grieving. That's why he's like a wall of bricks sometimes, and why he's emotional and raw at others.

"When?" I ask, the word a whisper.

He says nothing again. Like he's helpless to find words.

I'm devastated to see how sharp it is still.

He is better than he was three years ago. I've seen it.

I also know that grief goes in waves. That sometimes the tide rolls out and you can see all these beautiful things left behind. Sea glass and seashells on the seashore. That sometimes the waves come back in hard and leave you breathless, drowning.

That sometimes you're blindsided by the realization of just how far away you are from the life you were supposed to have.

I understand that.

Finally, he speaks. "It's been three years."

"The summer I first started running the motel . . ."

"It had been nearly four months." I don't know if he'll remember any of this tomorrow. Or even in ten minutes. I want to give him something, because I intruded on his space, and he gave all this to me.

When his guard was down.

I feel bad about it now, because I didn't imagine it was something like this. I didn't think about him being a man lost in *after*. And I should have.

I know what it's like to have been an entirely different person *before*. How did I miss it in him?

"You know I had . . . I had a relationship that imploded. I needed to get away. But it wasn't just him. It was . . ." I swallow hard and I look at my cake.

"I lost a baby," I say. "A girl. Just three weeks before my due date. We . . . had a nursery. It was really beautiful. Pink." I touch the pink fabric on my swimsuit cover-up. "I like pink."

He still says nothing, but I don't find it a hard or uncomfortable silence. He isn't silent because he is *afraid* of my grief. In LA I was surrounded by that kind of silence. Like people were afraid if they spoke too loud, they would break me. Like there could be anything worse than losing your child.

Christopher cheating didn't break me. It just pushed me out the door.

Half of why was that I found other people's discomfort with my pain unbearable.

It's one reason no one here knows this. One reason I've never spoken the words out loud.

I've never had to.

Chris told our friends while I was in the hospital.

He called my dad to let him know there was no grandbaby after all.

I had never even told my mother I was expecting.

Maybe it had gotten back to her through my dad, but I doubt it.

This is the first time *I've* ever told anyone.

"I don't know how to get over it," I say. "I left it behind instead."

It's silent in the room for a long moment. He shifts in his chair and picks up the cake. "Well. If you ever figure out how to get over it, let me know."

That's honest. I appreciate it.

"I'm starting to fear that getting over it is a myth," I say.

"Yeah. That sounds about fucking right."

"Yes, it does," I say.

I pick up my cake too, and we sit there, painful truths pulsing between us as we eat the most delicious buttercream I've ever had in my life.

This is also about fucking right.

Death and cake and a beautiful man whose heart I can never have, and probably wouldn't know what to do with anyway.

Even though it's difficult for me to swallow every bite, I do. I'm not sure at this point if it's my grief or his. His is a surprise. Mine is all too familiar, though I don't often let it take such concrete shape.

I just think of before.

Before, I wasn't even sure that I wanted children. Then I was pregnant, and we had decisions to make, and I had decided that I *did* want the baby.

So much.

Chris said he did too, but sometimes I think he wished he did.

For me.

At least, that was part of the rage I had internalized, and definitely part of the more hateful things I said to him. That he didn't want to be a father anyway. That this was convenient for him, because what he actually wanted to do was pursue his career and go out every night, and if we had our daughter, he wouldn't have been able to do that.

He would have left it all to me.

Maybe it was true. Mostly, I think it was me needing to make him hurt the way I did.

We finish eating our cake, and I stand up. Then I extend my hand. "I'll take that."

I take the clean plate from him.

He probably wants me to go, but I'm not sure I want to.

"Can I ask what . . . triggered this?"

"You just asked," he says, his words a little fuzzy.

"Sorry. I did. So . . . why tonight? Or . . . yesterday. Joshua Tree. That's what triggered this, isn't it?"

He nods. "Yeah."

I don't need to know everything tonight. I take his hand and lead him to the bed.

"Lie down," I say.

He looks at me. Somehow that look cuts through everything—all the pain, the grief, the long-held secrets—like a knife, and I feel the stirring of desire.

I feel an electric need to move toward him. To take the difficult feelings and turn them into something else. It feels like it would be easy. To take hold of him and let go of the pain. To find ourselves connected, not sitting across from each other with all that distance between us. Not when we both know.

But he is very drunk, and he's in pain.

He's also looking at me with absolute, undisguised need. Normally I find him tough to decode, but the alcohol makes it so I can read him.

It makes it so he can't disguise it quite so well.

I see the desire on his face, open and obvious.

He wants me. Even now. It kills him that he wants me. I'm not the problem. It's his desire for me.

And how very broken he still is.

"Go to bed," I say.

To my surprise, he obeys me. He strips his shirt off, revealing rangy, well-defined muscle and dark chest hair. I'm only human, and in spite of the uncomfortable pack of emotions running around inside me, I look at him.

I can't help it.

I move away from the bed quickly. I hold on to the paper plates like they're a shield. His eyes are already drifting closed. He really is that drunk, and I can't get rid of the feeling that the information I got tonight was stolen.

"Stay," he says, his eyes closed, the word barely audible.

My heart clenches. I can't deny him. I can't deny myself.

I lie down on top of the covers beside him, and I put my hand on his chest. I feel his heart beating.

And now I know it's broken, like mine.

CHAPTER NINETEEN

When I wake up, I'm cold, lying on top of the covers in his bed. Though, I suppose it's my bed, no matter how I look at it, since the motel is mine.

I don't know why, but that thought amuses me and gives me some measure of levity. Enough that I manage to sit up. If I didn't let myself think absurd things, I might get dragged back down, through the mattress, through the floor, into the darkness.

I look over at him. He's sleeping, but not peacefully. He's going to have a murderous hangover when he wakes up.

It's barely five in the morning, and I decide I'm going to go have a shower and get the day started.

I open the door to his room cautiously and slip outside. The sun isn't up, and none of my residents are outside.

I realize they will have seen me go into his room and not reappear. I didn't even bring my phone.

I left everything sitting out in the courtyard.

I cautiously tiptoe back to my room, which is unlocked, so stupid.

I push the door open and see my purse, my phone, and my keys sitting on the table. I pick my phone up and see I have a text from Elise.

I collected all your things. I assume something happened. I hope it was good. Text me when you get in so I know you're okay.

I send a text back.

I'm okay. He wasn't in a good space. I didn't feel like I should leave him. I'll explain everything later.

Even as I send the text, I'm not sure I can explain everything. I'm not sure I can explain his pain or mine. I'm not sure if I even should.

What he told me is clearly something he has a difficult time with, even all these years later. He chooses not to talk about it for a reason, and it feels wrong to do it for him.

I also don't want to lie to my friend.

I am gouged beneath the ribs for a moment by the realization that I haven't been honest with Elise. I've never really thought of it that way.

I thought of it as editing. Leaving my backstory out of it.

It seems reasonable, in many ways.

It's beginning to feel less reasonable.

I strip my clothes off and make my way into the bathroom, standing beneath the hot spray of the shower until I'm satisfied that I won't be able to wash away everything that happened last night.

I won't be able to find that place again. Where Rancho Encanto doesn't contain my past and I'm not carrying it with me.

There's so much more I want to know. About him.

My brain is spinning with the implications of everything.

I get out of the shower and slowly get dressed. I look at myself in the mirror and feel horrified by the face staring back at me. That woman, with her limp dark hair and wide brown eyes, looks exhausted. The circles beneath her eyes are a new feature.

I suddenly feel every one of my years and then some.

I know I'm only thirty-two. It feels old right now.

I go back into the living area of my room and stare at my tree. It's half-decorated. I haven't worked on my book for a couple of days.

I feel like I have stepped out of my real life and into something else. It's not my life in LA, not the one I left behind, but it isn't the life I've been living for the past three years either.

I wrapped myself around Nathan Hart, and he wrapped himself around me, and it was like nothing else existed.

Except it does.

It all exists.

I'm overwhelmed by that thought. It tumbles down on top of me like a load of bricks.

It all exists. LA and Christopher. My loss, and this place. Nathan, who he is here, and whoever he is when he isn't.

I move to the Christmas tree and look at the half-assembled ornaments that are around in an array.

I have to get it finished. It won't take long, but with everything else going on, I've been slow. All the little flamingos have hooks in them, and they are ready to be placed. I know that transit will disrupt some of the decor, but I want everything as mapped out as possible. To be sure I have enough to fill in all the empty spaces. I've tied one hundred perfect pink bows.

I pick up one of the flamingos and place it on one of the pink tinsel branches.

When I hear the knock at my door, I know exactly who it is.

I close my eyes. I bitterly regret that he's going to see the tired woman I was just looking at.

When I open the door, I'm hit by several realizations. The first is that he looks exhausted. But he's still beautiful. His dark hair is pushed back off his face, and there are shadows underneath his green eyes. He isn't clean shaven—dark whiskers cover his square jaw. He's dressed in a white shirt tucked into olive-green pants. He looks rugged. Sexy.

Maybe I look okay to him too.

He is also holding two cups of coffee.

"Can I come in?"

"Please," I say.

I move away from the door and take one of the coffee cups from his hand. "I assume that one of these is for me."

"Yeah," he says. "I brought that to go with my apology."

"Apology?"

"Yes. I shouldn't have gotten drunk like that. I shouldn't have ghosted you. I shouldn't have trauma dumped on you."

I'm shocked by that. I laugh. "I think I was the one who trauma dumped, actually. You were clearly going through something, and I decided to hit you with my personal tragedy."

"No," he says. "That's not . . . I didn't intend to drag you into my shit. This wasn't ever supposed to be that."

"Come on, sit down," I say, moving over to my small bistro table and taking a seat, shoving the chair across from mine out with my foot.

He sits. But he looks too large for this room. Too tall. His shoulders too broad.

"So what was this supposed to be?" I ask.

"Good fucking question, Amelia."

A muscle in his jaw tics, and he looks down at his coffee.

"I have time. Elise is working the front desk."

"Right. Well. I don't know. I don't know what it was supposed to be. I know what it wasn't supposed to be. I wasn't supposed to do this but . . . I'm tired. I'm tired of feeling heavy all the time. I'm tired of grief. I'm tired of living a life I didn't choose. Mostly, though, I got tired of not having something I wanted." He lets out a long, heavy breath. "I want *you*, even though I didn't want to want you."

I feel like he has taken a very small razor and sliced a part of my heart. Not really in a bad way. I hurt for *him*, for what he's been feeling. And the inconvenience of wanting me, because I feel exactly the same way.

I didn't want to feel something for the gorgeous disaster of a man who checked into my motel that first summer. I felt something for him all the same.

It had been the wrong time. It all still feels like the wrong time.

If it were the right time, he and I would both be a little bit less . . . *this*. I think.

"I have to start at the beginning," he says. "Except . . . I don't want to pile all this on you."

"It's not piling anything on me," I say. "Nathan, I feel a lot of empathy for you. I care very deeply about what happened to you. It doesn't make my grief worse, though. I'm not scared of your grief either. I've already felt the worst . . . the most hopeless, dark feeling that I wouldn't wish on anyone. I get why people can't handle it when they haven't experienced that. Because they don't want to know. They don't want to know what you can go through and survive. They don't want to know how horrible it can be. The stuff you have to keep on living with. But I already know. You're not traumatizing me. Life did that already."

It's true. I've never realized how true that is. I can remember clearly one of my friends saying to me afterward that she would never have been able to be as strong as I was. It didn't feel like a compliment, even though I knew she meant it as one. I had no choice but to keep breathing. To keep going. I didn't feel strong; I felt weak and broken. I still do.

That's the real tragedy of it. You go on.

Nathan already knows that.

"Okay. I'm not exactly sure where to start."

"Start wherever you want. I'll put it together. I'll ask questions if I have them. You just . . . Tell me whatever you can."

He's silent, but then he sets his coffee on the table, moves it one inch to the left just slightly. Then looks up at the ceiling. "My wife and I went to Joshua Tree for our honeymoon. Nine years ago. We stayed here. It was different then. She wanted to go somewhere that was different than Bainbridge Island. I couldn't understand why she didn't want to go to the Bahamas. She wanted to see the desert, so we did."

Joshua Tree.

That was why yesterday had been so difficult. He didn't need to connect those dots for me. I am all too familiar with what it's like to wish the grief were old enough to not intrude and to have it push its way in anyway.

"She's . . . she was an Olympic horse jumper. One of the youngest to ever win a gold medal. She did it while she was sick. She didn't tell anyone. Nobody but family. She worked her whole life for that. Her life ended really shortly afterward. One thing she asked me to do was to write her story. She didn't want me to be sad, she just wanted her story to be out there. I told her there was no way I was going to be able to do that at home. With all the . . . the ghosts of the memories and everything. She told me she would find me a place. So she did. You had the rooms listed, newly refurbished. The Hemingway Suite. She thought that was hilarious. She told me not to drink myself to death. She told me to work on it here. Between my other deadlines. That's what I'm doing. That's what I've been doing. I didn't choose this place, she did."

He sits there for a long moment staring straight ahead. "And when I walked in and saw you behind the counter, I thought it was some kind of cosmic joke, except I have a hard time believing in anything cosmic at this point, because what was the purpose of any of this? I don't know."

I have as many questions now as I did before. More. They're bubbling up inside me. He's given me a small piece of his story. His devastating, destructive story that turned his intensity to anger, that turned his depth into a pool that's drowning him.

I can only imagine that *before* he loved as fiercely as he does everything else.

He lost his wife. Of course it destroyed him.

Because he is the decent hero of a man I believed him to be. Not a cheater, not a basic, sorry excuse for a husband. He's wrecked, though, because of that, and it kills me.

"I'm sorry," I say. Because again, I know that sometimes it's the best thing. The only thing. Everything is insufficient, but saying something is better than saying nothing. "She sounds amazing."

"She was."

I'm surprised I don't remember a news story about this. Nathan is relatively famous, and she was an Olympian, and young, and there have been large swaths of time in my life where I've clicked on a lot of sad news articles, crying over strangers. I'm inherently interested in people, and curious about things even when they might make me sad.

I couldn't be, though, when I lost the baby. I wasn't reading sad news stories, or any stories at all.

I think we were both losing everything around the same time.

I want to ask him so many things. How he met her. Who he was before. I don't want to push him away either. We have two weeks left. I want every minute, but I want *him*.

This is all part of him.

"Can I . . . ask you about yourself?"

He clears his throat. "We've slept together, Amelia."

"Okay. So. Were you . . . Did you used to be . . . ?"

"More fun?"

"Sure, that's one way of putting it."

"No. Something about my humorless military father and never living up to his standards. Being a kid who'd rather read than do a ten-mile ruck didn't really make me his favorite."

"Do you have siblings?"

"Two brothers. Older. Not disappointing."

"You look like you could run for ten miles," I say.

"I can. But I've learned that you can do things you aren't suited to, and you can do things you don't like. You can even become great at them. Even if it never really fits."

I sit with that for a moment, thinking about my old life. I liked it. I'm not sure I could say it didn't fit. I don't think it would now, and that makes me feel strange.

"Do you have children?" I ask.

I'm trying to get a picture of who he is. He's been a fantasy object for me. An author photo. I know what he does, and I know some of the ways he is now.

I think, if I'm honest, I didn't really think as deeply about him as I pretended to. Because I didn't want to imagine who the man was beyond the walls of my courtyard. I wanted him to be this extraordinarily sexy, grumpy, complicated man I couldn't have. Now he is here, a whole man. One with wounds and the life and pain I hadn't known about. One who had been in love.

I study the lines on his handsome face, knowing that. He isn't just rugged to be a fantasy for me. He has lines on his face because he's lived a whole life that has caused him pain. And so have I.

I look tired because I am.

Because I packed up everything and moved to this place and tried to keep my reality from intruding, but it does, and it is. I haven't actually left anything behind.

It's all here with me, at my bistro table.

"No children," he says. "It wasn't ever the right time." He laughs. "God, that seems so stupid now. I mean, it's not a big regret I have, it's just the arrogance that we all have about time."

I nod. Except my loss didn't make me feel that way about time. I wonder if I'm sitting in the arrogance of believing I have an endless amount of time to be here in this place, in an emotional stasis, because I've certainly never thought beyond the motel. I've never thought deeply about how I would change and grow.

I've just been in this eternal present.

"Why wasn't this . . . I mean why wasn't it in the news? I know you keep your name separate, but I have a hard time believing this didn't get dug up."

My questions seem fractured, out of order. But I'm trying to fill in the holes of the story he gave me.

"The success came after things went to hell," he says. "Which is . . . not to say I had none before, but no one gave a shit about me personally. My wife got diagnosed with cancer, and suddenly the next book had a concept that was hardcover worthy, and then it got optioned, and even more shockingly got made. All in that eighteen months she was getting treatments, and horrible prognoses, and put on hospice, and I was in fucking hell. The show started airing two months after she died. She got to see a couple of episodes before, though. She . . . she really liked the lead actor too."

The things he's said about success make the worst kind of sense now too.

"God," I say. "That's . . . horrible. Actually, that is really horrible."

"Yeah," he says. "I mean, I guess I could have lost everything instead."

"I guess at least with the success you knew what to keep doing."

"Yeah, that's true. I think if I had lost everything, there was a time when I might have just stayed at rock bottom. I can see another version of myself working at a bar and drinking myself to death."

So can I. It scares me. It guts me.

"I'm writing Sarah's book as Jacob Coulter because that's what the publisher thinks will sell. That's the bargain I made to be able to do it. My name and my pseudonym are going to be unavoidably connected when that happens," he says. "Some documents just got unsealed that were sort of the last of my legal worries and . . . there's no point keeping them separate anymore. That's part of why I decided to go ahead and just finish the book. Her book. I mean, also, the publisher was after me for it. I've taken a little bit longer than I was supposed to. I'm trying to do an honest job. I don't want to write about her through the lens of husband, who had certain opinions about who she was, but I need to tell her story. She left behind a lot of journals. Some of them are about my failures."

He's silent for a moment.

I can't imagine how difficult that would be. I can also understand that as a writer, as someone who loved her, he wants to be honest.

"Nothing major," he continues. "But it might surprise you to learn that I'm sometimes emotionally unavailable."

I can't help it, I laugh. "I'm shocked to hear that."

I don't know why, but I feel a little bit validated that even the woman who married him found him difficult to access sometimes.

Sarah.

He's writing her story, and I can't imagine what that's like. To immerse in your own grief like that, in the life of the person you lost.

Of course, the person I lost hadn't even lived a life yet. It was all hope extinguished before it could ever really ignite.

"So you're finishing the book," I say.

"Yeah. Just . . . feels a little like another death, that's all."

"So it was the perfect time to sleep with some random motel girl," I say, trying to keep my tone light.

He looks at me. "You're not a random motel girl."

Tears fill my eyes, even though I wish they wouldn't. I wish that my emotion weren't so close to the surface. I wish it didn't mean so much to me that I wasn't random.

"We're grief magnets," I say. "The perfect foundation for a fling."

This feels a little bit fake. This feels a little bit like we're both trying to find a way to muscle out of the heaviness that's settled between us.

There has been so much honesty between us, and now a little bit of a lie. But I allow it, because it feels easier.

Maybe I don't really want to know all of this. Maybe I want him to go back to being a fantasy.

He's still gorgeous to me. That's not the issue. It's just now that I know this, I want to know more.

"Are you still going to read one of my books?" he asks. "For the event."

"Yes."

"Then you have to give me one of yours."

"Happily," I say.

I go to my closet and pull a box of one of my books out, selecting one of my forty-eight author copies. Honestly, it was exciting at first, and now it just feels like too many. I hand him one of the slim paperbacks.

"Looks interesting," he says.

"Spoiler alert, she doesn't stay a virgin secretary for very long."

He raises his eyebrows. "That makes me wonder why I haven't been reading romance all along."

It's strange. Because now I have all this context for him. There's a little more ease between us in some ways. Like we were able to just shed a layer.

I think maybe we have a chance at saving this. I don't want to let him go. I'm not ready for that. I need him right now. I'm not going to examine how deep a thought that feels. I want him with me when Christopher shows up.

I just feel like I want him with me.

I know him now. Much better than I did. I want him still.

I move to him. He puts his hand on my hip, and his eyes are hot, and I know. He feels the same way. We didn't break this with our grief, with our reality. I feel new because of that. I was so sure everything here would be ruined. That this perfect pink place would disappear, like the nursery I painted over before we sold the house.

But it isn't. I want him.

I don't have to sleep with him to forget. I remember. All the difficult things we just talked about. I also remember what it feels like when he touches me.

I sink down onto his lap, and I press my hands against the sides of his face, his whiskers sharp against my palms.

Then he's kissing me. Not tentatively. He gives no quarter, and I'm glad for it. He doesn't treat me like I'm broken. That is the most beautiful thing of all.

Because I don't want to feel broken. I don't want to feel like something less than the woman he wanted before he knew the truth. Something inside me feels like it puts itself back together as he kisses me.

I don't feel hollow anymore. I don't feel broken.

Not in every way.

He stands up, taking me with him, and he presses me against the wallpaper. He strips my clothes off, even as he holds me firmly against the wall. My heart feels like it's going to punch its way through my chest.

I push my hands beneath the hem of his shirt.

There's an edge to this now.

But it's a different one. It isn't the edge of mystery; it isn't the air of all these unanswered questions. I know the answers. And he knows mine. Whatever he was to his wife, he's this to me. Whatever I was to Chris, this man still wants me.

That, I find, is even more powerful than mystery.

Everything has been exposed. Everything has been brought out into the light. Here we still are.

I want to be marked with it. I want to be changed by it. I bite his lip, and he growls. His rough hands move to cup my breasts, his thumbs moving over my nipples. I've never felt anything like this. This deep, unending need. It's like being suffocated. Lungs burning with the need to draw breath. That's how badly I need to come. My body aches with it. I'm suspended on the edge of a knife, and when has it ever been like this? Never.

He lays me down on the bed naked and goes to his knees on the floor. He drags my body to the edge of the mattress and licks me like he's never tasted anything so sweet.

I am lost in this, in him. Nathan Hart turns edging into an art form. A glorious form of torture that I need to end, but that I also need to continue.

He is taking every thought in my head and unraveling it. He is turning me into a creature of feeling, and not one of words. I find this to be the most freeing thing of all. Because I live my life with such a strong narration. I'm a writer, and I find a way to tell a story all day every day. There is no story here.

There is Nathan, and there is me.

And everything he's doing to me.

I dig my heels into his back, and he pushes two fingers inside me as he continues to torment me with his wicked mouth.

I let go.

I'm falling, and I don't even want to catch myself. I shatter then, and he is there.

I push myself off the bed with trembling arms and sink down onto the floor in front of him, undoing the button on his jeans, lowering the zipper.

"My turn," I say.

I move him onto the bed and then position myself in front of him. I wrap my hand around his cock and lean in, swallowing him. He is the most beautiful man I've ever seen. I've never wanted a man more.

Not in spite of everything sharp, hard, and ugly.

Because of it.

This is something beyond reason. Something beyond desire as I previously understood it.

I can do this. I'm *great* at it. I can make him growl. I can make him forget. I can make both of us forget. That there's anything beyond this room. That there's anything beyond what we share here. That anything could be more important.

We didn't ask for the things that happened to us. We didn't choose it. We can choose this. We can revel in it. Luxuriate in it. So I do.

I move my tongue along the length of his shaft. I take him in deep.

He grips my hair and pulls.

I take it all in. The taste of him, the way my scalp stings. The deep, hollow feeling inside me as I anticipate more. Everything.

He pulls me back. His eyes burn into mine. I reach for a condom, thankful there's one close enough, and he puts it on as quickly as possible as he drives himself into me. As he tortures both of us with slow, measured thrusts.

I bite his neck. And he loses it. There is no sound. Nothing beyond our bodies, our fractured breathing. My desperate pleas that he give me what I need.

When we shatter, we do it together.

When it's over, he presses his forehead to mine and kisses me. It's so different from last time.

He doesn't turn away from me. He doesn't leave.

Instead, he gets up off the bed and goes into the bathroom, and I hear the sound of the shower.

I lie there on the foot of the bed. Naked and satisfied. But already hungry for more.

He returns a second later. "Shower?"

I feel a strange rush of euphoria. "Yes please."

There's something unintentionally intimate about this. Showering with someone is part of sharing a life with them. But there can be something commonplace about it, and this isn't commonplace. I'm so aware that I am standing there looking at his naked body. So aware of growing slick and hot from the water. He puts his hands on me, slides them over my curves. I do the same to him, my fingertips tracing the lines of his well-carved muscles.

When he kisses me, it's deep, his tongue sliding against mine. His body fitting against mine perfectly. I'm pressed against him from my lips down to the floor.

Suddenly, neither of us can take it anymore. Both of our hands reach for the faucet, we turn it off, and we find ourselves in bed again, tearing desperately at a condom packet. I roll it on him, and he's inside me before I can take my next breath. It's fast, and furious.

We're both undone by the time we finish.

"I guess the shower was pointless," he says, his chest rising and falling heavily with his breath.

I laugh. "I don't know, I would say it was pretty productive. Even if I'm sweaty again."

I don't say it, because it's a little bit terrifying, but I don't mind having his sweat on my skin.

I want to bury my face in his chest and inhale the scent of him.

I want him closer. Inside me without a barrier.

This is unhinged thinking, and I know it. This is me being drunk on sex, and on the emotional release of dredging up old trauma.

Maybe that's what this is. The two of us acting like survivors of a natural disaster engaging in life-affirming fucking.

I find that to be the most comfortable explanation available.

We *have* survived three natural disasters. Death is natural. Still, much like a fire burning down your house, it doesn't *feel* natural.

It feels wrong. It feels too hard.

But this doesn't.

I'm suddenly drawn back to the moment. To the clock on my nightstand and the time.

"I actually have to go man the front desk so Elise can take Emma to school."

"Yeah. I have . . . you know, deadline."

I look up at the ceiling. "Right. Those."

"I pity your hero. Didn't you leave him unsatisfied?"

"Saving all my love for you," I say, flippantly, but it lands heavy, and I feel my face get hot. "You know. Metaphorically."

He clears his throat. "Right."

He gets off the bed and starts hunting for his clothes.

I do the same.

"I'll see you tonight," he says.

And I smile. "Yes. I'll see you tonight."

CHAPTER TWENTY

I don't know why I feel like I'm engaging in a walk of shame out of my own room, but I do. I move quietly around the courtyard, making my way to the reception desk, slipping into my pink chair.

I ask Elise to stop by the office when she gets back from dropping Emma off, and then I type in the password for my computer.

My Word document is still there, minimized. My crickets chirp at me, and I feel disoriented. Like I forgot what my real life is. Like I've forgotten everything except the last all-consuming twelve hours with Nathan.

The door to reception opens, and Wilma walks in, followed by Lydia. They each have a copy of my most recent book in their hands.

"Good morning," says Wilma.

"Hi," I say, typing a couple more words officiously in my manuscript.

"We just came to tell you how wonderful we think your new novel is," Wilma says.

"Yes," says Lydia, smiling.

"I don't think you did," I say. Because I know them, and I know that they're up to something.

"It is good," says Wilma. "But what we wanted to ask you about is what exactly happened when you went into that man's motel room and didn't emerge until the early hours of the morning."

My mouth drops. "Are you spying on me?"

"No. You were *very* indiscreet." Lydia looks at me meaningfully.

"It really is such a boon to your generation," Wilma says. "We couldn't be so obvious when we took a lover. You know, back in Charleston in 1959, I bedded a man who worked at the newspaper, and his endowments—"

"Wilma," says Lydia. "We want to hear Amelia's story, not about your days as the town bike of Charleston."

"They were good days," Wilma says, with a smile. "Tell us about how he is as a lover, Amelia."

I want to be offended. I want to dig in and say that he in fact isn't my lover. That nothing happened when I went into his room.

The truth is, nothing happened in *his* room.

But I can still feel the impression of his hands on my body from the morning spent in my room, so I feel that my protestations would ring hollow.

"I just felt like I was entitled to a little bit of fun," I say.

Wilma laughs. "I knew it. And I knew you had electricity."

The door opens again, and in walks Elise.

"We'll let you gossip," Wilma says, patting my hand as she and Lydia exit, clearly taking credit for my sex life.

My crickets chirp again, and I jump.

I look at my newest reservations while Elise stands there, waiting.

Then, I finally turn my full attention to her.

"Is everything good?" Elise asks.

I experience a deep feeling of guilt. Because I'm not going to tell her everything. Not now. His secrets are his. Mine are still . . . complicated. It's going to be a big deal when she finds out that I've kept all of this from her. I don't think she'll be mad at me. Though I think she might be hurt. I feel like maybe I need to be careful about choosing my venue. Or maybe I still don't want to talk about it freely.

Maybe that's closer to the truth.

"Yes. I . . . Everything is fine."

"You had sex with him again, didn't you?"

"I did, Elise. I did." I pause for a moment. "So, this is where I tell you that my ex-boyfriend is an actor, and he's in a lot of Christmas movies, and he may or may not be booked to come to A Very Desert Christmas."

I brace for impact.

There is no impact. Elise is just staring at me. "What?"

"That's relevant," I say. "Because Nathan has agreed to be my . . . my fake boyfriend so that when Chris shows up . . ."

"*Christopher Weaver* is your ex-boyfriend. Your terrible ex-boyfriend . . . The one from LA."

"Yes, he is. I'm sorry I didn't tell you. But I was blindsided by the whole thing, and frankly, still kind of in denial."

"Well, I don't really blame you for that."

"Who could?" I ask. Except, she could have, and I know it.

"So, you're actually engaging in the plot of one of these Christmas movies in order to deal with this?"

"Kind of. Except he isn't going to fall in love with me. I don't need to fall in love with him."

For some reason, those words get stuck in my throat.

"This is a recipe for disaster," she says.

"No," I say. "Because I am full up on disaster. There have been enough disasters. Who the hell does this kind of stuff happen to?"

"Women in the kinds of Christmas movies your ex stars in?"

"Exactly! It's ridiculous."

Elise examines the edge of her currently bright-red thumbnail. "Just . . ." She looks up at me. "Be careful, okay? This feels like a very dangerous, potentially volatile situation, and I don't want you to get hurt."

"I'm not going to get hurt. Don't worry about me." I try to internalize that. I try to bolster myself. I've had my heart broken in such a terrible, complicated way. The breakdown of my long-term relationship was so complete and so deep. I know that I haven't given Elise the whole story, so she doesn't really know what I went through, or why everything felt extra sharp, extra hard, but I know.

Nothing else could ever hurt me that bad.

But I also know how I feel about her. About how much I want her to take a chance on Ben. On happiness. Even knowing everything she's been through. I suddenly appreciate that I've been a little bit cavalier with her fears.

Thinking that you might love somebody again after you got broken apart by another person really does feel like the riskiest thing imaginable.

Nathan is temporary. When he leaves Rancho Encanto, I'm never going to have to see him again.

We can dump all this pain into each other and then never have to deal with the consequences of it. We can indulge in pleasure and really, really feel like we deserve it because we know how bad so many other things have been. It's ideal, in many ways.

That's not how it is for Elise.

Ben is her best friend. If she takes a risk and it goes badly, she'll lose her support system. It's easy for me to say that he'll be there for her no matter what. I think that he will be.

But I can also understand why that's not so easy or clear cut for her.

"I'm really sorry that I was being pushy about Ben," I say.

"Oh, it's okay," she says. "It's probably fair. Somebody probably should be pushy with me. I'm . . . I'm tired of myself. I have two best friends. You and him. I can't tell him . . ."

"You know that he feels the same way."

"I do," she says. "That's the scary part. Because if I jump in, I'm going to be jumping in all the way."

I can understand why that's scary.

I haven't given over any control to another person for a very long time. I haven't even been trusting enough to tell the people around me my entire story.

"This whole being a person thing really sucks," I say.

"You write romance," Elise says. "Doesn't that make you uniquely qualified to comment on this stuff?"

"Yes. If I were writing your romance, it would be a friends to lovers, and you would have a happy ending, complete with a wedding epilogue."

"I like the way you think, but I'm concerned life doesn't work that way."

"That's why I don't feel uniquely qualified to comment, even with my romance pedigree. Those who can't do . . . write, or something?"

She taps the counter with her bejeweled nail. "So, you have a terrible ex who's a movie star."

I hold my hand up. "He isn't a movie star. He is a fixture of mid-budget TV movies."

"Okay, but still. Doesn't that make you . . . not believe in happy endings?"

I think about that for a moment. "No. Though I do think that sometimes in books, happy endings take a different shape than they do in real life. In books, they're kind of a fixed state. But I think in real life . . . we continue to have conversations. We continue to change. We continue to live in the happy ending, even as life happens around us. I think in books, the characters deal with all their issues, and that's when they can be together. I think in real life it's not that simple."

"Great. So you just have to do everything while dealing with all of your immeasurable issues and trying to love somebody."

My heart squeezes. "That's what I think. But, at least you have somebody that you love."

She nods. "Yeah. Somebody that you might lose."

I think about her daughter. Her beautiful, perfect daughter.

Emma.

You can lose anyone you love. I am so painfully aware of that. My thoughts get tangled up, and it takes me a long time to talk again.

"I think that's life too," I say, slowly. "We can always lose something. Hell, we can always lose everything. I think the truly miraculous thing about life is that we keep loving anyway."

Not necessarily romantic love. Not even necessarily the love a mother has for her child. My own mother's love certainly wasn't enduring, and I'm not sure if I'll ever get the chance to have a child that I get to keep with me.

I'm grateful for my family at the Pink Flamingo. I love Elise. I love my life.

Even though I don't want to examine the full implications of it right now, everything in me is telling me to reach out to Nathan. To grab hold of him. To keep on connecting to him.

Even knowing how everything could end.

"You're so funny," Elise says, looking at me. Her words make me startle.

"What?"

"I don't know, Amelia. Sometimes I feel like I still don't really know you." She shakes her head, and her earrings jingle. "But you're usually right."

"I'm sorry. I've tried hard to be a good friend. Though I've been trying to do it while I . . . I got hurt badly before I moved here. I was still kind of a mess. This place, you, have been so important to me." I feel tears pushing against the backs of my eyes. Pressure building. "You've been the friend that I needed. I'm sorry if I haven't always given back as much as I've gotten."

"Amelia, you share everything you have. Except your own feelings. You've given me your time, your advice. You've been wonderful to Emma."

I think, not for the first time, that it's probably helpful that Emma wasn't a baby when I moved here.

I'm uncomfortable with babies.

"I'm going to try," I say. "I'm going to try to be more normal. And not . . . I just wanted to leave everything behind."

"I get that too," she says. "That's actually one of the hardest things about Ben. He saw the person I was with Emma's dad. I'm so careful. I always have been. I wasn't with him, and I'm embarrassed. I think I don't . . . I don't fully understand why he should care about that woman. That woman who let things get so bad with her ex. Who didn't like herself enough to walk away when it was so obvious she needed to."

"Stop," I say. "Okay. I think we both need to stop blaming ourselves for bullshit that stupid men put us through."

Nathan makes me feel beautiful again. His hands on my body . . . It gives me an appreciation for myself that has been gone for a very long time.

"You know that Christopher cheated on me. I've been carrying around this feeling that I wasn't enough. I'm just done with it. He doesn't get to decide how I feel about myself. He doesn't get to keep being in my life when he is so resolutely out of it. It is so hard when you love somebody in good faith and they twist it because they'll never hurt the same way you do."

She nods. "He never loved anybody but himself."

"So he doesn't get to decide how much you're loved now. If that's with Ben, then great. If it's just you and Emma, then great. If we turn into old spinsters in this motel, then great. But he doesn't get to decide what you accept. He doesn't get to decide your worth. Neither does . . . Neither does Chris."

"So, does that mean you're thinking of trying for something more with Nathan?"

I shake my head. "I'm not the deciding factor there. There's a lot going on with that one."

"Yeah. Well. He definitely seems like a lot."

She pushes away from the counter. "I have a grocery order coming that I need to grab. Thank you. For taking the time for my nonsense in the middle of yours."

"There's room for both of us to have nonsense at the same time," I say.

I really believe that. Suddenly, my life feels so much more connected. So much more integrated.

I brought my pain with me, and it hasn't destroyed me.

I've given Elise a new piece of myself, and I'm shocked to find I don't feel reduced. Instead, I feel more whole.

I feel happier.

For the first time since everything started to crumble at that meeting, I feel like things might be okay.

CHAPTER TWENTY-ONE

Spice—what online communities call sex to get around censors.

I'm planning nightly dive-in movie spectaculars with a different Christmas film every night. I was excited about this before Nathan and I started our fling. Mostly because I don't really want to cut into my time with him. But I can't swerve on my plans. I promised everyone this would happen, and we chose the movies for it last year.

I don't expect that Nathan will come out for it, even though our entire relationship has changed in the last week and a half.

His relationship with the rest of the world hasn't.

It's complicated because at some point he's going to step out as Jacob Coulter, but he isn't being Jacob now. It feels right that this morning Sylvia called to say the newly announced event has sold out already.

Each and every chair sold.

All that heaviness, and success right in the middle of it.

It seems to be Nathan's story.

I'm trying to remain cheery while I set up the projector. I've run this motel for years without him participating in any of my events. I don't need him to do it now.

Jonathan and Joseph have already taken their seats, along with a couple of their friends who have come to stay and visit them for the holiday. Albert has arrived in a red turtleneck and red plaid pants, along with red-framed glasses to match. He looks every bit as dramatic as he is, but he is *seasonal.*

Lydia, Wilma, Ruth, and Gladys have their cribbage boards out, and Alice is set up with a keyboard next to where I'm putting the projector. She's going to play while Ruth sings.

Our short-term guests have also turned out for the festivities, along with Ben, who is sitting on a blanket with Emma and Elise.

I look to see how close Elise is sitting to him.

They give me hope. My current situation is far too temporary to feel *hopeful* about it.

Even if so . . . I'm not sure what hope looks like in our situation.

Maybe I don't need to. Maybe I just need to get the movie started.

I make my way to the computer that's going to stream the film, and Alice and Ruth begin to play and sing. Everyone sitting around the pool joins in, a rousing rendition of "Here Comes Santa Claus" filling the air.

Which then transitions into "Santa Claus Is Coming to Town" and "Rudolph the Red-Nosed Reindeer." Perfect, because we're watching the 1960s Claymation classic about Rudolph.

I hit "Play" on the movie, and the crowd cheers.

A few of the kids are floating in the pool, almost every adult opting to stay dry. I intend to join the kids now that everything has begun.

But then, I turn and nearly run smack into Nathan's broad chest.

"Oh," I say.

"You look startled," he says. "Is it because this movie is creepy?"

I let out a shocked laugh. "This movie isn't creepy. It's adorable."

"It has an elf that pulls teeth."

"He's a dentist," I say.

"It's creepy," he says.

"It's a classic," I counter.

"Classics can be creepy."

"Well this one isn't. And no. I was shocked to see you. Out of your room. With all these people here."

"It seems stupid not to join you," he says.

I try not to read too deeply into that, but one of my big problems is that I read too deeply into just about everything. Maybe it's because I'm a writer. Or maybe I'm a writer because I do that. It's hard to say. But either way, this is different. The biggest thing that's changed is the fact that he and I are . . . I can't even call it sleeping together. He hasn't spent the night with me since the night I slept near him when he was passed-out drunk. We have sex in the night, he goes back to his room, we have sex in the morning. It's a lot of sex and very little intimacy. Except . . . There's plenty that feels intimate. I can't deny it.

"You really came to watch the movie?" I ask.

"I didn't realize it was this movie," he says.

I push his shoulder. "Well, what's your favorite Christmas movie?"

He has to think about it. "*Home Alone*," he says. "I thought that if my house got broken into, I could handle it too."

I laugh. Because of course. I suppose every boy in the nineties thought the same. Then I wonder, growing up in his house, how much more important that would've felt. Given that his dad is all about the military and he has older brothers who were super involved with it as well.

Or maybe it's just a favorite movie and not childhood trauma. But I find myself wanting to dig deeper and deeper into him, who he is, every day.

I've never really thought that I was well suited to casual sex. Maybe because my emotions are never casual no matter how much I want them to be.

But I still don't regret this. I'm determined that I won't.

"Is he Elise's boyfriend?" Nathan asks, gesturing toward Ben and Elise.

"I'm hoping that he will be. They're friends." I give him meaningful side-eye. "For obvious reasons, she's determined not to disrupt that."

This feels like a potential minefield. Stepping into conversations about relationships and why people might not want to be in them.

"It's complicated," I say.

"Is it?"

"Yes," I say slowly. "Just, you know, the eternal complication of people being afraid of getting hurt."

He nods. "I mean, I am familiar."

"Of course," I say.

"If you have the chance, though," he says, "you should take it."

Our eyes meet, and my stomach gets tight. I know he isn't talking about us. He's talking about them. Maybe talking about his wife. But for one moment, for the space of a breath, I wish he were talking about us.

My thoughts race, and I try to sort them out. Try to stop myself from this intrusive line of thinking that I didn't even realize existed so strongly inside me. This potential to fantasize about a future beyond this week.

I shouldn't. I know better.

I hope he doesn't see all these thoughts playing through my eyes. Because this is about Ben and Elise. Two people who have known each other for years, who live in the same place. This is not about Nathan and Amelia. Two people who do not live in the same place. Who wouldn't even be able to blend their lives easily if they wanted to.

I don't even know enough about his life to have these kinds of thoughts.

That I feel like I know him as well as I do is about sex. I'm too smart to let myself believe that sex is knowing someone.

I know the way his skin smells. I know how he tastes. I know how he looks when he loses control. That's a kind of knowing that goes deep.

I knew Chris for years. It took a pregnancy for us to even really behave like we might be forever. To buy a house, to set it up and get ready to bring a new life into the world. We were having a baby, and we hadn't even talked about getting married.

Now I'm letting little drops of fantasy about *forever* invade me regarding a guy I've been sleeping with for nine days. I feel like I should be more realistic than that.

There's that word again. *Realistic.*

Maybe I should be happy about these fantasies, actually. I guess it means I'm still able to hope with some part of me on a level of delusion that might be disturbing. But at least it's hope, I suppose.

"Life's too short." I realize that might not be the best choice of words, but he doesn't even flinch.

"I agree."

But I feel a wealth of complication in that statement. Just because he thinks life is too short to avoid certain kinds of happiness, I don't believe he applies that same exact thought to himself.

He has clearly decided that his own life must contain a measure of sadness now. I wonder if I've done the same.

"How would you write it?" Nathan asks.

I do a double take when he says that. "Um . . . I mean, classic friends to lovers, right? He's been in love with her forever, but because he's sensitive to her past, he won't compromise the trust they've built, the relationship they've built. He loves her, but he also loves her daughter, and he's a father figure. She's skittish, and she leans on him, but she doesn't fully see what he could be to her."

"Why not?" he asks.

"She doesn't let herself. It's self-protection."

"Seems valid."

"It is, but . . . she's protecting herself from happiness too. Of course, she'll have to have a dark night of the soul before she realizes that. My fictional heroine, if I were writing the story."

"Yes, obviously."

"Right, so she has to lose him. She has to lose everything so she can see that's the cost of holding on to fear."

"Why?"

"See, this is why I do think romance novels are realistic, Nathan. Things just happen in a different order. In real life we have a spate of issues, and we don't know where they all come from. But they always show up. We date the same people who are the same kind of wrong, we fall into the same bad patterns with work, with personal habits. We fail our friends in the same ways, and we have the same fights with our significant other. Over and over again. Each and every time we have to hit these mini crises, and if we want to move past them, we have to drain a little poison out of the wound. A little bit each time, and next time maybe we won't fall as hard."

I take a deep breath. "In romance you drain the poison out. In one big cathartic fight. One catastrophic loss. The loss of the person who showed you that you needed to heal, and you have to let the poison go to be happy. It's the same process. It just takes a little more time."

We look at each other, and I can feel the truth of our own wounds between us. We both know why people don't just do that. It hurts too much.

It's the same reason Elise won't drop her guard and give herself what she wants. The sad truth is, you protect the wound, and it begins to protect you. So you guard it at all costs.

"I'm not writing it, though," I say. "Elise really went through it with her ex. I think it's all complicated when you have a child."

"I can see that."

Neither of us really knows, though. Because I know what it's like to love a child, but I never got the opportunity to take care of that child. At least outside of my body.

He loved his wife. He still does—I can see that. Though it's a different kind of love. One that's about partnership more than simply caring for another person. Though, then I realize that of course he *did* take care of her.

My breath leaves my body in a gust.

You say vows to somebody when you marry them. In sickness and in health. He did that. He fulfilled his marriage vows. Maybe that's why there's a strange sort of finality to so many things he says. Maybe that's why when he says things like life is too short, he doesn't mean himself. In some ways, I wonder if he feels like he's done. He ran the race. He completed the task.

Why would he ever want to do it again?

It's not a wound so much as a sense of completion.

It isn't really as sad or hopeless a realization as I might've thought.

I'm standing here staring at a very good man. One I would never want to ask more of. One I would never want to ask to sacrifice himself like that ever again.

"How did you meet *Christopher Weaver*?" he asks me, saying Chris's name like it's consequential. I'm actually kind of glad he did ask. I can't pretend that Chris isn't something I'm going to have to deal with.

Especially since he's acting as our moderator.

I can't pretend that he wasn't part of my life for all those years.

"When I moved to LA, I had a roommate. She was taking writing and acting gigs. Chris is just an actor. I mean, not just. I mean only. They ended up at a lot of the same table reads and things. Sometimes they made it into commercials or movies together, sometimes not. She got to know him, and they had a little bit of a friend group. I got brought into it. It was nice meeting somebody who was in the same industry because he understood how difficult it was. But we weren't competing with each other."

"What made you decide to write for TV?"

"I grew up just a few hours away from Hollywood. We did a class field trip to this studio. We went to a writers' room. I've always loved books. Movies." I gesture to the screen. "I love stories. Growing up . . . I was really lonely. My house was just a desperately sad place to be. I have a mother who is deeply uninterested in me. Books, movies, TV shows, they gave me a chance to live a different life. A different reality. If I watched a sitcom, it was like being part of the kind of family that I didn't have. Sometimes even watching dysfunctional families helped because I could imagine myself navigating those situations. I could think of myself as a character when my mom was being ridiculous. When she didn't come to my Christmas pageant or something. It was a way to deal with it. To imagine I was in an emotional Christmas special when I looked out in the crowd and saw an empty chair instead of my mother. Or my father. Though, he lived an hour away so . . ."

I was always thinking of myself in stories. Now I think of how I'd write someone else in them.

"He knew how your mom treated you," Nathan says.

"Yes. He did. It's . . . It's complicated. They got divorced when I was really little, and my mom hated him. He left her, and he found another woman suspiciously soon after who it turns out is the love of his life. He's still with her all these years later. My dad loves me, but I'm a complication. A piece of his old life."

"You're not a complication," Nathan says, his expression suddenly grave. "That's the most absurd thing, Amelia. Your parents should not treat you like a complication."

I feel run over by this. No one has ever said anything like that to me. People usually agree with me that it sounds like my dad is a decent guy who was in a difficult situation. I feel a little like Nathan has torn a favorite teddy bear out of my hands. A talisman that I find comforting. I like to pretend that I have one good parent.

He's just made me question that.

"I get it," Nathan says. "Really. Because my dad is a dick. So it's easy to have an issue with him. My mom was sweet. Supportive, except she never stopped him from talking to me the way that he does. She never stood up for me. I wouldn't need her to do it now. But when I was a little kid? I needed somebody to be on my team. She wasn't. I can come up with all kinds of excuses about why. Shouldn't somebody stand up for you? I mean, we didn't choose our parents. I guess they didn't choose *us*, the people we are and the people we grow into, but they *did* choose to have us."

There's truth to his words, however uncomfortable they are.

"No, I understand what you're saying," I say.

"I didn't really ever think of it this way either. Not until I met Sarah. I remember, the first time I took her home to have dinner with my parents . . . she asked why we all just let our dad talk to us that way. Why we let it be his show. He's not abusive, we aren't walking on eggshells around him in that way, but we definitely all let him have his moods. We let him dictate so much of what happens. She came in and pointed out what a mess that was. She also pointed out that at a certain point, everyone is at fault for continuing to allow it."

"It sounds like she was great," I say, my throat tightening. I'm not sure that I mean it, though. Because from the grave, this woman has now disrupted a narrative about my life, about my family, and at the same time, I feel . . . maybe a little bit jealous. It's a weird feeling, and I don't like it.

"I'm just saying, sometimes it takes someone from the outside to see a situation clearly. It sounds to me like nobody did right by you. Not really."

"Well. Maybe not. Though, it's why I got into writing."

"You probably could've done it without the trauma."

"Maybe," I say, forcing a laugh. "But maybe not."

"I'm just curious why you didn't start with books," he says.

"That felt like a whole different world," I say. "I felt close to Hollywood. I did not feel close to publishing. But, I have to say, in the end, I'm happier. I actually prefer less collaborative writing. I like being able to have my own life. I feel like every bit of you can get swallowed up in LA."

"Yeah, I've never been tempted to get involved."

"Even with the TV adaptation of your series?"

"I leave that up to the professionals. Who are not me."

"Well, I'm not sure I would want to go back now," I say. "I'm enjoying what I'm doing too much."

"So you found the right kind of writing for you," he says.

I nod.

I look around the courtyard. I take in the feeling of rightness in this moment. "I think I ended up where I was supposed to be."

Even as I say that, something inside me wants to reject it. It makes it feel like I'm saying I was meant to lose my baby. I struggle with that. I don't think I was. And yet, this place feels like the right place for me. Maybe it's just the right place for me now. Maybe it really is a matter of the Amelia I was before.

The Amelia that I've had to become.

I wrinkle my nose. "Life. It is so very . . . life."

"No argument."

I lean back against the wrought iron fence that surrounds the courtyard. "How did you meet Sarah?"

I know a lot about her. Just from what he's said. I know she was strong. I know she loved him. She defended him against his family. She accepted the Nathan of him.

"At a bar," he says.

I don't know quite what to do with that. "Really. Not . . . a high-end equestrian event? A publishing gala?"

He chuckles. "No. It was a friend of mine from the military's bachelor party. She happened to be there with a group of friends. We started talking because I had been drinking. And . . ."

"You being a little bit drunk is a key part of the story?"

He nods. "Yes. Because I otherwise don't go making conversations with strangers."

I'm fascinated by this. By Nathan. By the fact that this . . . this sort of difficult, locked-box aspect of him isn't from his recent grief. But I do wonder if it made him double down on it.

"We didn't have anything in common," he says. "Her family is nice. Well adjusted. She grew up surrounded by horses. I'd never had anything to do with them."

I look at him, but I don't say anything.

"I found myself living on a ranch, basically. I had her horse for two years after she died. He was never happy afterward. I think he might've died of a broken heart."

Tears sting my eyes. I can't think about Sarah's brokenhearted horse. It kills me.

It also kills me to know that there's no way a horse loved Sarah more than Nathan did, but he still has to be here. He's still breathing. Her parents are.

"She never really minded. She just seemed to take me at face value. I frustrated her sometimes. I mean, we were married for years. So of course I did. But . . . she was really the first person who didn't try to change me. That's a pretty rare thing."

That makes it even harder for me to fight back tears. I can't think if I've ever been in a relationship where I didn't feel like I had to change. Maybe that isn't fair. Because I changed myself pretty substantially when I moved to LA. Maybe that's something I do. I left Bakersfield and I wanted to start over. I wanted to be a more interesting character.

I go back over all the things I just said to Nathan, and I realize it's true. I find it much easier to recast myself in a different role when I go somewhere new. I'm afraid of myself. Or at least parts of me. And I would never have said that before this moment, but it's how I feel.

If I can't think of myself as a character playing a part, then maybe I'm just a sad girl who isn't important enough to have her mom show up to a Christmas pageant. Or a girl whose dad was happy to move away to be with the woman he preferred, the kids he preferred.

Maybe I'm the girlfriend that didn't matter enough when I couldn't be the support system my boyfriend needed me to be. When my pain was bigger than my ability to be there for him.

Then I'm definitely not the interesting stranger who moved to a new place and refurbished this beautiful pink motel.

I'm just Amelia. Amelia Taylor, the same as I've always been. Never quite being enough.

He's here. Right now. And all these people are here with me.

So maybe it's not quite as terrible as I think it is.

"Are you okay?" he asks.

"I'm working on it," I say. "Every day."

"I guess we all are."

"I do think there's something wrong with you," I say. "This movie is great; I will hear no arguments."

"You haven't watched any of it."

"I've seen it *many* times. How else is a kid supposed to spend a lonely Christmas Eve while her mother is out drinking and meeting men?"

He winces. "Really?"

"Yes. But that . . ." I shake my head. "That doesn't even bother me."

It's true. The stuff with my mother, it hurts, but I've accepted that about her. For the most part. I remind myself of that. My mother being a narcissist has nothing to do with how important I am. It's just that nothing can ever be as important to her as she is. A lot of the things with her do feel like old healed wounds.

I leave them be now.

"Well, you're not spending Christmas alone anymore," he points out.

"No," I say. "I'm not. Everyone is with me." He's with me.

We end up sitting with Elise and Ben and Emma for the rest of the movie. Ben and Nathan talk, and I'm more fascinated than I should be, watching him make conversation with someone else. It's a rare sight.

Then Alice comes over and asks if he's read any of my books. Albert finds himself engaged in a lively debate—meaning that the cribbage ladies, Alice, and Nathan, to my surprise, begin to argue with him about the function of genre fiction.

"Everything has a structure," Nathan says.

"But some are more predictable than others," says Albert.

"Let me ask you this," Nathan says. "Why is a sad ending more unpredictable than a happy ending?"

Albert sputters. "It just isn't realistic."

"Why is tragedy inherently more realistic?" Nathan asks.

Given what I know about his life, I find this question to be revelatory. That he would dig into this. Into this conversation.

"Everybody dying is easy," Nathan says. "I'm not an aficionado of romance novels, though I have now read a couple and listened to Amelia give some fascinating commentary on the topic. I have to say, both of the books I've read have felt pretty real. It shows people dealing with issues and living. That's what we all have to do, deal with shit and keep going. If you want to kill everybody off and let them be dead, then I would suggest that you actually want a more digestible reality." He pauses for a moment. "That's the messy part. Bad things happen and people have to go on. There's a whole genre of books that show you how to do that, and you want to dismiss them?"

I believe that. I agree with it. I have to stop myself from cheering when he says it. Because that is the truth. It's the living that's the hard part. He knows it. I know it.

"Well, everybody has their opinions," says Albert.

Nathan's mouth kicks up into a half smile. "Considering that I also write genre fiction, I would say that my opinion is founded in pretty deep understanding."

I smile, because I know he's going to do it.

"Have I read anything you've written?" Albert asks.

"Oh, you probably haven't," Nathan says. "I bet Gladys has."

Gladys's eyebrows shoot up high over her glasses.

"My pseudonym is Jacob Coulter."

I delight in the bomb of excitement this drops in the middle of the gathering.

By the end of the evening, he has signed books for Wilma, Gladys, and a couple of our temporary residents who brought books on vacation with them.

I laugh all the way back to my room that night, hanging on to his arm. "You didn't have to do that," I say.

"Everyone here is going to find out soon. I'm shocked they haven't yet," he says.

"I guess they're not looking at the Very Desert Christmas website," I say.

"When the memoir publishes, I'll probably have to do publicity. It's going to be the real me, my real life, and there's no getting around that."

I look up at him. "You really love her."

He nods slowly. "She was the love of my life, Amelia. I think her story is really inspirational and important. Even if it wasn't, I have the opportunity to publish it. I have enough trust with my publisher, so they're letting me do it. Treating it like it's kind of a big deal. Who wouldn't take that opportunity?"

My chest feels sore. "Anybody would," I say.

"That's what I figure."

I don't have to ask him why it's taken this long, because I can see how hard it is. All of it. I reach out and touch his face, and he kisses me.

He kisses me, and the sadness of the previous moment is wiped away. All I can think about is the joy. The way he talked to everybody. The way he stood up for romance, really because he was standing up for me. He sat for a movie he doesn't even like. He talked to my friends. It feels like freedom, that I can just enjoy this. That I don't need to believe that this means it's forever.

He was lovely to me, now. Just because.

He's not earning anything. He's not saving up points, and neither am I.

He likes me. I'm not the love of his life, but he likes me, and that matters.

He kisses me deep and hard, and I kiss him back.

I feel a sort of giddy happiness inside me, but this kiss isn't giddy. It's dark and rich, like everything with him.

He is the flourless chocolate torte of men. Powerful, overwhelming.

Except I don't feel like I can overdose on him.

Every bit I have just makes me want more. That's the only part that scares me a little bit.

I try to ignore that particular thought. I try to just be in the moment. To just be kissing him. To luxuriate in the feeling of his hands as they move up and down my body. As he grips my hips, as he pulls me forward and lets me feel how hard he is.

He is the most beautiful man I've ever seen. It's the hottest sex I've ever had. I tell him that. Over and over, in clumsy, broken words against his mouth. Against his neck and his chest as I kiss my way down his body and take his cock into my mouth. As I try to show him with my tongue, my lips, just how amazing I think he is.

One thing that hits me hard is that I felt this way before I knew his story. Whatever his feelings are for me, this passion existed before he knew who I was either.

It is something that goes beyond emotion. It's elemental. It's chemistry. I am undone with it.

It makes me feel special just for existing. It makes me feel like I don't need to be a character or a new creation.

Because it's nothing other than us. Who we are. At our very essence, apart from anything we've done, anything we've experienced, anything we could ever do.

It isn't being the love of his life. But it is pretty amazing.

I take him to the edge, and then he makes it his mission to take me too. Over and over again.

I gasp as I find myself bent over the vanity in the corner of the bedroom. As he thrusts into me from behind. We're back in that dark, swirling chemistry that captured us first.

I can see him in the mirror. The intent look on his face. The concentration. The torment.

We aren't teenagers experiencing the first taste of passion. It's all the more powerful for it. Because we have lived life, experienced consequences. Heartbreak. And we're still here. And this is as powerful as it ever was. It is inevitable.

I flatten my forearms on top of the vanity and lower my head because I actually can't stand to look at him like this. It makes me feel too much. It makes me feel like if I ever don't have him, I might die. And he's already so deep inside me that I feel like I need him in order to breathe. To *be*. That isn't what I wanted. So I try to just feel. But feeling is complicated. It isn't just my body. It's my soul. My heart. Everything. So when my climax finally takes me, I shatter completely. Shaking, trembling, calling out his name as he does the same with mine.

When he carries me to the bed and lays me down, he stays with me.

I don't sleep. I hold on to him, and I hope he doesn't leave. At one point during the night, he gets up out of bed, and I hold my breath. Waiting to see if he's going to get dressed, waiting to see if he's going to go. But he gets back into bed with me and holds on to me. And I hold on to him.

Only then do I drift off to sleep. Because something has changed. When I wake up, I know Nathan is going to be in bed with me. I don't have to imagine that I'm in a TV show, or in a book, because right now my reality is better than any story anyone could ever make up. Drifting off to sleep with that feeling is the best one I can remember.

CHAPTER TWENTY-TWO

It's Never Just Sex—sex in romantic fiction works to build feelings between the main characters, whether they want it to or not.

When I wake up in the morning, he's still there. Sunlight filters through the curtain and reaches the edge of his bare shoulder. I touch it with my fingertips. Afraid that maybe he'll disappear, maybe the light will disappear.

Both stay.

I trace a line down his skin, following the trail of the sunbeam. He opens his eyes, and my breath catches. I remember seeing him for the first time. Those eyes startled me then. Now he's here, in bed with me. Looking at me. I know him now. Yet, looking at him isn't any less impactful. Maybe it's even more so.

"Good morning," he says, his voice full of gravel.

"Good morning," I murmur back.

We lie there for a while, in the quiet, in the realization that we've spent the night together. Or maybe that's just me. "Shower?"

He nods. He gets out of my bed, naked, and I admire the broad expanse of his back, the fine musculature there. He is so hot. Genuinely. So incredibly hot.

And also, his ass, which is glorious.

He turns and looks over his shoulder. "Are you checking me out?"

"Yes," I say, scooting out from beneath the covers and climbing slowly out of bed. Then I head into the bathroom and turn the water on. I feel a strong arm wrap around my waist, and I find myself pulled against his naked body. He kisses my neck, and I sigh.

This feels good. It also feels significant. I know we aren't supposed to be significant. But we are. I realize, with no alarm or fear, that this is changing me. I don't know if a fling is supposed to change you.

Very little in my life has gone the way people think life should go. There have been a lot of good things, but some really terrible things too. I don't know if it's supposed to be this way, but I'm grateful for him. I try, as I put my hand over his forearm, to hold him where he is holding me, to be grateful for whatever happens after this. I need him. I know that I do, that I did.

I need this.

I want to believe that maybe he does too. Maybe this is the only way he's going to get through finishing this book. Maybe this is the only way he's going to be able to move forward.

I hope so. I hope that even if I'm not the love of his life, I'm *something*. Because he certainly is to me.

We shower, and he offers to go get real coffee. I feign offense at the slandering of my single-cup coffee maker but can't deny that I prefer drip or espresso. When he comes back, he's got his laptop with him.

"I had an idea," he says, sitting down at the table. "For an opening scene."

"Oh," I say. "One of the thrillers?"

"Yes. New series," he says, his movements quick and decisive. I've never seen him creatively enthused before, and I love watching it.

He gets his computer out and puts it on my table. I take this as an invitation to get mine.

"Well, why don't you do that, and I'll work on getting my word count."

That's how we have our coffee. Sitting across from each other at my tiny bistro table, typing away, intermittently scowling at our screens. He looks up, over his laptop, his expression somewhat bewildered. I don't ask, so he goes back to work.

"Is it good?" I ask him after a few minutes.

"I am a *genius*," he says, taking a long drink of his coffee.

"Same," I say. "Though, if you ask me in ten minutes, I might tell you it's the worst thing I've ever written."

"The beginning is the best part," he says.

I shake my head. "False. The beginning is the worst part."

"No it isn't," he says. "You get to begin with all kinds of explosive action, and you don't have to shape it into a narrative for a while yet."

"No," I say. "Beginnings are terrible because there are so many things you still have to figure out about the book, about the characters. Every time I start, I'm overwhelmed by all the things I don't know."

He shakes his head. "That's a problem for the future."

"My preference is to gather it close and make it my problem for *now*," I say.

I like this. I like that we think of it differently. I feel like maybe I'm seeing a little bit of him. Separate from this project. Separate from this tragedy. Separate even from the way that he sees himself. He isn't as taciturn or difficult as he seems to think he is.

He's just been made to feel like he is.

He's not an extrovert, but that's fine. I don't mind it at all. I'm not especially shy, but I need time to think. He asked me a while ago about spending time alone. It's true, I have avoided it for the last few years, but even when I'm alone, I'm often thinking about my stories. Not about myself. I think naturally, I would choose to have more mornings like this. Quiet, working on my book.

With someone important sitting close to me.

We work like that until it's time for me to go man the desk for checkout, and he goes to his room to work on the memoir. He brings me lunch at around one o'clock, and we eat sitting in my room again.

It gives me a taste of what life with him could be like, but I'm not trying to get like that. I'm trying to just appreciate what he gives to me right now.

I look at the tree. It's nearly finished. Pink and sparkly and ready to get transported to the site.

"I have just a few flamingos to finish up," I say. "Then I'm going to wrap it in Saran Wrap, and I need to get it over to the A Very Desert Christmas location."

"I can help with that," he says.

"With hot gluing flamingos?"

"If you need it," he says.

"I would love that, actually."

"My pleasure."

I laugh. "Somehow I doubt it."

"I mean it. Christmas has pretty much meant nothing to me for three years, but it's impossible to be a grinch when . . . flamingos."

"The kids are coming here for one of their rehearsals. I'm thinking I should have them all do a tree. They deserve something fun. They're going to school in a hollowed-out Walmart. They've been through all the same trauma as the adults, but they're little. I feel so bad for them."

"The kids should definitely do a tree," he says.

"I'm going to have to get some supplies."

We spend a chunk of the afternoon on the flamingos. Then a plumbing crisis in one of the rooms takes up some of my time. He tries to help, and I tell him I absolutely cannot have a guest helping me with a motel disaster, regardless of whether the guest and I are *fraternizing*. (He objects to that term, and I tell him that's his problem.)

He and I share a long look at that, but he lets me take care of it on my own. It's getting dark, and I'm a little bit hungry, but I decide that it's time to get the tree out to the A Very Desert Christmas site, and afterward there can be food.

Nathan helps me wrap the pink tinsel tree and get it loaded into the back of my Jeep.

I drive the short distance up the road to the site, and I'm awed by what I see.

Most of the trees are already there, lit up, with lights strung over the top.

"It's magical," I say.

This is the new home of my Christmas memories. My childhood ones really aren't good, and a lot of the things pertaining to my life in LA feel tainted now.

But this doesn't.

The community has experienced hardship. I guess you can't keep the bad things out no matter how hard you try sometimes. But what they've done in response has turned it into something new.

It's a miracle, Christmas or otherwise.

We open the Jeep, and he lifts the tree out, not taking my help. He hefts it over his shoulder and moves with fluid grace ahead of me.

"As much as I'm enjoying watching this display of masculine strength," I say, "you don't know where this is supposed to go."

He turns and looks at me, and I grin back at him.

"Then where should I put it?"

"I'll show you," I say, happily scampering in front of him as we make our way through the grove of lit trees.

I search for my number, and then find it.

"This is the spot," I say.

He sets the tree down and begins to unwrap it. It is a glittering pink monstrosity in the midst of all the green. I love it more than I can say.

"You're running the auction for all these?"

"Yes, I'm the auctioneer, and I handled the sign-ups for all the entries." I look around and start laughing. "I almost do have a Christmas tree farm."

"What?"

"Oh, I just keep thinking, parts of this feel like one of those Christmas movies, but often someone owns a Christmas tree farm. Here's mine, I guess."

I take his hand, and we start to walk slowly through the trees. Lit-up Christmas trees, reindeer, and cacti are mounted on posts that provide scaffolding for a net of white lights that are overhead, like stars that have been brought down lower just for the occasion. The lights are so bright in the grove, it blots out everything beyond them.

It's like we're the only people in this bright, glittery world, and I want to believe it.

Just for now.

"There's the one Elise made for Ben's mechanic shop. This one," I say, pointing to one with mermaids all over it. "This one is from Bob Riker at the antique store."

There's a tree with coffee-themed decorations from the local coffee place, and there's one with woodland animals, which I quite like.

"One thing I don't understand about your story," he says. "How did you end up here?"

I stop and look around, at the lights, the trees. I draw strength from them. "I moved out of our house as soon as I caught him cheating. I was in a hotel; it was so *temporary*." I take a breath. "Three months after we lost her, I had a job opportunity out of town, and that was when my flight got canceled and I found out he was cheating. Just three months after. Her nursery was still set up. So I . . . I couldn't deal with it; I left that night. I didn't even really have a fight with him—it just felt like . . . my whole life was already ash, and he was making sure that was all it was. That there was nothing good or redeemable left there. So I was in a hotel, with one suitcase of stuff, and I was dreaming about another life. A new one, where I could just leave. Where I didn't go and tear down her nursery piece by piece, but I could start over. I saw a real estate listing for this motel." I laugh. "I put an offer in that day. I used my savings. When we sold the house, I put it into renovations. It was basically just a facelift, so they only took a couple of months. The Hemingway Suite . . . I'd just gotten all that posted not long before Sarah would have passed."

I realize that it's chance that we ever met. That I saw the ad. That he'd gone on his honeymoon here, so this was where his wife looked. That she saw the room I designed and thought it would be perfect for him.

It makes me feel like somehow part of me did make it for him. It makes me feel like in some ways I got to meet Sarah, even though I never will.

Sarah is why he comes here. She wanted him to, and so he did. He does. Year after year to work on that book. I came here because of the listing in the paper. We would never have met if those things hadn't happened.

We would never have met if our lives hadn't crashed and burned. But it doesn't feel like something that happened because of tragedy. It feels like a small miracle. An oasis in the middle of the desert, which in many ways is what Rancho Encanto is.

"I wanted something different than a city," I say. "It was competitive. The pace was too fast. I liked it for a long time. I just couldn't after we lost the baby." I frown. "I couldn't find myself there. Because everything around me was still trying to be the way it was before. I wasn't the same, though. I couldn't be. I think that's what happened with Chris. He wanted things to go back to how they were before that happened. He wanted to pretend it didn't. At least, that's how I felt. So I thought since I couldn't be the same in that place, where everything else was exactly like it had been before, I needed to go to a place that was totally different, where nobody would know I was different."

"I think that Sarah didn't want me to die in my office. I think she wanted me to have to make this drive. To get out. To see people, even if it was just because I had to stop to pump my gas."

"She knew you really well," I say. "That's an amazing gift. I say that as somebody who was in a relationship with someone who didn't really know them." When I say that, I realize how true it is. I also realize how much of that is my own fault.

"Why didn't he know you?"

I want to blame Chris. But that's not real. It's not even fair. It's been three years, and the truth is, as much as I don't really want him here, I can't hate him anymore.

I'd rather be honest, because that might be the only thing that helps me.

"I don't think I wanted him to."

It was my slow-draining poison. The wound I already had by the time I got to him.

"Not on purpose," I continue. "I wanted to blend in with everybody there. With that life. I didn't want to be me. I'm realizing that more and more recently. I didn't want to be this girl from a small town who hated driving in the traffic and felt sad and lonely whenever I thought about my childhood. I wanted to be . . . interesting enough. Smart enough, cool enough, to be with him. I think . . . The thing about grief is . . . it makes you so tired. It makes you way too tired to put on a facade. I have always felt things deeply. I spent my life hiding that. Pretending I didn't care whenever my mom was . . . herself. Pretending it didn't bother me when my dad couldn't make it to things because he lived far away. Pretending that I didn't feel second best to his family. I carried all that for so much of my life. But then Christopher and I lost the baby and I couldn't do it anymore."

I let out a long, slow breath, and I look up at the diamond-studded sky. "I think maybe neither could he. There were no masks. There was no bright, shiny veneer of anything. We just didn't have it available to us. He needed someone to cater to him more than I could. He needed things to be okay on a surface level, and I needed to be devastated. We just couldn't find each other. I think . . . I don't know. He didn't know me. If it would've been like Sarah, if he were dying, he wouldn't have known what road map to leave me behind. I'm very sorry that your wife had to do that. I just think that what she did was extraordinary. I can see that the way she loved you was extraordinary."

It makes me feel crushed to say it. I'm happy for him. And at the same time, sad for myself. Not about my relationship with Chris. Not about what we had or didn't have. About the fact that I'll never be able to love Nathan like that. Knowing him. Inside and out. His every breath. What he needs.

We wouldn't have met if not for our tragedies. But it's those tragedies that hold us separate now.

We're meant to be, I'm convinced of that. We're meant for this moment. It's just that the moment is destined to be shorter than I want it to be.

Maybe it's a happy ending of a kind.

Endings move on a continuum. One thing ends, something else begins. If I were writing this in a romance novel, readers would riot. They wouldn't consider these few weeks a happy ending.

Time moves different in romance novels—we talked about that earlier.

Time moves differently, but the feelings are real, so maybe this is real enough.

A few weeks to heal each other. To make each other laugh. To be skin to skin with another person.

No happy ending lasts. Not really. It ends the way that his did. Eventually.

It ends like Alice's, whether it's weeks or fifty-seven years.

So maybe I should just be thankful we have this.

"You didn't move closer to your dad, though," he says. "Or back to where any of your friends from high school were."

"No," I say.

I moved to be alone. Maybe I'm not any better than he is. It isn't like I've let the people around me *know* me. Not really.

Just him, and he's leaving.

"Maybe we're the same, you and I," I say.

"I don't know if I would go that far," he says.

"Maybe not," I conceded. "Though I think we might both be very good at figuring out how to be alone in a crowded room."

He nods slowly. "But not in an empty field of Christmas trees."

I think maybe that's one of the most romantic things I've ever heard.

"Are you hungry?" he asks.

"Yes," I say.

"I have an idea." He gets out his phone. "What's the address here?"

"They're not going to deliver to an empty field."

"You don't think they'll do that here?"

"No," I say.

He places an order for pizza anyway. Then he goes back to my Jeep and takes a blanket from the back.

It takes thirty minutes for the food to arrive, but it does arrive. Nathan takes the blanket out to the middle of the trees, under all that brilliant light, and spreads it out.

Hands down the most romantic picnic that has ever been conceived of.

I sit there with him, eating pizza, surrounded by eclectic trees, glowing in the lights.

"Perfect," I say.

He looks at me, and Christmas lights reflect in his eyes. "I need you to know, if you haven't guessed already. You're the first woman I've been with. Since losing Sarah."

I probably did know that. If I paused to think about it, that's what I would've guessed. But hearing it from his mouth makes my heart do all kinds of things.

"When I . . . The first time I came to the motel, I was a wreck. I was four months out from losing her. It was the absolute worst time of my life. I planned on never even noticing another woman again as long as I lived. I walked into that office, angry that I was there, mad that I felt beholden to a ghost to do what she said instead of staying home in my office. Knowing that if I did stay home in my office, I was going to lose my fucking mind. At least what was left of it. I walked in, and there you were. So goddamned beautiful. It was like an out-of-body experience. Because I couldn't feel my body anymore. I just . . . I couldn't believe that you were real. I was so fucking resentful that my wife had sent me to a motel owned by the only woman I wasn't married to who I'd thought was beautiful in . . . God, years. Every time I saw you, it got more intense. I didn't feel disconnected from my body anymore, and you weren't just beautiful. I wanted you."

I realize something then.

Us sleeping together, this, it was inevitable. Coming back in December was him moving it forward.

He could've waited until next summer, and I know that it has to do with the book. But in many ways, it has to do with two things.

His impatience for it all to be over, and his need for me.

Both things are true.

He wants this done so he never has to come back, and that's the reason he was finally able to sleep with me. He isn't coming back.

He's also impatient. So he came back early.

He's here at Christmas for this. For me.

It's because he wanted me. The whole time.

"Goddamn. I don't know what to do with this," he says.

He sounds helpless and in awe at the same time.

He sounds angry, and happy.

It's the strangest thing. Yet extremely real. Realism is overrated, honestly.

We finish our pizza, and then we're just sitting, underneath the lights, the stars. I lean against his shoulder, and I take a deep breath. I smell his soap, his skin, the pine trees. I've never felt happiness that hurt so much. Like Christmas itself, I guess.

I start humming "Have Yourself a Merry Little Christmas."

It's a song that always makes me sad. I don't know why. There's a melancholy to it, or maybe it feels that way to me because Christmas was always a little bit lonely.

He takes my hand and pulls me into a standing position, brings me up against his chest. And before I realize it, we're dancing. Slowly, without rhythm, to my song.

He looks at me, and my heart expands. Everything falls away. Everything but him. Everything but us. This is the single most romantic moment of my life, even though the road I had to walk to get here was an awful one.

Right now, it's all beautiful.

I want to stop time. I want to live in this moment as long as possible. I remember sitting in my pain and wishing that time would move quicker. So that I could get past it.

Time is my enemy either way.

In Rancho Encanto, time hasn't mattered quite so much. It's like I've been sitting, staring at a blank page, unwilling to write any new words because once I do, my foot will be on a particular path.

A blank page has limitless possibilities, but at the same time, it's nothing.

I can't do nothing anymore. I have to choose what story I'm living.

At least now there's a reason for this song to be painful and bright all at the same time. Because it will always be Nathan's song.

This place will always belong to him. This moment.

This will always be a happy ending of a kind.

One that didn't last as long as I wanted it to.

But was happy all the same.

I hang on to him, and we sway even after I stop singing.

Time just keeps on moving.

CHAPTER TWENTY-THREE

I'm at the site for A Very Desert Christmas, and the chaos is extreme. It's nothing like when Nathan and I were here last night, dancing in the silent night with only my voice as a background track.

This is a cacophony.

There is a choir of children rehearsing, there are donkeys. There's even a camel. The pageantry is nearly obscene.

The cheer is aggressive. And I'm here for it.

I'm rooted, now, in the quirky over-the-top nature of Rancho Encanto, and it couldn't come at a better time.

Reigna was pretty excited about how the children's choir was coming along. I'm not a music director, but there is a shrill quality to the performance.

Alice is playing the piano with gusto, and I have to admire her energy.

The nativity scene next to the singing children is also quite a sight, complete with Mary, who is played by Lorena from the Coffee Wagon, and the baby Jesus, who I'm sure is played by Lorena's new baby, while the part of Joseph is being filled by what looks like a bag of flour. I'm going to have to ask for some more information on that. Is Joseph permanently a bag of flour? Is there an understudy? Is the understudy gluten-free?

I hum as I look at my clipboard, moving through each space to make sure that the map is right and everything correlates correctly.

I've already double-checked that the trees are all numbered and my list is right so everything matches at bidding time, and I had a look at the area for our book event, where the chairs are set up and ready to go, so now I'm doing final spot checks on everything else.

We want to make sure all the guests have an easy time navigating through the different activities and shopping opportunities.

The different food trucks excite me most of all.

Every business has offered to do food at cost, with employees donating time, so that any profits can go toward the fundraiser.

I'm amped for the handmade noodles at the truck on the end. Unfortunately, not every truck is serving today, though some are because they'll get some money from those of us hanging around hungrily getting things set up.

I hear my name, and I'm sure that it's Nathan. I think I must be hallucinating even as I turn around. This man who wouldn't even come out of his room a couple of weeks ago is standing here in the middle of this half-assembled nonsense.

"What are you doing here?"

"I couldn't pass up the chance to check it out with everything in place. I wanted to cast an eye on the venue for the panel to figure out if I needed to bring anything else."

Except, he stopped now. With me here, with everyone here.

I want to believe he feels the same pull toward me that I do toward him. Toward something more. Something deeper.

I also . . . don't know what I would do if he did.

I'm not sure what to do. If I should move to him and display any kind of intimacy or not.

So I just stand here, clutching my clipboard when I want to be clutching him.

"This is . . . interesting," he says.

I laugh. “You have no idea.” I gesture toward the camels. “There’s livestock, which frankly even surprised me. I don’t have anything to do with the entertainment portion.” I pull a face. “I mean, obviously. Or we would’ve gotten anybody except . . .”

“Yep,” he says.

“At night this is going to be amazing,” I say. “I mean . . . it’s . . . it’s so glorious out here.”

I look off at the mountains, steep and purple, the sun casting gold over the craggy rocks and cacti.

“Yes,” he says.

He’s looking at me, though. Not the view. My heart expands, then contracts.

“Thank you.” I don’t want to seem like I’m thanking him for saying I’m glorious, in case he wasn’t. But my heart hopes.

That’s new. I’m not sure how I feel about it. The hope.

“Come on,” I say, moving us over to where the kids are rehearsing. “I think we are legally obligated to get an early look at the show.”

As we draw closer, the high-pitched singing grows louder, and at least that does something to dispel some of the tension in my chest.

“So this is what I’ve missed avoiding Christmas services with my parents all these years,” he says.

I laugh. “I don’t know. Maybe they aren’t this elite at your parents’ church.”

There is chaos as Mary moves into her position with flour bag Joseph, and the donkey jumps, and then a camel snorts and startles.

Reigna throws her hands up and yells, “Cut! Oh, hello, Amelia,” she says. “I’m so glad you stopped by to see rehearsal.”

“This is very impressive,” I say.

“Very. I can’t wait until Christopher is here to read for us.”

“I didn’t realize you were doing a whole manger scene. I thought that it was going to be . . .”

"Oh, it will be inclusive," she says. "We have a manger and will be doing a display with the menorah and a kinara. Of course, many portions will just include Santa as a secular symbol."

"I see," I say.

"I thought of everything," she says.

But the resolute refusal of the donkeys to behave makes me question this. Alice is sitting at the keyboard, and when she sees me, she waves.

And winks.

She is a scoundrel, which is why I love her.

"From the top," says Reigna.

The choir begins to sing "O Come, All Ye Faithful," and that's when everything falls apart. One of the donkeys gets loose and begins to run around the choir, which makes the camel startle again. Half the manger scene is knocked to the ground.

One of the children in the choir, whom I recognize as Lorena's oldest, gets jostled and falls over and starts crying, and Mary mobilizes. She stops in front of me, and suddenly, I find myself being handed baby Jesus.

"Can you hold her for a second?"

She races to her other child, and I find myself frozen. I haven't held a baby since . . .

I feel Nathan get still next to me. I'm horrified by the wave of grief that threatens to swallow me whole. Because it's been more than three years. This isn't my baby. I've seen babies. I've been around them. I've even seen Lorena's baby before. But I've never held her.

My throat feels too tight. My body strung out.

Nathan knows. He knows why I'm standing there, losing touch with reality. Losing touch with the ground. I know he doesn't know what to do. Neither do I. I can feel that he's about to take the baby for me, when suddenly, there is a gentle touch on my shoulder.

"I've got her," says Alice, looking up at me with startling clarity in her blue eyes.

Like she sees me. Like she sees what's hurting me.

She pats my shoulder and holds the baby close.

"You go on," says Alice.

Nathan takes my hand, squeezing it slightly as we walk away from the scene.

"I'm . . . I'm sorry I . . ."

"You don't have to apologize," he says.

He walks me to my Jeep and stands with me, saying nothing. He reaches out and touches my face. "I wish I knew the right thing to say."

"I don't think there is a right thing. I spent so much time wondering if there was something . . . anything . . . that my friends could've said. That Christopher could've said. But we experienced the same loss, and we couldn't even find a way to talk about it. So I don't know how anybody else is supposed to talk about it with me."

"What a dick," he says.

"I don't know if he was. Maybe he was. I . . . He wanted me to be fixed. I couldn't figure out how to be. I . . . I keep thinking I'm okay, Nathan. I keep thinking that I'm done grieving. Then it hits me, in this terrible wave. What's wrong with me? Why did I make that about me?"

"You didn't. You lost . . . Amelia, I've experienced loss. I understand grief. I know that it comes in waves that you can't anticipate. I know that it tries to drown you sometimes. I get it."

I wrap my arms around my body and try to hold myself together. "I just didn't expect that. I don't think about it all the time. That's the thing. It's the Chris trigger. He's . . . He's engaged, and he and his fiancée are having a baby. At least, that's what he said. That does hurt. It means he found a way to move past this that isn't quite how I did it. I've just been here. Hiding."

"Yeah. Well. I'm not exactly the person to ask about letting go of your grief. I've spent nearly three years working on my dead wife's memoirs."

I laugh, in that way you laugh when nothing is funny and everything hurts. "I mean, that is pretty impressive. I'm just the grief hide-and-seek champion. Except I think it's finally catching up to me."

"What can I do for you?"

"You shouldn't have to do anything for me."

"But I want to." He takes a deep breath. "I haven't wanted to do anything for anyone in a very long time. So please let me. It's been a really long time since . . ." He grits his teeth. "I know this might surprise you, but I'm kind of a hermit. Back home."

It doesn't surprise me, but it hurts me. I wanted to believe he had a network somewhere. That he falls apart when he comes here because this is where they went on their honeymoon. Because he's working on her story.

"I write, and generally, I don't associate with anyone," he says. "I have my deadlines, I start the next book. I have old friends. Friends that were hers and ours. My in-laws. They love me. Which, actually . . ." He swallows hard. "It's a terrible thing to watch them grieve. Because . . . She was everything to them. Their only child. I don't think my parents would be half as sorry to lose me. But here I am."

My heart twists. "That sounds suspiciously like survivor's guilt."

"We aren't supposed to be talking about me," he says.

"Why not?" I ask.

"You're hurt."

"The whole world is hurting."

"Don't do that. Don't minimize this. You don't have to. You don't have to be fair. Who made you feel like you had to be?"

I close my eyes. "You already know the answer to that. Like I said. We went through the same loss."

"You didn't experience it the same. It felt differently to him. Or maybe it didn't, but he expressed it differently. I haven't learned . . . I haven't learned anything. Writing my wife's memoirs, you would think I would learn something. About grief, about processing this. I haven't learned a damn thing. Except that it's not the same for me as it is for some people. A guy I went to high school with lost his wife, and a year later he got married again. I can't imagine that. Do you have any idea how terrifying it was when I found out my wife was sick? Living in the dread of . . . when she was going to go . . ." He shakes his head. "I can't imagine ever putting myself in that situation again. I mean . . ."

"When you feel so happy, and then you just lose it. It comes from nowhere."

I understand that. I felt like everything was coming together when I got pregnant. That something was going to be healed by it. Instead, something got broken. So much worse than it was before.

"Yes."

"Anyway. This sucks," I say.

"Yeah."

His agreeing with me is right up there with *I'm sorry*.

I've thought for a long time *I'm sorry* doesn't fix grief.

But right now, I think maybe that isn't true. Because having him with me right now makes me feel like something might be fixable in me that I didn't think was.

"You want to go home?" he asks.

I nod. "Yes."

He opens the car door for me. "I'll see you back there."

I feel good, knowing someone is going to be waiting for me. Even in the middle of this strange, unsettling wave, I know I can reach for him.

And that changes something.

CHAPTER TWENTY-FOUR

Found Family—when the protagonists create deeper bonds with their chosen community than they had with their family, and these bonds help the protagonists to heal.

I've done my best to recover from the earlier upset, and I'm ready to lose myself in Nathan. I had my word count to hit—several days of it—and admittedly, I throw myself into it a little bit more vehemently than maybe I need to.

I need the distraction. When I'm done in the office, I walk outside, wrapping my arms around myself. Alice, Lydia, Gladys, and Elise are sitting in the courtyard.

Alice looks at me, her eyes kind and soft. And I stop.

I want Nathan. But something makes me linger at the courtyard.

"Join us," Alice says.

I hesitate, then ultimately open the gate and head into the swimming pool area.

I can tell she's acting with caution but that she wants to ask if I'm okay. Suddenly, I feel . . . tired. Tired of holding my secrets in. Tired of carrying the weight of all this. Like it's something I'm ashamed of. It's not that. I'm not ashamed; it's just that sharing hasn't made it go away. If anything, it feels closer to the surface. I'm not broken, but . . .

Nathan understands grief. He wasn't thrown off by my reaction to it.

He didn't think it was odd that this many years later I'm still affected.

I'm searching for something, and I don't even know what it is. So I sit down.

"How did the rest of rehearsal go?" I ask.

"Fine once we got the camel settled down," Alice says, smiling. "I love that I can still experience new things even at ninety-five. That's a gift if you ask me. Though I'd like my next new experiences to include fewer barnyard animals."

"Is a camel a barnyard animal, really?" Lydia asks.

"It depends on where the barnyard is, I think," Gladys says in a sage tone.

Alice looks at me with those laser-focused eyes. She doesn't want to put me on the spot, and I know that. For some reason, right now I don't feel on the spot. I feel safe.

"It's okay," I say to Alice. "You can ask me."

The others in the group look at Alice and me intensely.

"Amelia," Alice says, in the most gentle tone I've ever heard from her. "Did you lose a baby?"

I nod. Wordlessly.

"I recognized that look on your face," she says softly. "It was the same one I saw looking back at me in the mirror after I lost my little girl."

Her little girl.

"Alice . . . I didn't know."

Alice does something I don't expect. She smiles. "Oh, it's amazing to think, it's been so many years. So many I don't count up how old she would have been." She lets out a gentle sigh. "Because there is no *would have* or *could have*, only what *is*. I do think, though, about how long I've loved her."

My heart feels sore.

Elise reaches across and grabs hold of my wrist, squeezing me tightly. She doesn't ask me why I didn't tell her. I don't know why I thought she would. Instead, she just holds on to me.

"It happened before I came here," I say. I tell them the story. About how the pregnancy was unexpected but I wanted it more than anything in the world.

About my pink nursery.

"I named her Emma." My voice breaks. "It's a beautiful name." I look at Elise, and I feel something fracture in my chest.

I haven't said her name like that since I got here. Then after I'd been there a year, I met Elise, and I wanted her to be my best friend. She had the prettiest little girl with the same name as the one I'd lost.

It felt wrong, to make it a sad thing.

I didn't want to make it a sad thing.

I didn't want my *life* to be sad.

I feel exhausted and angry. I don't understand why I have to deal with this. I never do this. I never get angry. About my terrible mother, my fucking awful ex-boyfriend. About the baby I lost that I wanted so much. More than I wanted him.

I feel it, so deep, so real, so hot and destructive.

Anger.

Anger because I have had to deal with so damned much. Anger, because I didn't know how else to handle it but to lock it away inside me.

I wipe tears away from my cheeks. "It just feels so pointless," I say. "I wanted to leave it behind. Because I don't want to carry it with me anymore. If I can't carry my baby, why . . ."

I break then. I didn't do it when I told Nathan. I do now. As these women, who have been so good to me, who have done things for me that my own mother never did, hold me. They all put their hands on me, and let my sorrow fill the silence.

When the wave subsides, Gladys finally speaks, her sharp brown eyes sparkling. "I lost two pregnancies before I had my son. You feel so alone sometimes when those things happen. Ashamed."

Alice nods. "Yes. Especially in our time. Women were supposed to be mothers. I failed at that. It made me useless for a long time. I didn't want to feel *different*, I didn't want to be different. What was the point, after all?" She sits in silence for a moment. "But I *am*. I'm different, and my life is different than I planned for. Different doesn't make it wrong, or bad, or failed. When I accepted that, I found a lot more peace."

I don't know what to say to that. So I listen. I'm hungry. Hungry for the wisdom of women. I wonder, for the very first time, if maybe that was why Christopher could never really understand.

Because I carried that baby. Because I was the one who had to give birth and come home with empty arms.

The person I would've wanted to talk to, my own mother, wouldn't be there for me. I hadn't even told her.

So I'm desperate now. For this woman to look at me and tell me I can be okay. She understands. She knows.

To sit with someone else who *knows* is the most healing thing I never knew I needed.

"It changed me," Alice says. "For a long time I resisted that. I wanted to pretend like none of it happened. I went to the hospital thinking I would come home with a child, and instead I lost my dreams. I wanted to forget. I wanted to go back to being myself." She lifts her shoulders, as if she's shrugging off a weight. "I couldn't. It wasn't until I realized that I could keep her with me, and I could let it hurt, and I could let it heal, that I actually began to find myself again. I've had a beautiful life. That loss . . . It wasn't beautiful. I wouldn't wish it on anybody. I don't think loss like that is *meant to be*. I don't think terrible things are so easily explained. Her life was real, a momentary thing. It was up to me what I decided to do with that love I had for her. I decided . . . slowly, over the course of time, that I could let that love be a gift. That I could remember it well."

I thought of how she had taken the baby from me. How she could hold her when I couldn't.

"We never had children," Alice says. "Not after that. Though, we had such a wonderful marriage, Amelia. Filled with so much love. I don't dwell on what isn't. But I *remember*."

Gladys seems to consider Alice's words before she looks at me again. "A child is a promise of a whole world," she says. "When you lose a pregnancy, a child, you lose that world. That doesn't mean it wasn't real. It doesn't mean it didn't matter."

That truth settles deep inside me.

My Emma's life is an unwritten story, but I can still write her into mine. The truth of what loving her means to me will underlie every syllable, every sentence. How can it not?

It *matters*.

She matters.

So do I. The loss I felt, the way I grieved and am still grieving. It matters.

I feel surrounded by this wisdom, held close by it. By these different experiences of motherhood. Elise, who has her Emma. Gladys, who had loss before her son. Alice, who found joy in a different world than she'd first dreamed for herself.

This, I realize, is something I was missing.

Sitting with women and asking them how they live. How they love. In spite of everything.

Because of everything.

I am in awe of the fierce strength in these women.

It makes me see a strength in myself I haven't seen before. It makes me see the real truth of what Elise and I were talking about earlier, that life is made up of pain and loss. That the happy endings happen between the unbearable.

And we keep going, until we find more happiness. However it looks.

Looking at Lydia, Gladys, and Alice is looking at loss. Of all different kinds. They're all widows now.

I realize now I'm not simply looking at loss. I'm looking at lives well lived.

Well loved.

I look around and realize that while I tried to leave things behind, I didn't leave everything behind. I brought the pink with me. I brought that hope.

I lost the world where I would watch my Emma grow.

My love of her, the hope of her, came to this new world with me.

Everything that's ever healed me, hurt me, shaped me has come to this world with me.

When I'm a mighty oak, like Alice, I'll be shaped by all of it.

It's my pain, which means it's up to me to try to decide what to do with it.

For a child that never breathed.

She changed me, and I'm glad she did.

This experience changed me. Maybe when I'm older, I'll hold someone else's baby with ease the way Alice did. Maybe someday I'll hold my own like Gladys.

Maybe someday I'll sit in this courtyard with a young woman experiencing this same loss and I'll hold her hand and speak with the confidence of time.

What I'm certain of, for the first time since everything fell apart, is that I'll be happy.

Truly happy. Because the lines on these women's faces are not all from tears.

They have smiled, and they still do. After loss. After hardship.

Alice is an oak.

Because of the love in her life, but the loss in it as well. It isn't an easy thing; it isn't a simple thing. It is only doing the very hardest work, it is only being willing to take the next step forward when you cannot see where it's taking you. It's letting your face smile again so it can make new lines that are forged by happiness and not just sorrow.

I can do that. I can.

I realize I've been missing something all along. I thought I left my grief behind.

I brought it with me, and I tucked it away. I kept it hidden so I could keep it safe, because I didn't know what my life would look like without carrying my daughter in that way, but I can do it in a different way.

I can do it like Alice. Who had to let herself be changed.

I can do it and not stay in the same place. I don't have to leave her behind entirely to find happiness. That's been the lesson of the last few weeks. I'm learning how to be. This new version of myself, not a fake one. Not one who was born the day I walked into Rancho Encanto. Not the woman I was in LA either, or the girl I was in Bakersfield.

I know what it costs to hope now. To strive for happiness. It is so much heavier, but I imagine when I was younger. When I hadn't lost anything. I've been afraid to imagine my future. Now I'm not. Someday I'll be like Alice. I'll look at a young woman, and I'll know. I'll have the right words for her. Maybe that's the only gift I have right now. The hope that someday I will be able to do for someone else what Alice did for me. I'll take that hope.

That healing. It makes sense in this moment. This village I've created.

Part of me aches, knowing I do still hope I can have that fairy-tale happy ending.

But part of me feels like it can rest. Because *this* is a happy ending. If it's all I ever have, it's a pretty damned good life.

A good world.

I dragged myself here. Wounded. Bleeding. Exhausted.

I've been afraid to start this new chapter. I've let the page stay blank for far too long. I was scared of what it would look like to start writing Amelia again. This changed version of me who won't be able to keep the subtext of grief out of this new chapter. Maybe out of all the chapters after.

I feel different about it now. I feel an acceptance of it. More than that, I feel ready to start. To see where it takes me, how it changes me, who I become.

My life doesn't have to be a blank page.

It's time for me to start writing my own story.

CHAPTER TWENTY-FIVE

I don't go to Nathan's room that night, and he doesn't come to mine. I think he understands that I need time. Time to go over my realizations, time to come to some new conclusions.

When that man walked into my motel almost three years ago, I thought he was a wreck.

I thought I was living in some kind of accepted space. I was in the after of a painful experience, but I knew it, and I was moving forward.

I was wrong.

I'm just as much of a wreck as he is.

I find a strange sort of comfort in that.

I'm a wreck, but I'm ready to be less of one. I'm ready to make some changes.

The next morning I send him a text, and he's at my door with coffee twenty minutes later.

"Are you okay?" he asks.

I sit with that for a moment. "I am. I . . . I'm better, I think. Better than I've been for a while. Who knew, I just needed to . . . talk about it."

I know it isn't that simple. It isn't just talking about it. It's actually sitting in the wisdom of other women. It's being in that community.

"You know, I think I understand why women got accused of witchcraft so often," I say.

"Really?"

"Yes. Because our wisdom is powerful. It upends the rules. Changes how you see things. About life, about yourself. At least, that's what happened to me last night."

"I'm definitely not going to argue with you about the wisdom of women."

He looks like he wants to say something more, but he doesn't. I don't push him, even though I want to.

"So," I say. "I have kind of a wild idea."

"What is that?"

He turns his full attention to me when he asks that question, and I think that kind of focus could become an addiction. I remember Christopher half looking up from his laptop when I'd talk to him, and it isn't like I wasn't distracted sometimes too.

This is just different.

This is something totally new. That's all.

"I want to drive to Bakersfield today."

I don't fully realize that that's what I'm going to say until the words exit my mouth. Because it was only a germ of an idea spinning around in the back of my mind from the time I got out of bed. I really hadn't decided I was going. Much less including another person in my psychosis. Now I've invited him, and I can't go back.

"Your mother?"

"Yes. I am hurt. By the whole lack of relationship I have with her. By everything. I try to pretend I'm not. I try to pretend it doesn't matter. I . . ." I take a deep breath to ground myself.

"I don't know if I can explain it. I've told myself and told myself that it's okay. That she is just who she is. She can't help it, she has a personality disorder. Whatever. I think to an extent, that is a really healthy thing for me to do. I'm not taking her issues on board, I'm trying to make my own life, but the problem is that I'm hurt by it. I don't know if I just need to tell her that, or what. It feels like I deserve something. I don't know. Or maybe I just need to see the house that I grew up in.

Maybe I just need to see her. I'm very good at running, Nathan. The thing about running is it's not closure. It's just leaving things behind. But if you run too fast, you leave the door open, and all kinds of shit follows you. Whether you mean it to or not. Letting shit follow you isn't the same as working it out either."

"Right. I mean, I'm familiar with shit."

"I know."

"Actually, I really do want to go on this journey to your childhood trauma."

"That is the nicest thing anyone has ever said to me," I say. "So . . . come along with me as I drain some poison."

He smiles at me, and I want to save the image of that forever. It's gone too quickly.

"I'll drive," he says. "I get better gas mileage."

"No doubt," I say.

We bring our coffee and head out to his car. It is a very cute car.

We get in, and I quiz him on his music preferences. And scowl in judgment about all of them, even though I have never met a genre of music I didn't like. Unsurprising, his tastes are more *discerning*.

"I love pop music," I say as we head down the two-lane road that will carry us to the interstate.

"It's not for me," he says. "It's too . . . bright and happy."

"That's why I love it," I say. "It sounds light, and it sounds easy, but sometimes the lyrics are devastating. That's . . . life, isn't it?"

"I think you're putting too much thought into '. . . Baby One More Time.'"

"You can never put too much thought into Ms. Britney Spears," I say.

"I didn't know anyone felt that strongly about it."

"Have you never been on the internet?"

"No," he says. Which makes me laugh because I know he's lying.

As we drive, my phone rings. I look at it, and then I feel my heart slam against my breastbone.

Chris.

Of course. He'll be rolling into town this weekend, and he was asked to moderate the panel. He's trying to do . . . whatever this is. Damage control of a kind, maybe. I suppose I would know if I answered.

"You can get that," Nathan says.

"I don't want to."

"Why not?"

"Fucking *Fuck*," I say.

"Oh. It's him?"

I look over at him, and I see the tension in his forearms, the way his hands tightened on the steering wheel.

I'm satisfied by the fact that Christopher creates this level of tension in him as well.

"You do realize you have to see him this weekend?"

"Yes," I say, redirecting. "But it won't be on the phone. It won't be because he decided to break years of silence. It won't be in a moment with no one there so he can say whatever he wants. I'm going to stand next to you, and I'm going to introduce you, and I'm going to say that I own a motel here. That I write books now. That I'm very happy to see him. Then I'm going to congratulate him on his new life, and his new fiancée, and his new baby." My eyes fill with tears, and I'm not even sure why.

"You don't have to do that," he says.

"No, I don't, though I think it would make my life a lot better if I did. I think I would feel better. I think I would feel like I had drawn a line under it, or something."

"Is that how you feel?"

"No." I'm aware there's a terrible irony to that because we are currently speeding toward Bakersfield, where I intend to say some very stark things to my mother, and I'm still not sure what I want to say to Christopher. Or if I want to tell him the truth. I'm not even sure what the truth is.

I sit there, staring at the road and the way it rolls in waves over the farmland, dry and difficult.

"I don't love him," I say. "I know that. I'm sure of it. I think I wouldn't be with him even if . . . even if Emma had lived."

This is my first time saying her name to Nathan. This is my first time trying to honor that world while I'm living in this one. It's given me a good place to put it. Sometimes I think that is maybe the best thing you can do with grief. Because you're going to live with it. It's going to be with you. How do you carry it so it doesn't get too heavy? I don't want to forget her. I don't want to believe that the loss was meant to be. I can accept that there was the potential for a life, for a world, that there is no longer a potential for. That I live in a different world because of that loss. I can honor that while living. While I write myself a new story, while I put myself into a new world, full of new possibilities.

"You think so?"

"I know so," I say. "The problems that we had, they would've been the problems no matter what. The things that he . . . I was so broken when I lost her. I couldn't be the woman he wanted me to be."

I stare out the car window at the cracked, faded road. The yellow grass and rocky hills. "Fundamentally, the way we deal with hard things is so different. I was too . . . lost. In my own grief. I'm not saying it was something I did wrong, but I could never have found a way to meet him in the middle even if I had wanted to. Even if it had occurred to me. He certainly didn't try with me. He was frustrated. I was lagging behind him as far as he was concerned. He wanted to get back to the way things had been. Then, when I couldn't meet his needs, rather than continuing to try with me, he found somebody else. That's the bottom line. I'm not saying he can't change now. I'm not saying he can't make a different decision with this woman he's engaged to now. But unless he's dealt with the thing that made him treat me the way he did, he'll do the same thing to her. Even if we hadn't lost her, I think eventually he would have cheated. Not because there's something wrong with me."

Those words are a revelation. A breakthrough. "There's nothing wrong with me," I say. There is no noise, except the tires on the road. I let out a long breath. "There is *nothing wrong with me*."

"No," Nathan says. "Of course there's not."

"I felt like there was. For . . . always. *Always.* How could I not? My dad left because he loved another woman so much that he had to be with her. And not with me. My mom can only love herself. The way I carried a baby was wrong. The way I grieved that baby was wrong. At least as far as he was concerned. I'm not the problem, though. I'm not."

"Amelia," he says. "I consider myself incredibly lucky to have found somebody who accepted me the way that I was. The truth is, somebody who's been made to feel like you do, all of your life, someone who felt the way I did because of my dad, we are way more likely to keep repeating that cycle in every relationship we have. Because we'll take anything."

His wisdom is surprising, and definitely true.

"Did you take anything before you met Sarah?"

"Yeah. I had a history of it. I'm over six feet tall and I have a job. So I never had trouble finding women to date me. I had trouble getting them to accept that I wasn't what they initially fantasized I might be. They thought I was G.I. Joe. That I was going to be their military boyfriend fantasy. Then I spent more time reading books than they wanted me to. I didn't want to go out. I didn't do the party thing. I didn't . . . I didn't give them what they wanted. For a long time, I let that affect me. I figured . . . it was something wrong with me, because . . ."

"You always got treated like there was something wrong with you."

This is Psychology 101, and I know it. But having it laid out for me like this, having it spoken so plainly, and about my issues, is both jarring and revelatory.

In the back of my mind, there is always this little wheedling voice that says I was the commonality in all these relationships. The truth is, my parents taught me to take nothing. They taught me that sharing the deepest parts of myself didn't matter. That my feelings weren't important. That the things I cared about weren't important. Then I met a man who treated me better than that, because Chris had. For a long time he had. When I met him, I wasn't critical of some of the other issues.

I should have been. "Thank you for coming with me on this four-hour car ride of childhood trauma."

"There's nowhere else I'd rather be."

I choose not to dig too deeply into that, but I also choose not to question it. I let that assurance wash over me. I feel something stirring deep inside me. I don't want to give words to it. I don't even want to give it a voice. It still echoes loudly in my head and my heart all the same.

I try to accept the fact that he and I are on that happiness continuum. It's not forever. Even so, I feel different. Something is shifting inside me. My ability to just accept, to just float, doesn't seem to exist in quite the same way that it did.

I've decided to swim. I can feel myself on the edge of a waterfall. I have to make decisions. About everything. I have to decide how I'm going to deal with Chris. I have to decide what I want to do with Nathan.

First, though, we're going to talk to my mother.

I make a squeaking noise that's nearly a scream and cover my face with my hands.

"That's the mood?" he asks.

"Until further notice," I say.

He nods. "Fair."

"I need some music."

"How about some Britney Spears."

We are propelled by pop music all the way to Bakersfield. By the time we get there, I feel nothing. It's an out-of-body experience, driving past the same fields I remember from childhood. The same buildings.

It has changed, but not that much.

I'm different, though. I have changed so much since I was a kid here.

I felt insignificant and lonely most of the time.

It's never been Bakersfield that's the problem. Just the way I felt in it. I realize that strongly as we drive through town and make our way toward the street my mother still lives on.

I don't know if she'll be home. It might be an exercise in futility.

I could have texted her. I really didn't want to.

I didn't want her to rehearse. I didn't want to have any contact beforehand. I just . . .

We roll up to the front of the house. The grass is dead. It's been so dry. There's one palm tree in the front yard that's still alive.

The house is in desperate need of a new coat of paint. There's a car in the driveway with the hood popped. It's up on cinder blocks. There's another car that looks functional.

I take in the little details of disrepair. They speak of solitude.

If I lived near my mother, if we had a relationship, I would take care of some sort of landscape to make it look nicer. I would've helped her fix her car.

I would have helped arrange to have someone paint the house.

I realize that I came here to yell at her. I came here to tell her what a terrible mother she was.

Everything in her life already speaks to that. She's been cut off. By everyone.

I feel that. Deeply in my soul.

The pain of it. In that moment, I feel sorry for her.

Because there is nothing wrong with me.

There is something desperately wrong with her, and she's never been able to have a relationship with her daughter.

Yes, it gave me issues. I'm angry about it. I have every right to be. What I'm angry about is the lack of a mother who can give me the things most mothers can. I ache for a person who doesn't exist, and no amount of confrontation is going to fix that.

I came here to say something to her that would satisfy me.

"What does your dad's house look like?" I ask Nathan as we sit there in front of the house.

"It's nice," he says. "He has the lawn cut every week. In fact, he has landscapers. He can afford to keep everything looking great."

"Do your brothers help him with things? Projects?"

He shakes his head. "They're busy with their own lives."

"Have they helped you?"

"They're busy with their own lives," he reiterates.

Suddenly I'm just . . . over it. Everything.

"It's awful," I say. "This isolation. For what? This . . . this selfishness. In your case, this idea that a good son looks a certain way. Well, even your father's good sons aren't there for him, because they're self-important just like he is. If they only knew you. Because I started reading your book, Nathan, and it's amazing. The observations that you make about life in the military . . . They're so compelling."

He snorts. "People don't really read for that."

"I do," I say. "You're smart about people. You pay attention to them. You write about them in interesting and compassionate ways, and it says so much about who you are. It is incredibly stupid that your dad doesn't care about that. You could give your family insight into their own experiences that they probably don't have."

He barks a laugh. "They would just say I don't actually understand because I only served four years."

"Look what you did with it. Look what you're doing with it still. You had a woman who loved you. Do they even have that?"

"My brothers are married," he says.

"Well," I say. "Still."

"They have lives that are just like my dad's," he says. "My parents were married for forty-five years. I don't think they knew each other. That's a really scary thing, Amelia. Maybe you would have stayed with Christopher. If you had a child, maybe he would've cheated on you, and you would've stayed. Or maybe he would've hidden it, or you would have pretended to let him hide it because you didn't want to break up the family, because you didn't want to destroy the facade. You can be married to somebody who doesn't know you for a very, very long time. I saw that, in my parents' marriage. People accept the worst kind of bullshit."

"You're better off," I say. "You're . . ."

I start to say that he's *happier*. But I'm not sure he is. He's locked himself away from his family, and that's a win. Except he's locked away completely.

Not now, though. Right now, he's with me.

"Well," I say. "This is what my mother has. Because she's alienated her only child. Looking at it . . . I honestly just feel sorry for her. I don't want this. If I have children someday, if I . . . have children I actually get to . . . raise, I don't want this. I guess I should be glad I can look at her sad lawn, and her dilapidated house, and I can recognize what it means to not be a mother. I can recognize what I don't want. I . . . I was so lucky last night to get to sit and talk to Alice and Gladys. To get to listen to them share their wisdom with me, because I did not ever get maternal wisdom from this woman. Right now, this is wisdom of a kind. I know what I don't want. I know who I can't ever let myself become. I've been an observer for so many years. I have the people at the Pink Flamingo. I have to make sure I don't isolate myself from the people who care for me."

He looks grave. I realize I've stepped on something touchy here.

"People care about you," I say.

"If they don't anymore," he says, "it is definitely my own fault."

"Nathan," I say. "You're not a narcissist. You lost your wife. It's different."

"Maybe," he says. "The end result might be the same, though." He huffs a laugh. "I'm the crazy guy who lives alone on an island. I will be Old Man Hart before I know it. The kids will be afraid to get a ball off my lawn."

"Well, they should get off your lawn," I say.

"I'm sure I'll be shouting that while shaking my fist in . . . Hell, I probably only have ten years."

Time.

Time just grinds relentlessly on.

And kills the grass and fades the paint. And turns your hair silver. And makes rifts widen. Makes pain turn into a dull ache.

Not now. Not with us.

"I'm not going to get anything from this," I say to him.

"You don't think?"

"No," I say. "I already know there's nothing I can say to her. I already know I can't . . . I can't say a set of magic words to her and make her suddenly care about all the pain she put me through. That's not realistic. What I wanted to do was tell her all the ways she failed, but she's just going to turn it back around on to me. That's who she is. She'll resist character development at every turn, trust me. I'm glad I came here. I see it clearly now. I see myself clearly now too."

"We drove all this way," he says.

"Yes. That's already more than she's ever done for me. I have put more thought and more effort into this relationship than . . ." I clear my throat. "I think I just need to let it go. Because I'm living my life. A life I'm choosing. I can't make my childhood hurt less. All I can do is decide where my energy goes. And it's not going to be here."

He nods slowly. "Good for you."

"Yeah," I say. "Very good for me." I feel like I needed the drive, I needed to sit here. I needed to look at this house and feel nothing but pity for the person who lives inside.

I needed to feel, profoundly, that this isn't my home. I grew up in that house, but it's not my home.

Rancho Encanto is my home. It is maybe the only place I have ever felt at home. I'm done keeping my roots shallow. I'm going to let them grow deep.

"It's good," I say. "We skipped fighting. We skipped the screaming. We skipped the inevitable blame game. Some people don't change."

"But you're changing," he says.

"I damn well am."

We're silent for a moment. "So, is your dad the kind of parent it just makes more sense to be no contact with, or is he someone you can reason with?"

"The complication with my dad was always my mother. I loved her. He sucks. She put up with it. I still talk to him, and I still go over for dinner on occasion. Because she would want that. She wouldn't want him by himself—she never did. That's why she stuck it out."

I wish I could have dinner with his dad. I wish I could tell him what a wonderful man Nathan is.

Then I realize I'm wishing for things that extend far beyond what we've agreed to. As we make our way back to Rancho Encanto, instead of shutting that down, I let it simmer inside me. I let myself consider what that might mean.

I feel like I'm getting closer to giving those feelings a voice.

Like I don't just know how I would write it.

I know how I want to say it.

CHAPTER TWENTY-SIX

I wake up before Nathan the next morning. It's early, the sun is rising, and my courtyard is flooded with pink. Not just Pink Flamingo pink, but the rose from early-morning sun. Nathan is asleep in my bed, naked. He looks beautiful. I stand there and look at the room. My motel room. My home.

He fits.

At least for me. I don't know if he could ever fit for him.

I'm tired of being hurt.

Though, the truth is, I've never fought for a relationship either.

That thought settles over me like a blanket as I get dressed and quietly slip out the door.

The air is cool, and it smells damp. The sun casts a sharp wedge of light over half the pool, the water a glimmering jade. That's when I see Alice, sitting there at the same table she was occupying the night she told me about her child.

I know why I woke up early.

I push the gate open and walk forward. "Hi, Alice."

She looks up, and the wind catches her white hair, a smile brightening her face. "Good morning, Amelia."

"Can I sit?"

"Of course," she says.

I didn't go in and talk to my mother yesterday. There is nothing for me to learn from her. There's nothing that matters.

Not there, in that sad, dilapidated house. I won't learn anything by shining a flashlight in the dark corners of my childhood. Picking over the bones of all my disappointment.

It occurs to me that life has done a decent job of bringing love to me. Even when I wasn't looking for it.

"I wanted to thank you. For the other night."

She shakes her head. "No thanks are required."

"I want to thank you. I have a mother, and she can't love anyone but herself. When I needed her the very most, she wasn't there for me." I close my eyes. "Not just one time. So many times. I needed wisdom, and I didn't have a mother who could give it. I needed love, and I didn't have a mother who could give it."

"You know," Alice says, "people say dreadful things sometimes. They don't know they're dreadful. They say them without thinking. They say them without considering who they might be talking to. I have heard, countless times, that a woman doesn't know love until she has a child. There are a great many women who don't really know love, even when they have children. Amelia, I have known love. Great and deep and terrible. Beautiful, destructive. Self-sacrificial. Selfish, sometimes. I've lived so many lives all in one. It is a life's work to look back on all your years and see that what you are, what you felt, what you experienced, was enough all along. Even now, here I am. With you. Here, in this place. It's new. Even at ninety-five, there are still new people and places to see and be in. Believe me, my girl. I know love." She puts her hand out and presses it over mine. "So do you."

I feel like this wisdom is unearned. Like I haven't lived enough to hear it.

I want her certainty. I feel like I do know love.

More importantly, I'm starting to realize what I want it to look like in my life.

Maybe I still want everything. Or maybe this is the first time I've actually wanted everything.

With Christopher I wanted whatever he would give me. I was determined to bend myself into whatever shape worked. Until I couldn't do that anymore.

Until my feelings were bigger than his.

Choosing those feelings, choosing myself, has been the best thing. It's what brought me here.

To this moment.

To Nathan.

"I . . . Alice," I say. "I don't want to say the wrong thing. I just feel like I need to tell you that you've been the mother I needed. The one I never got. When I went to see her yesterday . . . I tried to go see her yesterday. I didn't want to go in. I didn't want to have a conversation with her. There were a lot of good reasons for that. I didn't realize until just now that I have experienced what it's like to have a good, loving woman in my life. One who supports me. Cares for me. One who has the wisdom for me I am aching for. One who sees me. So I just wanted to thank you. For being something she couldn't."

Alice squeezes my hand, and I'm quite certain I see tears in her blue eyes. At least, as certain as I can be because of all the tears in mine.

"A life as long as I've had," Alice says, "is filled with all kinds of possibilities. So many doors you can walk through. So many worlds. I'm happy with the world I spent all these years in."

"Can I ask you another question?"

"Of course you can."

"You loved Marty so much. You built a life together. A beautiful one. He was the love of your life."

"Yes," she says.

"If someone is the love of your life . . . there's no . . . is there no one else you can love after that?"

"I don't believe that," Alice says. "You have to understand, I'm a woman from a very specific era. My husband was a wonderful man.

When he died, I could wear shorts, even though he never liked them. I could get a bichon frise, even though he always said they were terrible dogs. I didn't have to ask anyone permission for anything. I didn't have to consider someone else's feelings. I wanted freedom more than I wanted romance. *Freedom* was something I hadn't had in my life before. I'm not saying that he was a controlling man, or a bad one. It's just that even in the nicest relationships, you have to consider each other. I wanted to be selfish. Like I said, I am an oak. I don't wish to choose to bend around anything new, but that's not to say there's anything *wrong* with bending your life around someone."

She pauses for a long moment. "I think the most important truth is that I didn't meet anyone who could hold a candle to the love of my life. I didn't meet anyone who made me want romance more than solitude. I did meet a man who made me forget myself. Who made me lose my head. I had a couple of love affairs after Marty died."

I feel scandalized by this. "Did you?"

"Yes," she says. "I didn't want to share my life, but that didn't mean I wanted an empty bed. The truth is, had one of those men been special . . ."

I feel hollow.

"They still wouldn't have been the love of your life."

"No," she says. "Not the love of the life I lived with Marty. As we've already discussed, Amelia, the loss of someone is the loss of the world. It's also the loss of who you were before."

I know this. I think about it all the time. The before and the after.

"Marty was the love of my life, of my youth, the one who held me after our greatest loss. The one who formed so much of who I am. When he was gone, I had to find a different life. It stands to reason that for the new woman I was, shaped and changed by my grief, there could have been a love. There wasn't, and I'm happy with it. I was never motivated enough to search for it."

I'm stunned by this.

"That . . . makes so much sense," I say.

"Of course it does. I'm very wise. Because I'm *so old*." She smiles at that.

She *is* old. And it's beautiful. Wonderful. Just like her.

"Alice, I am going to write you the smuttiest book as a thank-you."

"Make sure it's substantial." She holds her hands out as if she's measuring a salmon she caught.

"I can do that," I say.

"Does this have anything to do with that handsome gentleman in room thirty-two?"

"Maybe," I say. Though I realize there's no point in hiding anything from Alice. "Yes."

"You should never be anything less than the love of someone's life, Amelia. So the question will simply be whether he's smart enough to snag you or not."

Or a million other things. I'm not going to argue with her. Instead, I'm going to hold all the wisdom she's just shared with me close to my chest.

I've had two of the most important conversations in my life in the last couple of days. With her. I want to hang on to everything I can.

For the first time, I wonder if it's a gift that I'm not yet a mighty oak.

That I can still change and bend, because that's the time of my life that I'm in.

Because I'm thirty-two. Because there are so many more doors left open. So many more worlds.

I suddenly don't feel afraid. Of whatever is going to happen with Christopher, or whatever might happen with Nathan.

I decide to go back to my room. I decide to get back in bed with him.

The parade is in just a couple of days, followed by the reading of "A Visit from St. Nicholas," performed by Christopher.

It will all take care of itself. For now, I'm just going to be in this world that's only me and Nathan.

CHAPTER TWENTY-SEVEN

Plot Moppet—a small child in a romance who exists solely to drive the plot forward or cause a shift in the romance between the main characters.

Rehearsal for the children's performance is happening at the Pink Flamingo today. It's amazing to think that only a couple of days ago I might've struggled with this. There are some shards of glass still embedded in my heart that cut a little bit, but I've figured out how to carry them better. I have my found family to thank for that. And so many things. Even the meddling.

Maybe especially the meddling.

The courtyard is in absolute shambles. There are children in angel robes, in stocking caps and scarves that they don't need. There is a mitten floating on the top of my pool.

Alice is warming up at the keyboard, and the notes of "O Holy Night" are plinking through the air at an extremely high volume.

Angel, Sofia, and Emma are passing out snacks and generally acting as if they are the tiny managers of the motel. Which I suppose is fair, since they live here. I get a small kick of secondhand joy from seeing them own their environment like this.

Being seen as being on the inside is the kind of thing that makes you feel really special when you're a kid.

It's been a while since I let myself really look at children. Appreciate the pureness of their joy, the small things that make them happy.

The ruckus is loud enough that I know Nathan isn't getting any work done. So when the door to room 32 opens and he steps out, I'm not surprised.

I do, however, feel the need to apologize.

"Sorry. Probably impacting your writing time."

"I'm not worried about it. The big project is almost done, anyway."

My heart squeezes slightly. "True."

There are a few players missing during this rehearsal. There are no live animals, and Santa Claus is not in attendance. Neither are Mary, Joseph, or baby Jesus.

As rehearsal gets started, Emma comes over and grabs hold of Nathan's hand. He looks at her, then at me, surprised.

"Nathan," she says, regarding him with sincere eyes. "You should be the donkey."

"I should be?" he asks.

I've seen him be kind to the children, but I haven't really seen him interact with them. Not like this. But Emma and Sofia are fascinated by him, and I can't blame them. He's tall and imposing. Fascinating. A *pirate*, Emma thought.

"Amelia," Sofia says. "You can be a camel."

"Why am I a camel?" I ask.

"Because you are," Sofia says, as if that is the most sensible thing and my arguing with it would be foolish.

Nathan and I are both brought to an area I assume is the designated stable.

"You have to be on all fours," Emma commands.

Nathan looks at me, and my face gets hot. "There are children present," I say.

"I didn't say anything," he says.

He doesn't deny the children's demands, so then I feel like I can't. Which is how we find ourselves on our hands and knees on the Astroturf.

For the entire Christmas song set.

"It's very creative," he whispers to me.

"I think they're singing in five different keys."

"You have to give them credit for flourish."

During "O Little Town of Bethlehem," one of the little girls climbs onto Nathan's back, as if it's her job to be ferried by the donkey, and as if he is, in fact, method acting as a donkey.

He smiles and complies, making big clopping sounds and movements on his hands and knees.

I break the rules and sit up, watching him as he trots the small child around. He has a crowd of children around him, shrieking in delight, and now I know he's going to get asked for rides endlessly by the smallest children.

He would make a great father.

That thought is like a punch to the gut. I'm not supposed to hope for things like that. I'm not supposed to hope for a child and *forever.* I'm supposed to be at peace with where I'm at.

It's a fine line. Being at *peace* and hiding from your demons.

I know that's true. I know that I would have to put any heroine through the fire on this one. I would have to confront her with the things she really wants, the things that hurt the most, the things she needs to heal from.

I would have to make her talk about her deep wound. I would have to make her go and find some kind of peace with her mother.

I would have to . . . do so many of the things I'm already doing.

There have been a lot of pivotal moments over the last couple of weeks. Over the last few months. Over the last three years. This quiet, happy moment in the courtyard feels somehow the most altering.

Because I'm not just looking at my sadness. I'm not just examining my grief. I'm looking at potential happiness.

I'm looking at something that could be.

It's like I had writer's block and suddenly the words are flowing. But it's not a page, it's my life.

I stand up, and I realize that my hand is pressed to my chest.

Alice moves from behind the keyboard and makes her way to me, her hand resting on my forearm. "It's okay to want that," she says. "I hope you know. It's okay to want everything."

"What if I can't have everything?"

"You'll survive. You'll keep on living. You'll smile again. You'll dream again. You get to be my age, and you realize that you had everything that was meant for you. So you might as well want it all, then see what comes."

Maybe it's greedy, standing here in the motel courtyard with so many people who love me, to want Nathan Hart to love me too. To want him to love me most of all.

I would let a fictional woman want all of this, so why can't I?

I want him. I want everything.

The scene before me is devolving into utter chaos, but I have one more surprise. It's the reminder I need to kick myself into gear.

"Okay," I say, raising a hand. "Children. Who wants to help me decorate a special Christmas tree?"

The kids scramble over to where I'm standing. "I have an extra tree for the auction that's happening at A Very Desert Christmas. I would love to auction it off and donate the money to help build you all a new school. I have all kinds of decorations, and I want you guys to just put as many on the tree as you want."

I retrieve the tree from where it's lying on the outside of the courtyard. It's a silver tinsel tree, synthetic through and through.

Then I retrieve eclectic bins of ornaments. This will not be a tree with any theme other than childlike abandon.

The kids go to town on it, and the end result is a loud, glorious disaster.

Nathan helps lift small children up to hang ornaments near the top.

I like him.

I like him *so much*.

I've listened to his pain. I have licked him everywhere.

I feel a deep, profound connection with him. We recognize each other, at the deepest places we carry our pain.

But along with that, I can confidently say that I just like him. And that, I feel, is incredible all on its own.

It feels like something too big and bright to be contained.

I don't want to contain it.

I just want to feel it.

When the kids are finished, the tree is like a great glowing horror, and they are overjoyed. They circle around the tree in excitement until their parents come to get them, and then Nathan carries it to my room for safekeeping until we can move it out to the auction site this weekend.

"That's not a Charlie Brown Christmas tree," he says. "That is something else entirely."

"It's joy," I say.

He looks at me, his eyes grave. And then he grips my chin and kisses me. "I think you might be right."

Joy. He feels it too. This big, beautiful, incredible thing. I want to tell him what I'm feeling. I want to tell him how much I like him.

Instead I kiss him. Instead, I let him take my clothes off. I say with my body what feels difficult to put into words.

We'll have time for that.

I have to believe we will.

CHAPTER TWENTY-EIGHT

Knowing nothing is happening Thursday and Friday makes me feel like I'm on vacation. Yes, I have my usual motel duties, and we have the dive-in movies. I'm not driving to Bakersfield, and I'm not confronting my old wounds and slaying dragons, so it feels nearly peaceful.

Nathan and I hole up in his room, unusual because I still feel weird about being in a guest's room, but here we are.

"This feels naughty," I say, stretching out on the end of his bed while he sits at his desk, typing and looking furious at the world.

He just looks that way sometimes. It's intensity. It's caring. It's part of who he is.

I've inhaled two of his thrillers, even with everything that's going on. They're like the man himself. Sharp, insightful, hard in some ways. His main protagonists are so emotionally invulnerable, I want to punch them in their rock-hard stomachs. There are no romances in his books. Sex, liaisons, but nothing I'd call a real romance.

Typical, and he isn't typical in so many other ways.

He turns and looks at me. "I'd report you to HR, but I think that's . . . you."

"Maybe." I roll over onto my stomach. "I ship Tanner with Monica, by the way." His main military man and his friend slash colleague are, in my opinion, crying out for some bedpost-rattling sex and a happy ending.

"Nope," he says.

"You can't tell me what I ship, Nathan."

He looks at me. "I can tell you what I don't intend to write."

"Boring!"

"Why is that boring?"

I throw my hands into the air. "Like, goddamn, Nathan, he's always saving the world, and she's there for him. Don't they deserve some happiness?"

"Some people can't be happy. They have missions." He turns back to his computer, and I wonder if he means him. I also wonder if he's working on Sarah's book.

I stand up and move behind him, wrapping my arms around his shoulders. He doesn't pull away or hide the screen from me.

"How is the mission?" I ask.

"I'm . . . done," he says.

It's so final and so strange, even to me. "Oh. Nathan, I'm . . ." I don't know if I'm supposed to be happy for him or if this is another form of losing her.

Writing about her, pulling her words from her journals and turning them into a story, would have kept her close to him. Now it's just done.

I take a breath. "Can I read it?"

He stills beneath my touch.

"I don't have to," I say, starting to pull away, but he puts his hand over my wrist and holds me there.

"You can."

We stay like that for a second, and I can feel his heart beating under where my arm rests against him. Hard. Steady.

I close my eyes. "Only if you're okay with it."

"I want you to read it," he says, and his voice is stronger now, surer.

He emails me the document, and I get my laptop and sit in his bed. I start reading, and I'm not sure what I expect from this book. From this faithful adaptation of a woman's life, written by the man who loved her.

But it's somehow more, somehow deeper than I could've imagined.

It isn't just Sarah I'm reading about, but Nathan. Because I can see her through his eyes. I can see how much he admired her. I can see her achievements through the lens of someone who loved her so much, and it humbles me.

I have never had a single person in my life who looked at something that I did in this way. I don't feel envious, not really. I'm in awe. That somebody like him can see a person that way even after everything he's been through.

That this kind of love and connection can exist in the world.

Nathan offers to get us lunch, and I nod in agreement as I shift positions and stretch across the bed with the laptop in front of me, my chin propped up on my hands.

He talks about how they met. How deeply she accepted him. There is honesty in these pages, about all the ways in which they clashed through the years. They're both active people. Nathan loves to hike. Sarah always wants to be outdoors with her horses, or entertaining friends, and Nathan wants to spend hours working on his book. She's proud, but she doesn't quite understand him. I realize that's the lens he sees her through as well. He is astonishingly proud of everything she does. He doesn't love horses, not like she does. He understands that it matters to her, and because of that it matters to him. They pour so many resources into her endeavors. It is a very real support.

He finds a way to love it because she does.

I find the capacity for that fascinating too. I also know what it's like, to be the partner who's slightly more introverted, and I'm not even as introverted as Nathan. But I didn't want to go to industry events all day every day in the way that Chris did. I had to be dragged to them sometimes, and it felt like putting on a mask to get ready to go. I can see a sensitivity in the way he and Sarah handled this with each other that I didn't experience in my own relationship. I think that maybe their commitment to being different and supportive is a very rare thing.

I think how much it must've meant to him, coming from a family where he was very different from his parents, from his brothers, and finding someone who not only accepted him but who did it while not being exactly the same person he was.

That is a gift.

I can't help but love Sarah as I read this book. Her drive is singular, to the point where, when she is diagnosed with cancer, her primary concern is still making it to the Olympics. She doesn't want anyone to know she's sick. There are times during her illness where that puts a massive strain on her and Nathan, even as he recognizes that this is *her* life and she has to be able to go out the way that she wants to. She doesn't want to extend her life for four or six months longer if she misses out on the things she loves the most.

She doesn't want to lie in a bed. She doesn't want a surgery that will make her worse and not heal her entirely.

I feel his tension in that, his acceptance, but I also feel her bravery. Her strength. There is so much certainty in her. Of course, her choice costs Nathan. It costs him time. He's the one left with the whole life to live after.

Even so, her decision isn't selfish, and he never comes close to painting it that way. Her decision is the sum total of her life and her legacy. The writing is his determination to honor it.

Nathan comes back with food, but I'm lying here crying very real tears as Sarah wins her final gold medal. Thin and ill, with people making comments about eating disorders while in reality colon cancer has ravaged her body. She doesn't let it affect her because she knows her strength. She was a very strong person in ways I'm not sure I've ever had to be. In ways I know I've never had to be. I'm not sure I've ever known who I am with the level of certainty that Sarah Hart did.

I realize that Nathan could only know her this well after she was gone. He knew her the whole time, but he got her side of it after. I can't help but feel a sense of tragedy in that.

Or maybe it isn't tragic. Maybe it's just a miracle to be known this way, no matter when it happens.

He sits in his desk chair, holding the bag with our food, and I keep reading, overwhelmed by a swell of emotion. The book doesn't end with her dying. It ends with that medal. I lay my head down and weep. He says nothing.

I can't say anything.

Not for a while.

When I finally do find words, I just want them to be the right ones. Our grief is different. My loss doesn't mean that I perfectly understand his. Or that I have all the right words. He had to love her while letting her do things that physically hurt her. He had to love her while watching her die slowly over eighteen months. And ever since then he's carried this great need to tell the story.

"I'm sorry if it's offensive," I say, "that I finished something that took you three years in just about four hours."

He shakes his head. "That's the best compliment I can get. I guess it's readable."

I laugh, watery and emotional. "Barely. It's really beautiful."

He nods, and I see heaviness in his eyes.

"You finished," I say.

He nods again. "Yes. I did."

There is a finality to it, as there is with everything he does. This certainty. He told the story. The story of this beautiful, defining relationship. The story of this person. Because yes, their love was part of it, and the way he loves her is key to it, but ultimately, it is the story of a singular woman and how she lived. How she made sure to leave on her own terms, even if she wouldn't have chosen to leave when she did.

"I can see why she's the love of your life," I say softly. "It was really a lovely relationship."

"Yeah. I'm lucky," he says.

But again, there's that finality.

It's like the fall of the guillotine.

Losing Sarah has separated him off from possibility, and that's what he *wants*.

He did it. He was her husband, and it's over now.

Now he's done this.

I'm desperate to know what that means for him. What will become of him now? Will he go back to Bainbridge Island and rot away in his office while he writes books about other people? Characters he will never give a romance to, because obviously he wants to avoid the implications of romance. I'm worried, because I know about my own tendencies.

Yes, I came here. I revamped the motel, I did make friends. I also know I spent a long time keeping parts of myself locked away. I have too much in common with him not to worry about his isolation.

"Maybe I'll travel the world," he says.

I don't believe him.

I can see that he doesn't see anything magical in the world anymore. He is fixed. He doesn't feel wonder. He is locked still in that old world, where all the joy has been leached out. Of course I selfishly want him to see a different possibility. A different future. Though, it's more than that. He can be done. Done with love, as much as I wish that weren't the case. I don't want him to be done with life. With the world. With magic. I feel a small amount of hope because he's had sex with me. That sounds silly. In reality, sex, the way we're doing it, is just to feel good. Just to feel close. It's alchemy between two bodies. I know there are cynical versions of that, but what we have isn't cynical.

"Well, you're done with *this*," I say. "I'm on track with my book again. We should go camping."

"Camping?"

"Yes."

"You have a dive-in movie."

"Yes, I do, and any number of people can set it up for me. Let's get out of here. Let's get out of . . . your head."

I want him to feel some magic. I want to. I need it.

"You have camping gear?" he asks.

I laugh. "Believe it or not, I do."

In the early days, there were renovations, and also, sometimes being contained in four walls felt too claustrophobic. Being alone with my thoughts without the feedback of birds or the sun or something other than the echo in my skull.

"Well, okay then. I can't see a reason not to."

I can't tell if that means he wants to or not.

I get off the bed and move over to where he sits. I grab his face, and I stare into those green eyes. "Okay, but that's not enough. I want you to come camping with me because I want you to see the sunset. Because I want you to see the stars. I want you to fuck me outside because that sounds amazing and I've never done that before. I want you to see that there are good things." My breath hitches. "I want *me* to see that there are good things. It's been a lot of pain for a long time. We deserve something."

It's on the verge of being a declaration, and he doesn't pull away from me like I'm afraid he might. Instead, he hangs on to my wrist and looks back at me.

"Those are some pretty damn good reasons," he says.

There's a desperation there. I recognize him for what he is. A man who hit a blank page in his life. A man who doesn't know what happens next. I can feel him almost reach out to me. I can tell what he's thinking. The *almost* is good enough.

"We deserve a little treat," I say.

He laughs at that. "Yeah. If anyone does."

I savor this victory, small though it may be. I give thanks for these two empty days. Because apparently Nathan and I needed empty days more than I realized.

We're both so good at filling time. With books and writing and, for me, the busyness of the motel.

Slowing down always felt too scary. Now I realize I was running from exactly what I needed.

CHAPTER TWENTY-NINE

We take my Jeep to my favorite camping spot nestled in the rocks and the Joshua trees, off the beaten path of the usual campsites. It's public land, and you're able to pitch a tent there, and there's a lot more solitude than in the official campgrounds near the park.

"It's beautiful out here at night," I say.

It's already getting late, and the sun will be setting soon. It's too dry out here to light a fire, and cooking in those conditions seemed too great a task, so we stopped at the supermarket on our way out and picked up a roast chicken, bread, fruit, meat, and cheese. Frankly, I am more than okay with the spread.

We pitch my small dome tent, and I don't really need his help, but he offers it, and I think it's relatively chivalrous, so I allow it.

"No campfire, I assume."

"Indeed not," I say.

"Fair."

We have our camp chairs and are seated in front of a large rock that serves as an altar upon which I would like to cast my hopes and dreams, rather than a fire.

The sky is pink, that rose glow on the mountains, the cacti, the Joshua trees an enchantment.

He is silent and looks around.

I hope he feels what I do.

I hope he recognizes the magic here.

Or maybe I just want there to be magic. But wanting it has to mean something.

I wonder, not for the first time, if the right thing to do would be to build a monument for my grief. Except . . . I want the monument to be my life. I want my daughter's life to matter. In that it made me do wild things, it made me embrace more of who I am.

I want that to be my tribute to her.

So maybe the rock sitting in front of him is magical after all. It must be, since I am suddenly filled with that certainty.

And the desire to be brave.

I don't want to be trite about finding purpose in tragedy, but my God, if you don't, everything just seems pointless.

I can't live in the pointlessness.

Like my life is a blank page that I keep on staring at, no words coming to rescue me.

I keep my eyes on the sunset, the glow there. I'm reminded of when I sat with him that night, and the glow in the distance was a fire.

"How is the fundraising looking?" he asks, stretching his legs out in front of him.

He must have been thinking the same thing.

"Good," I say. "I'm so grateful for everyone. Maybe someday I'll even be grateful Christopher came to help, I don't know. I really thought I left devastation and destruction behind, in my old life, and then Rancho Encanto caught fire." I look down at the ground and kick a pebble. "It's a lesson, though, isn't it? You can't make yourself safe. Existence is risk. Caring is dangerous."

"Very cheerful," he says.

"I mean it in a cheering way. In the sense that I wanted to be safe. But I see now that isn't possible. It's clarifying. It makes me want to do more, find more, reach for more."

"Like?"

Things I don't want to say out loud just yet. But there is one thing.

"I have this . . . itchy feeling," I say. "Like suddenly there are more ideas. Like I want to write more. Does that make sense?"

He looks at me, a strange expression on his face. "Yes," he says slowly. "What got you thinking about that?"

"Everything. Honestly. Everything. I don't know what I want to write about exactly . . . Everything I've been through, not like you. I think what you did is honestly so beautiful. You aren't asking people to come to any trite conclusions. You aren't saying anything trite. You're just sharing her. I think that's brilliant. I don't have anything quite like that. But I feel like I have access to more parts of myself all of a sudden, and it makes me feel more creative."

He nods slowly. "I get it."

"It's like I've been afraid. For a really long time. About what moving forward looks like. I don't like 'moving on' as a phrase, I've decided." I laugh. "At least I don't like it right now. Though, maybe I will tomorrow. I'm still figuring this out."

"Well, that I definitely understand."

Both of us have old grief, but neither of us has been living like it was old. Him, because he needed to write about it. Me, because I refused to process it. I'm sitting here feeling absurdly happy, even with everything that has been going on the last few days. Even with the Christopher of it all looming before me. I sigh heavily as I tilt my face upward and watch as the sky starts to deepen from pink to purple.

"When you were a kid, what did you want to be?"

"A writer," he says. "I used to wear glasses that didn't have lenses in them because I thought it looked literary. My mom got me a typewriter from a yard sale that didn't work."

It makes me like his mom a little bit.

"I just liked books," I say. "I thought that maybe I could just escape into one. I was in my head a lot. I pretended I was in stories because it made everything more bearable."

"I'm kind of surprised you didn't gravitate toward acting," he says.

"Yeah," I say. "I mean, I thought about it. When you're an actor, I feel like people own so much of you. The right to comment on the way you talk, the way you look, and I just couldn't handle it. I watched so many of my friends in LA audition, and I saw how brutal it could be. I saw with Christopher too, but make no mistake, it's a lot more brutal when you're a woman. I really gravitated toward creating the stories, not being in front of anyone or anything. I just, I don't know—I like the part where I get to control the world." I laugh. "Wow. That is . . . telling."

"I think it's fair. For a couple of kids who got dropped into lives they didn't connect with," he says.

"Yes. True. We didn't choose it. We had to be subject to the whims of our parents and all of that. God. No wonder we both wanted to make worlds we can control."

"You know, I thought I could like the military, actually," he says. "I could do what I was told, detached from everything. I liked the physical activity. I actually have conviction about . . . what we did. I couldn't write about it if I didn't. There's not enough hope out there sometimes. I know I don't seem like someone who's filled with a lot of it but . . . at first I was. That's why I write the books I do. I want to believe that the good guys can win. I want to believe that the good guys can actually be good, and not corrupt. I want to write about heroes who can overcome anything."

"I think that's why I like romance. You said it so beautifully at the dive-in movie when you said that it's so much more work to find the hope. It is. I'm not saying I have found it perfectly in my own life, but I believe in it."

He looks a little bit lost. "I want to. I . . . I'd love to give you a romance between Tanner and Monica. I don't know how to write that. Not right now. Because it feels . . . I feel like an explosion might happen and she might die."

"Nathan, you're literally in charge of the book." I almost laugh, but it's not really funny. He's being serious. That's how terrifying love feels to him. Even in fiction, fiction he controls, it could all go wrong.

"I know. It doesn't make sense." He clasps his hands in front of him. "Life makes it really hard to hope for things."

"That's why happy endings are so hard," I say. "But people don't value it. They think it's easy."

We sit there, looking at each other, and I feel this desperation welling up between us. I feel the weight of it. "It's not easy," I say. "And it's not . . . trite, it's not fluffy. I wish it was. The easy way out. The easy way out of what? What's easy?"

"No fucking kidding."

We sit for a long moment. "I think, even when everything was really dark, it had to be romance for me, because I needed to believe in something bigger than what I was experiencing. Better than what I experienced. I need to believe that somewhere out there in the world there were people who would take their trauma and overcome it. And I . . ." I laugh. "I have been writing something I wasn't doing. Over and over and over again. I was writing people who were digging deep inside themselves in order to be in love. It's all a metaphor, right? It doesn't have to be romance." I sort of want it to be. "It can be anything in life. I was writing people doing things I couldn't do myself. Healing is that damned hard." I let silence settle between us for a breath. "It is really beautiful out here," I say aggressively as the sky grows even darker and the stars begin to shine brightly.

"Yes," he agrees.

"Nathan," I say. "I don't think I believe in fate. Because I don't think that your wife was meant to die any more than I think I was supposed to lose a baby. I think they're just really bad things that happened. I don't believe in fate because nothing came along and pulled me up onto my feet. Whatever it was that brought us together . . . I'm glad of it."

That's a hard thing to say, because it was the difficult things that triggered us meeting.

"Me too," he says.

"Maybe you should travel the world," I say. "Only if you'll be happy when you're looking at all those different views."

He gives me a measured look. "I'm happy now."

There's nothing more for me to say to that. There's nothing more to say at all. We sit there as the moon rises. Then we go into our tent. He shows me what happy means. With his mouth, his hands. It's not a simple kind of happy. It's not light. Nothing between us ever is.

It feels good, though.

As I drift off to sleep, I realize that for the first time, I feel understood. In that deep way I had thought no one had ever seen me, he does.

If that's the gift I get from this, I make a vow to myself that I'll let it be enough.

I hold on to him all night, like I'm afraid of him disappearing.

CHAPTER THIRTY

"You're going to come to the parade," I say. I don't mean it to come out as a command, more as a question, but I'm not successful. I've had too much coffee, and I'm feeling emotional after coming back from our camping site and returning to reality.

After the night spent holding him and baring our souls and feeling understood in a way I never have.

Can't imagine why.

I'm also feeling . . . heightened in every way. It's like I have a running list of all the things I need to take care of in my mind. Seeing Christopher, talking to him, that's the first thing.

Talking to Nathan is another one.

Telling him what I want. Telling him I want him in my life. In this life.

This world.

That's important, and it's eating me alive from the inside out. It's all I can do not to turn to him and say something about it now. I'm trying to stick to the PEMDAS of emotions. Order of operations has to be observed.

I have to let go. *Really* let go. I have to close the door.

Christopher is something I don't need to make room for. It's not a pain I need to carry around all the time. Truly, it's not pain I feel. I'm angry. He isn't my mother. He's not a narcissist. He wasn't great to me. Our relationship didn't end well, and he handled all that badly. I think, though, that he isn't a terrible person. He gave me a lot in our time together. More than just pain.

Some of what was wrong with us was me.

Me not knowing what I wanted. Me not knowing how to tell him what I wanted.

So yes, it's worth it to have a conversation with him in a way it wasn't worth it to try to have one with my mother.

There is no point banging your head against a brick wall.

I let our relationship crumble. I didn't fight. There were so many reasons for that. I don't necessarily want to fight today, but I do want to . . .

I don't want this part of the story to be blank anymore. I want to fill it. With whatever happens. Whatever he says. I want to finish it.

"Yes," he says. "I'll go to the parade. Though I do feel obligated to tell you that in general I would rather die than go to a parade."

"You know, I get that feeling from you."

"I don't seem like a happy paradegoer?"

"You do not," I say, chuckling.

We decide against driving. Parking is going to be a nightmare.

So we walk, holding hands, down the sidewalk that only a couple of weeks ago we walked down as relative strangers.

I still think . . . maybe we were not so much strangers as I thought we were. We clearly recognized something in each other from the first moment.

I am bolstered by that as we continue on.

I smile when I see town. It is absolutely festive. There are lights wrapped around every lamppost. Tinsel intertwined with them.

There are cars parked up and down both sides of the street, and a section of it is blocked off for the parade. The smells of chestnuts, pecans cooked in sugar and cinnamon, churros, and popcorn are thick in the air. My stomach growls.

"Should I get you a treat before the parade starts?" He bumps my elbow, and my heart flutters. It's a casually affectionate gesture.

Given that we tend to run on high intensity or sexual chemistry, it feels new.

"Of course I would like a treat," I say. "Will you have one, or will your arteries seize up?"

He gives me side-eye. "It isn't that I never eat sweets."

That creates a slightly weird vibe between us, because I sat with him when he ate some cake when he happened to be drunk off his ass, so I'm not entirely sure if that is indicative of much of anything.

"Just very rarely," I say. "I get it. I think maybe you deserve a treat."

"Right. Because I'm your fake boyfriend for the afternoon?"

That hurts. It cuts a deep groove right into my heart, and I do my best to breathe past it. I do my best not to let it hurt me. After all, he's operating on the rules that we established at the beginning of all this. We're doing sex and friendship. At least officially. My feelings have changed, but we didn't agree to that. I'm hoping . . . I'm hoping he likes what we have enough to give me more.

To give me something more than just leaving and never coming back. I can't bear that. I can't face it.

"No," I say. "You're Nathan. And you're with me. I think you should get a churro."

He grimaces. "I can't say no to a fresh churro."

"I knew it. You're not a monster. No matter how much you want everybody to believe that you are."

"That's evidence that I'm not a monster?"

"I mean, I have other evidence, but there are children present. So I can't say it."

Silence lapses between us as we walk to the churro stand.

"Hey," I say. "If I . . . If I did want to write a different kind of book, with my newfound creative itch . . . could you help me figure out which agents I might want to query, and all of that?"

The truth is, I'm good at doing things myself. That doesn't mean I want to do everything by myself. I don't want my mother's barren lawn. I want connection.

"Yes," he says. "Sure."

I realize that's the test balloon. My first acknowledgment to him that I might want connection that extends beyond this week.

He doesn't say no. So.

We wait in line, and he buys the treats, complete with the chocolate dipping sauce. This feels relevant. Sweet. Like this might actually be a date.

In spite of what he just said about being my fake boyfriend.

I look up at him and smile. His eyes are so green. They make me feel more than I thought possible.

I think that maybe I didn't know love until he looked at me.

Maybe that's dramatic, the most dramatic, jarring thought I've ever had, but I let myself have it. Right now, I let myself.

"We better get in our positions for the parade," I say. "If I can't see the bagpipe players, I will be distraught."

"I didn't know you had strong feelings about bagpipes."

"Who doesn't have strong feelings about bagpipes? Positive or negative, they don't really lend themselves to neutral feelings."

"I'm neutral on them," he says.

"Literally impossible. They are the loudest instrument known to man."

"No," he says. "Decidedly neutral."

I think he's just being a contrarian. And I learn a new thing about him. He will not be told. Not about this, probably not about anything.

I tuck it away deep inside. I love that I learned something new about him.

In spite of the fact I've now seen him naked countless times.

The very sad thing is that I probably could count how many times I've seen him naked. It's only been a couple of weeks.

I just want it to feel countless. I want it to feel like more. I want it to feel like forever.

This shift inside me doesn't even surprise me anymore. I've accepted it.

I know what it's like to let the same pain twist around inside you for three years. I know what it's like to hold on to things.

I know what it's like to marinate in something for so long that it becomes an integral part of who you are.

This certainty coming after such a short amount of time is one of the nicest feelings I've ever had. As a person who is a champion in rumination, it's like the clear skies of Rancho Encanto. Wide open, bright. Nothing obscuring the truth.

"Okay. It really makes a person want to get a bagpipe player to come play 'Amazing Grace' in your personal bedroom," I say.

"I have noise-canceling headphones."

"You're ridiculous."

"Maybe."

He smiles. It turns out, I'm wrong. Everything wasn't bright and clear before. It is now. All the brighter for him smiling. Something has shifted inside me, and I know it's never going to go back.

We take our positions, and Sylvia walks out to the middle of Main Street, a microphone in her hand. "Thank you," she says, "for coming to the tenth annual A Very Desert Christmas!"

The crowd cheers uproariously.

"As you know, Rancho Encanto suffered a tragedy this year when a fire burned down our elementary school and left more than a thousand people without shelter. This event is raising money for the community, for those who lost their homes, their livelihoods, and their school. We want to extend a thank-you to those who have come, who are shopping in our community, staying here, and donating to the cause. The parade is about to begin, so, everybody, sit down and get ready for the show!"

"I'm expecting Disneyland levels of entertainment," he says.

"Adjust your expectations," I say.

It turns out I didn't really need to say that, because the parade begins, and the first entry that comes into sight is the banner that says A VERY DESERT CHRISTMAS, carried by four little girls dressed as cacti.

Music starts to play loudly, elevator Christmas music, but I love it all the same.

"Obviously I meant you needed to adjust them and make them higher," I say.

He laughs, but that is quickly drowned out by the line of bagpipers who are playing "God Rest Ye Merry, Gentlemen" louder than I have ever heard it in my life, and this isn't even the first time I've heard these particular bagpipers.

After that there's a float, which is essentially the North Pole on a flatbed truck, sponsored by the hardware store. There is a homemade snow globe with people dressed like elves inside it, and an old farm dog dressed as Rudolph the red-nosed reindeer.

There is a section of old-fashioned cars, ballet folklórico, Irish step dancing. I polish off my churro, and Nathan gives me half of his. I want to call him a quitter, but I also want his churro, so I decide against harassing him.

During the parade, I realize that he has moved behind me and I'm leaning against his chest. Leaning against him. He's holding me up. I sigh and let myself melt against him. I'm not afraid of the other shoe dropping. I'm not afraid of anything, not just now.

The parade ends with an aqua-colored convertible with Sylvia sitting in the front, and . . .

I blink. Christopher's sitting in the back, waving.

He is dressed exactly like he would be for one of his movies. Flannel shirt, scarf, despite the fact it really isn't that cold, and a stocking cap.

I fold myself just slightly against Nathan's chest because I don't want Christopher to see me. Not right now.

Nathan becomes an even more solid wall, and I know he understands who this is.

His hold on me tightens, and the beauty of being held by him, protected by him, surpasses the stress I feel in that moment.

He whispers in my ear. "Are you okay?"

"I am," I say. "It's actually the anticipation and awkwardness at this point. He's tried to call me twice. I haven't answered. Maybe that's stupid. I don't know."

"None of it is stupid. I think you're in one of the few unique situations that a person could have in the world."

"My ex-long-term boyfriend becoming a made-for-TV movie actor and showing up at my new hometown? Fair." I look up at him, and I know he knows this, but I want to say it anyway. "I don't want him."

He nods. "Good."

I take that *good*, and I hold it close. I turn it over in my mind like it's a particularly shiny rock I want to look at from every angle. We walk from there to the site for the Festival of Trees and move down the line of food trucks, where I order something from every one.

"There really is nothing like girl dinner," I say.

He lifts his brow. "And that is?"

"Having little bits of everything you might want. A great, eclectic triumph. A symphony of taste. Girl dinner is art. *Sometimes* it's RITZ crackers and cheese, but it's actually one of my very favorite things about being single. The ability to just have a meal that's pieces of everything."

"You can't do that when you're with somebody?"

"When you're with somebody, you have to consider them."

"They could also consider you," he says.

It's a reminder of why I like him so much. Putting it mildly.

"When you write a hero," he says, "does the heroine get to choose the food?"

I ponder this for a moment. "Yes," I say. "She does."

"Don't accept less for yourself than what you'd write," he says.

His words echo in my head until we filter down to the A Very Desert Christmas venue, where a crowd is already amassing.

We head over to the location for our event, and the line waiting for us is beyond what I'd imagined. I'm not sure what I did imagine, but it wasn't this.

There's a big sign outside the tent pavilion for Nathan's event, and it has both our faces on it. I stand next to the sign and spread my arms out, smiling. "We should get a selfie."

"I've never taken a selfie in my life, and I'm not going to start now."

"Why doesn't that surprise me?"

We move into the tent, and there are stacks of books in there. More of his, fair enough. He is Jacob Coulter, and I am not.

I take a deep breath, and I fully come to terms with the fact I'm not just going to see Christopher in a parade. I'm actually going to see him, talk to him, interact with him.

I feel so much more okay than I expected to. It's still weird.

"Are you good?" he asks.

"I am," I say. "I mean, nobody is totally good right before a socially awkward interaction, but that's all it is. Genuinely."

Nathan nods and goes up to the front, where all the chairs are facing. I see it again, his relative ease with this kind of thing.

"You're a strange man," I say, and I mean it in the nicest way.

"I am?"

"Yes. You are. Sometimes the least personable human being on the planet, but also the most. You are utterly insensitive. On the surface. Usually, if I get past my knee-jerk reaction to the things you say, I realize they aren't clichés, they aren't platitudes. You're actually saying something important. You value your privacy, but I can see that you do well at things like this."

"At something like this," he says, "we're talking about the books. I can do books, Amelia. Writing is the only way that I've ever found to make sense of anything. I'm not talking about myself when I'm talking about my stories."

"You are, though," I say. "They're the deepest part of you. The part I think not even you see sometimes. I mean, that's why we have to write, isn't it? I don't think it's a coincidence that I started writing romance after the biggest romantic implosion of my life. Helped me sort through everything. Everything."

"Save it for the panel," he says, giving me a slight smile.

"No, because I'm not talking about that in front of Christopher." I take a fortifying breath. "Wow. This is going to be interesting."

The tent begins to fill. Then Christopher comes in at the very last minute. I realize why. As soon as our eyes connect, I see his guilt. I see his fear. He has no idea what he's walking into. He knew he was asked to moderate this panel, that I was on the panel—even if he didn't know my pen name, he knows what I look like—and he's been stressing about it. Of course he has. I wouldn't pick up his phone calls. That kind of amuses me. I didn't really mean to get revenge on him that way, but apparently I did.

Nathan steps forward and holds his hand out. Aggressively. Not in a friendly manner. "Jacob Coulter," he says.

"Christopher Weaver," Christopher says in response. Then he looks at me. "Amelia . . ."

Nathan moves back to my side and puts his hand on my lower back in an extremely possessive gesture that can't be misconstrued. Christopher's eyes dart between us.

"We'll talk after," I say.

Because now there's just the panel.

Christopher is, of course, charming as he introduces us to the crowd, introduces himself, and reads Nathan's—Jacob's—and my bios.

When we start talking, it's like Christopher disappears. Nathan and I already know how to talk about writing. I ask him a hundred questions that I've already asked him. We go back and forth, talking about genre conventions and process, why I love a daily word count and why he would find it oppressive.

This is where his passion has always been, even when he can't find it. He manages to talk about his feelings without sharing anything personal.

"Why do you write romance?" he asks me.

"Because no matter how terrible things have been in my own life, I wanted to believe there was hope. That's what we all want to believe.

Don't we all want to learn how to write a happy ending in our own lives? That's what I've been doing. Learning how to write one. Figuring out how people other than me, fictional people, find happiness after the darkness. What's more important than that?"

"Nothing," he says.

When we finish the panel, we're both busy signing books. I've never done a book signing before. I enjoy it more than I thought I would, even if it takes a little bit to get used to signing a pseudonym.

It takes a few tries for Belle Adams to feel natural. I'll have to ask Nathan for pointers later.

It hits me then that I've found something in him I never imagined was possible. I've found a man who learns about the world the way I do. Who processes his feelings using the same method I use. We might write differently—me with my word count, him with his brooding—but there is something so common between us that I've never found with another person.

Writing is how I learn about the world and myself. People who are like me and people who aren't.

Very few people would ever understand that, but Nathan does. He had to write a whole book about his wife, about her life, in order to sort through everything he experienced. He writes books about the military that help him make the good guys better than they are. He worries about writing romance, because he's scared it will hurt him, like the one in his real life.

I get it. We get each other.

Yes, we connect with our grief. We also connect with how we see the world. How we filter it. How we figure out everything we feel by writing it.

He's also so good in bed it's unreal. He makes all the other sex I've ever had seem like sad warm-ups, while he's the main event.

With him, it's like in my books.

Straight out of my fantasies, off the page and into my bed.

The next time someone tells me sex in romance is unrealistic, I'll pity them.

When we finish the signing, Christopher is gone, and I realize he had to go do his reading.

Maybe we won't get to have our conversation. Maybe it doesn't matter. I thought it was important, but my big realization was just . . . I'm glad I spent the day with Nathan. Talking about what we love, our books. Meeting readers and interacting with them.

Nathan is being occupied—against his will, maybe—by a pair of zealous women who are each holding a stack of his books and talking to him very intently.

"The thing is," one of them says, "if you think about it, Tanner wouldn't have done that."

Nathan is nodding. "I did write it that way, though."

I stand up from the table after everyone is gone, and I start moving some of my remaining books back into a box, when I see Christopher come into the side of the tent.

"Amelia, do you have a minute?"

"Oh. Yes." I straighten. I glance over at Nathan, who is still getting a lecture on the mistakes he's made in his own series. I got an email like that once, but he's basically getting the full screed in person, and he's handling it well.

"Is . . . Jacob Coulter your . . . fiancé? Husband?"

"No," I say, and I don't offer an explanation. "Congratulations. On the engagement."

I don't know if I mean it, but I'm glad I can say it.

"Thank you," he says. "That's not how I would've chosen for you to find out about that."

"It's okay," I say. "Who could have predicted we would end up in the same place at the same time quite like this?"

"Yeah, that's . . . My agent used to know Reigna? I guess she taught him how to do the soft-shoe."

I nod. "That sounds about right."

Silence lapses between us for a moment. "Congratulations on the books. You always kind of wanted to do that."

"Thank you."

It's desperately awkward for a second. I start trying to grab words and piece them together. I start trying to figure out what I should say to him. What monologue will fit just right. The triumphant scene where I make him grovel for all he's done wrong.

Then he takes a deep breath. "I'm sorry," he says.

Whatever I was going to say is just . . . gone. I didn't expect that.

"What?"

"I'm sorry. I handled everything with us in a way that was just . . . There wasn't a worse way. I'm sorry."

"Thank you." I don't know what else to say.

I forgive you seems . . . well, not true. I'm angry. He wronged me at a time when I needed him to do right by me more than I had ever needed anything. Whether it makes sense or not, I never felt like he was failing only me. He was failing our daughter too. Maybe that part isn't fair, but it hurt me then, so badly. Forgiveness is too simple for what I feel.

Still, I can appreciate the apology.

"I didn't treat you well enough," he says. "I couldn't understand what you were going through because I didn't want to. It hurt too much. I was in denial. Of everything. And you weren't. You deserved better."

I did.

I did deserve better, though I don't need him to tell me that.

I never expected to get an apology from Christopher Weaver even once in my whole life, and I like it.

But I don't *need* it.

The simple truth is, he's not my problem. He's not going to be in my life. I feel completely fine wishing him well and never having anything to do with him ever again. Not in a hateful way.

I just . . . I don't need him.

I don't want him.

He's not the thing that still hurts. He's not the great loss.

He's not the love of my life.

"I didn't really break up with you," I say. "I ran away. I regret running away. Though, I don't regret where I ended up. I'm really happy. I hope you're really happy."

"I am," he says.

"Good. I don't think we ever could have made each other happy."

"That's probably true." Though he looks confused by that. I realize it's the confusion of the partner who was getting more than he was giving.

I'm not even that mad about it.

"I'm glad you're here," I say. "Because I think not having closure on it, not even . . . an apology, or just getting to stand in front of you when I don't feel like I'm falling apart, was keeping me stuck. I just feel like I can let it go now."

I can let him go. I can let that life go.

It doesn't mean letting go of Emma. It doesn't have to.

"This place is pretty amazing," he says, looking around.

"Oh, I love it," I say. "I love it here."

I love my life. That's the bottom line. I realize he didn't ask me if I was behind him getting hired. I don't feel the need to tell him that I wasn't. It just doesn't matter.

"Well. I . . . Take care," I say.

There's a song about this. About the strangeness of when a person you used to be intimate with becomes somebody that you used to know. When it doesn't even feel intense enough for anger.

For longing.

Whatever was left of my feelings for him blows away on the wind.

I turn, and I see Nathan.

He's the only thing that matters.

I don't need to put him and Christopher side by side to know who I have stronger feelings for. I don't need to do a pros and cons list. I don't need to do a list about what love is, and how Nathan is different from Christopher.

If I did, though, the winner would be clear. It's too obvious for anything quite that literal.

"How did that go?" he asks, putting his hand on my shoulder.

"It was fine. It was fine. It wasn't dramatic. It wasn't painful. He apologized to me." We're walking away from the tent, and it's dark out now, crowds of people still milling around, laughing, drinking cider. "I don't know what I expected. I let my grief over the baby turn into this thing that was tangled up in him. I was angry at him. For a very long time. I mean, if I sat down and thought about it, I probably still would be, but not enough to yell at him. Not enough to let him have any more of my energy. I just . . . I don't want to be with him. I don't want that life. I don't . . . I just don't."

I laugh, and it comes out half a sob. "I have to do an auction!" I say. "In front of people."

"Are you going to be okay?"

I know he just means the auction, but it feels like a bigger question. I'm glad I can answer it honestly. "Yes," I say. "I'm going to be just fine."

CHAPTER THIRTY-ONE

The Grand Gesture—when one protagonist does something expensive—in time, money, or pride—to show the other protagonist the depth of their feelings.

It's time for the auction, and we've drawn a bigger crowd than I expected. Several people that are here were also at the book signing, and it makes me feel bolstered, because I'm not just running an auction cold. I feel warmed up after the book event.

The whole forest is beautiful, and everyone here had a chance to look at the trees they liked and write down the numbers for what they want to bid on when it comes up.

I look at my list in front of me and begin. "The Route 66 Tree, by Get Your Kicks Diner."

Bidding starts off strong. As we get deep into the auction, it's starting to get astronomically high. I'm shocked. Shocked that it's going so well and people are so invested in doing something great for the community.

Each tree starts fetching more and more money. My opening bids are starting over $200 almost every time.

The mermaid tree goes. The John Deere tree. The avocado tree, the kitten tree, and the peacock tree follow. Then there's a tree all done up with Elvis, one with Marilyn Monroe wrapped in glittery ribbon.

There's a tree covered in candy, and one in tropical flowers.

My favorite is the one the kids made.

Each one is a labor of love for the community. Work that the people who live here put in to rebuild this place we've chosen to call home.

Finally, it's time for the Pink Flamingo tree. It's so pink. So obnoxious.

So me.

I see Chris, pushing his way to the front row, and he raises his hand. "Five hundred dollars."

My eyebrows shoot up. It's a high opening bid.

He gives me a slight apologetic smile, and I'm frozen for a second. I guess since I didn't take his apology, he wants to give money?

"One thousand dollars."

I turn and see Nathan standing there, his arms crossed.

"One thousand dollars," I repeat.

"Fifteen hundred!" That's from Christopher.

Everyone in the crowd is watching them, all eyes fixed on the two men trying to outbid each other.

"Twenty-five hundred," says Nathan, looking over at Christopher like he might start a fistfight with him.

I blink. I feel like I'm in the middle of a Hallmark Christmas movie showdown. Much like every love triangle I've ever seen, it really is no competition. I know Christopher doesn't want me back. I know that's not why he's doing it.

But still.

"Three thousand dollars."

There's an audible gasp from the crowd.

All *I* can think of is that Christopher is going to have to explain to his fiancée that he bid this much money on his ex's Christmas tree if he wins.

I don't hate that for him, though I don't want his life to implode. Not when my life is going so well. But I wouldn't mind if his life were a little bit of a trial for him on occasion.

"Ten thousand dollars." Nathan looks straight up at me as he says that number, and I cannot believe it. It is by far the highest bid anyone has seen here, and if I had ever begun to doubt he was a millionaire *New York Times* bestseller, I don't now.

The crowd is cheering, people shoving at each other, shoving at Nathan.

He's definitely won. It's definitive. It's not just a bid, it's a grand gesture.

The grandest of gestures.

So I decide to give him one of my own. I step off the stage and straight into his arms. *"Sold,"* I say.

With that, I wrap my arms around his neck and kiss him.

People cheer. It feels like exactly what it is. That magical moment when things couldn't go better. As if it were *written*, and not a scene from life.

We part, and Nathan looks at Christopher. I can feel thwarted male pride emanating from Chris—love that for him—and triumph from Nathan. Love that for me.

Then Christopher turns to me. "I'm glad it's working out for you, Amelia. Take care."

"You too."

Just like that, Christopher Weaver walks out of my life again, but he takes something with him. Whatever power he had over me. It's just gone.

I look up at Nathan. "You realize that was over the top, right?"

"Yep," he says.

"Why did you do that?"

"I wanted to beat him. I wanted you to win. I wanted to give money to the town." None of those reasons are a declaration, but I like them all the same.

"I support it, but that was a lot."

"It wasn't too much for you," he says. Then he clears his throat. "Would you like some mulled wine?"

"I would," I say.

We get our hot drinks, and we keep on walking, until the crowd thins out, until we're well away from them.

I know it's time. Time for me to tell him.

Time to make my grand gesture. My declaration. Because everything has changed for me.

He changed it.

"I thought this was the main event," I say. "I thought this was what the month of December was building to. Me finally having to confront my past in a way I haven't wanted to. I've done my very best to leave it all behind. Honestly, since you came back . . . everything has changed. Everything in me has changed."

My drink warms my hands, but suddenly I feel cold. A little bit afraid. I'm making the decision. I'm doing it. I'm not letting life push me around. I am not adrift. I know what I want. I came here wounded, unable to see the future. Unable to even dream. I'm dreaming *now*. I want to keep on dreaming.

I want to write the rest of my story, not just let it happen around me, not sit there staring at a blinking cursor, on hold because I'm scared.

"It's like I was frozen," I say. "For all these years, because it was just too painful. The problem was, I was stuck in a thought that I had to heal from everything or heal from nothing. Where I thought I had to sort of deny everything that I had been through, or I was going to have to do this incredibly impossible work. But I don't have to get over it. I don't have to get over the pain. It's there. It's part of everything. It's part of love, it's part of life. It's part of being happy. When I look at the faces of all my darling old ladies, I see the lines. From happiness, from anger, from sadness. It's all there, and it's all part of them. We don't get out of life without it."

I take a jagged breath. "You have to do the work of healing. You just do. Because if you don't . . . then all you have is the pain. It's there, beneath the surface, whether you want it to be or not. I thought I had come here and run away from it all, and then all it took was me being handed a baby to dissolve. All it took was hearing that my ex was going to come and speak at this event, and I felt broken.

"It comes for you eventually. Even if you don't want it to. It can be a fire in your safe haven, or your ex invading your new life, but it will come. I wasn't building to a confrontation with Christopher. I was building to this moment where I could stand in front of *you* and say that I want more."

He freezes, the expression on his face one of near terror. "Amelia . . ."

"I don't want you to leave and never come back. I don't want to never see you again."

"I can't do that."

"You can. You aren't dead. And neither am I. We're alive, and that means not having to face the great and terrible truth that we can never see each other again. It is our choice. Because this is our world. It's the one we have."

"I can't give you anything," he says.

"You just bid ten thousand dollars on my Christmas tree."

"That's not what I mean. I'm broken. I can't fix myself for you. I can't do it for anybody."

"Maybe I don't care if you're broken. Because I'm not. I've decided. It's bullshit. I didn't choose to have the parents I had. I didn't choose for my mother to be a narcissist. I didn't choose for my dad to move away. I didn't choose to invest years in a man who was just a bait and switch, one who never loved me the way I did him. And I didn't choose to lose my baby. I didn't choose it. So I will be damned if I won't take a chance and choose good things when I have the opportunity to do it. I am not choosing broken. Not when I can choose whole."

I shake my head. "Nathan, we're not writing this, and I know . . . I know why you don't want to drain all the poison out at once. I know. Please do it. For us. Because I think you can be the hero that I'd write. I think you . . . I mean, you're real. We're real. I think we can have a happy ending, but it's up to us to make it happen." I take a deep, gasping breath. I need him to understand. "It is real, Nathan. It's realistic.

I've written it over and over again. People have to fight for it. They have to heal for it. But it's real."

My heart is pounding so hard it hurts, and my throat aches. I want to beg him, because I care that much. Because I want this for us that much.

"Amelia," he says. "You are extraordinary. I don't ever want you to doubt that. I'm not like you. I've been through loss one time, and it's enough times for me. I can't find that hope again. I can't even write a romance—how am I supposed to live it?" He takes a jagged breath. "I don't think you get to do this twice. I lived my whole life feeling like the odd one out. Feeling like I was speaking a different language to the people around me, and then I met someone who was fine with it. That is something you don't get to do twice."

"If you don't care about me enough, you can say that."

He looks wounded. Maybe he needs to be. For me, and not for anyone else.

"I can't take a breath deep enough, not anymore. I can't have a feeling that goes that far. I can't . . ."

I see the fear. Real, deep fear. He is terrified. At this moment, of me. Of himself. He is terrified, because his world ended. And to dream, to hope, to wish, to build something new is extraordinarily terrible, and I know it. It's also the only way. The only way to find a life that isn't shrouded in darkness, that isn't defined by loss.

"I'm glad you had that," I say. "Nathan, the most beautiful thing about your love story is that she had you. You were *her* happy ending, Nathan. She had you until her end." Tears make my words sharp. Short. "I am so glad. But you didn't end when she did. So you have to decide what your life looks like. You have to decide what else there is. I don't really want to be second best to someone who isn't here anymore. Who does? I'm not asking you to promise me forever. I'm not asking you to promise me everything. I'm just asking you not to end it entirely. Not to cut us off. I'm asking you to leave the door open."

He moves toward me, his eyes desperate, his hold on me rough. "When you leave the door open, there are too many things that can get through it. I can't do it."

He is desperate now. I think I'm even more desperate, though.

"I love you. I love you. I'm very clear on what that means. I'm very clear on what it could cost. I am very clear on how badly this could hurt me, but I am strong enough to handle it."

This is my third world, really. There was Bakersfield, the one where my parents broke my heart. There was LA.

Now there's Rancho Encanto, and I'm on the cusp of being shattered again. I already know I'm not going to run away afterward. I already know that whatever happens after this moment, I'm not going to burn myself to the ground and start over.

This place nearly burned to the ground. It survived. It will thrive because of all the love and care we've poured into the community.

So will I.

I love this place, because my family is here. My residence, my motel. My life.

It really is mine. That was why those other lives were so easy to leave—they mostly belonged to the other people in them.

But not this one.

"I'm telling you this, as a woman who really knows who she is now. I'm telling you this, and I'm scared. I am scared, because it's going to break me if you leave. I'm still going to keep breathing. I already know what we can survive."

"So don't," he says. "Don't do it again. Not for me, not for anyone. Don't do it again. Protect yourself. That's . . . If we only get one chance at love, then we only really have to have our hearts broken one time."

"That's not true," I whisper. "It just isn't. Because your heart can break in a thousand different ways. When the sun rises too beautifully, or a child that isn't yours cries. When you drive by a house that you've never lived in, but you wish that you did, or you see a life that makes you ache, even though it could've never been yours. When you hear a song that breaks your heart. When you look around at what you *didn't do*. It hurts so much more than any of the things you did. Because life goes on. And on and on. There is nothing you can do to protect yourself if you actually want to live and have there be any point to it. Your books are so good, Nathan. You put all this great emotion into them. You put your belief in heroes and put goodness into those stories because it's who you are. If you cut yourself off, you're not going to be able to feel it anymore. Maybe that's what you want."

"It is," he says.

"Why," I ask. "Why? When you could have . . ."

Everything. I realize I'm calling myself everything. I feel like what he and I have just might be the brightest, most brilliant star in the sky. When I feel him withdraw, when I realize he's going to turn away, I understand. I had thought a while ago that we might only ever have a happy ending of a kind. I told myself that to comfort myself, but for me that's never going to be a happy ending.

It's bullshit.

Continuums are bullshit.

I want him to be my happy ending forever, and anything else just feels sad.

Yes, knowing him made me better.

No, I'm not going to go right back to that devastated place.

But I hate this.

"I'll say this," I begin, "from one person who has known real loss to another. You have got to accept that this is your life. Maybe it doesn't have to be with me. I *wish* it was. If you don't love me enough . . . Hell, Nathan, maybe you had a love that was so much better than ours, so you can never feel it again if it's not big enough. I understand that. So maybe I'm feeling all of this alone, but someday, you're going to arrive at this moment again, and maybe it won't be with romance, but it will be with something. Something that pushes you past this protective little cage you put yourself in. I want you to remember this then. This is your life. It can be beautiful. You can honor her not just by putting out a book about her life. You can honor her by living yours."

His face is hard like granite, and I see all my heroes in his green eyes.

I see everything he's done to prove to me he could be mine.

"You caught Gladys when she fell," I say, my voice trembling. "You rescued Wilma's necklace and fixed the washing machine, even though they faked that. You danced with Wilma when she asked, you were a donkey for the kids." A sob climbs my throat. "I have never met a man who tried so damn hard to not be the hero of the story. You could be the hero, if you were just brave enough."

Then I'm the one who turns away from him. I said everything I needed to say, everything that exists inside me. It's not closure, because it's going to take a long time for me to get closure from this. In these stolen moments over the last few years, Nathan Hart has made me feel more than any other man ever has.

If I was confused about love, I'm not now.

I'm also strong enough to walk away because he's not giving me everything. I know what I want. I'm not asking him for everything; I'm just asking him to try, and he won't do that, so there is no more conversation to have.

He doesn't stop me. He doesn't call out for me. When I stumble out of the grove of trees, I run into Elise and Ben, who are in fact making out underneath some mistletoe.

"Well, it's about damned time," I say.

Then I burst into tears.

CHAPTER THIRTY-TWO

The Dark Moment—the part of the story where all is lost.

I am devastated.

For the first time, Nathan does online checkout. He leaves early. I'm both relieved and upset by it.

I wish I could talk to him again. I wish I could be with him again. Instead, I open the door to room 32 and sit on the edge of the bed for a long moment. This was his room. I thought maybe I was in a romance novel. All the tropes were there.

I tricked myself, honestly. I thought, *Great, time to start writing a new story,* and I was so sure I knew what genre I was in.

But as angry as I am, I immediately check myself. More has changed in me for the good in the last few weeks than in the last three years. I can't deny that. I can't deny that he was instrumental in it.

At the same time, I want to be wounded, and furious. At the same time, I want to feel like everything is over.

It feels like it might be.

It really does.

Instead of letting that crush me, I marvel at my own strength. At my own fearlessness. Because here I am with a broken heart. I chose to put myself out there, even though it was scary.

"I'm brave," I say into the empty room, and then I laugh, because what a hollow victory my bravery feels like at the moment.

Elise and Ben took me home from A Very Desert Christmas, and I immediately left them and went to my room to have a small mental breakdown beneath the hot spray of the shower, as God intended.

I am curious about how she and Ben got together, though, and I table discussion of my heartbreak so that we can talk about it. When I leave room 32, I find Elise, and the two of us go out for coffee and pastries while Gladys watches Emma.

"So," I say. "How did it happen?"

"*I* want to know what exactly happened with Nathan."

"My story is sad," I say.

"Well. I kissed him, and he kissed me back, and honestly, there wasn't much discussion to be had after that. We've both felt this way about each other for a long time. I'm scared, because I don't know what the future looks like. What I do know about Ben is he isn't going to transform into a monster. I've known him for such a long time. I also know what I want now. I know how to communicate. So, I'm ready to try this adult-relationship thing."

I grimace. "Well, I'm happy for you."

She looks down at her coffee, then back up at me. "He turned you down."

"Yes," I say. "It's not as simple as . . . I don't know. He was married, Elise. His wife died. He doesn't want . . . He doesn't want to get hurt again."

Elise is thoughtful for a long moment. "I understand that. I mean, not the same. I also understand being really scared about repeating the same thing you've already been through."

"She was the love of his life."

Elise nods. "Ouch."

"Yeah. It hurts. It hurts really bad. I don't want to begrudge this poor woman, this woman who died way too young, the love that he has for her. It feels petty to be jealous. It's just, she's dead and his love isn't doing her any good. It's just that she got to have him to the end of her life. And what about mine? What about his?" I feel guilty saying that.

"It's true, though," Elise says. "Just like my continued fear of Emma's dad doesn't keep him any farther away. What those really strong feelings do is keep you safe. I'm sure . . . He loves you, Amelia. I have never seen a man look at a woman the way he does you. Except when Ben looks at me. It's love. I'm sure of it. I'm also sure that he *can't* do it. Out of fear. Why do you think the guy spent three years coming back to the motel? He has feelings for you."

She isn't totally right about that, because I know the whole circumstance of it. But it does make me think. He took so many years to write Sarah's memoir because to finish it would be to let her go.

At the same time, I've been in his face, his life. This complication he didn't want. He's been keeping himself suspended in a place where he didn't have to let go, and he didn't have to embrace anything new.

He didn't have to embrace what could be next for him. What could hurt him again. So complicated and so simple, all at the same time. He was in this strange place where he was supposed to let it all go. Her and me.

He probably has no idea what that means for him. What that means for his life. I'm also sure that he thought it was going to be easy to let me go. That he didn't think I was going to fall in love with him. He probably didn't think he was going to fall in love with me. I believe he did. I sit with that certainty. *I believe he did.* That is maybe the saddest thing about all of this.

"Well, I can't chase him down. I guess at least I can say that after years of babying myself, I took a risk, and I got hurt. That's what I've been doing, coddling myself. In not telling you about . . ."

"Emma," Elise says. "I wish I would've known. This whole time. Just because . . ."

"You have been really wonderful. You could've gotten mad at me for not telling you, you know, anything about me."

"Of course I'm not mad. Not all pain is the same pain. We don't all feel pain in the same way. How you needed to deal with your loss, that's up to you. I can't imagine how much it hurt for you to end up here and meet my daughter who had the same name as yours."

"At first, I kind of separated the two. Now, I think it's lovely that you have your beautiful Emma. I love to hear that name. I do."

"I'm just so sorry about all of this. What can I do?" Elise asks.

"Take me to Desierto Encanto and help me pick up dudes?"

"Really?"

"No," I say. "Sadly, that has never been how I try to get over things."

"A real tragedy."

"Right? I'm no fun. No. Just keep being my friend. Because this is where I actually change instead of reverting to type. This is where I actually find peace, dammit."

Except really I'm sad. I contain multitudes in this new world, apparently.

The ability to be happy and sad and new all at once. "Don't let me fold in on myself," I say as we exit the coffee place.

"I won't," she says. "You live close. I'll come for you if you start to fall apart."

"Thank you."

I drive back to the motel, and it's nearly time for checkout, so it's time for me to get behind the desk. I open my Word document, and then I open a new one. I'm going to finish my book on time, heartbreak notwithstanding.

I have a new idea. A different one. One thing I don't want is to contract in on myself after this, as tempting as it is. I'm still going to write about love, because I still believe in it. Because I still feel like that's what he and I had.

I'm going to try something new. This is addicting. Taking risks. Putting myself out there. Suddenly I feel like everything inside me is worth it. Really, truly worth it. I am owed recognition. What I'm offering the world matters. What I was offering to him matters, whether he realizes it or not.

I sniff loudly into the silence of the reception area, and I tell myself that I'm not on the verge of tears.

I check out a wave of guests and prepare for the lull. Christmas is in two days, and for the most part, people don't check in this close to Christmas. I look out at this room that has given me so much joy. It still does. Because it's mine.

The door opens, and I look up. For a moment I think I might be hallucinating. There is no way Nathan Hart just walked into the lobby.

That's when I realize.

I thought it was the end, but it wasn't.

Because it wasn't happy.

CHAPTER THIRTY-THREE

"God," he says, the word coming out as a curse and a prayer.

He pushes his hands through his hair, and I can tell he hasn't slept since last night.

"What are you . . . ? What are you doing here?" I ask.

"I got however many hours down the freeway and turned around and came back. Because I can't . . . This is stupid, by the way," he says.

"What? *You?* I agree that you're a little bit stupid."

"No. This. I don't want to be in love with you."

"Great. Thank you."

"No. You don't understand. It hurts. Too much, Amelia." He puts his hand on his chest like it hurts right now. "I was never supposed to have to feel this again. I was never supposed to want something this bad, or to hope this much. But you were there. The minute I checked in that first year, you were there, and I knew you were dangerous, and I should have listened to that feeling. You were dangerous, and I couldn't . . ."

He shakes his head. "Sarah is dead. If I never checked into the motel again, she would never have known. She couldn't . . . she couldn't make me. You made me. You made me keep coming back. Every year I walked the tightrope between wanting to hang on to how badly it hurt to have my wife be gone, and how much I wanted to see you, and I strung all of it out . . . all of it. I let it get tangled around itself. Until I could hardly make sense of it. Dammit. Amelia. After last summer . . . I wanted it to be over. I wanted it to be over because I couldn't keep coming to see you. So I came back, for one last time, and I thought if we fucked, great. I could get it out of my system. But I didn't. You are in my blood. You are in my breath. You're in my heart, and that is the most unforgivable part."

"Nathan . . ."

"Every year, I would see you, and I could feel that there was a sadness about you. I could feel that there was something in you that was like me, but you weren't . . . you weren't dark. I wanted that."

"Well, you were. Intense, and terrifying, and I wanted you in spite of myself. Even though I knew full well that I couldn't afford to take on a project. I did not want you to be my project. I agreed with you. That maybe the sex was inevitable. It wasn't supposed to be this for me either. You think I'm any happier about it?"

"I thought that if I . . . I thought that if I said that there was a love of my life, it meant I wouldn't have to do it again."

"Is it so bad? Loving someone?"

"Losing them is," he says. "It's so bad. It tears you in half. Amelia, I can't . . . I'm in an impossible situation because if I walk away from you right now, if I never see you again, at least the grief won't be final. But it will be grief all the same, and I'm so tired of it. I am so goddamned tired."

I stand up slowly and walk around to the other side of the counter. "Then maybe try being happy. Why don't we try that?" I raise my hands and bracket his face. His dear, familiar face. I see those lines, all that pain. I want to make new lines on his face. From smiling. From laughing. From loving me. "I love you. I *do* know what it feels like to love and have it taken from you. It's not the same. I also know how expensive hope is, Nathan, I do."

"It's too much," he says, his voice gritty.

"Yes. It is. So you can go back home. You can go sit in your office, and you can know what will happen every day for the rest of your life.

However long it is. Or we could do this. You and me. I told you I don't need anything other than just the reassurance that I'll see you again."

I find myself being lifted off the floor, enveloped by his arms, and then he's kissing me.

And it is magical. It is beautiful. It is hope.

It is everything.

"No," he says. "That's the thing. I knew. I knew that it was never just a possibility with you. It was inevitable. It could be everything. That's why it terrifies me." He closes his eyes. "I love Sarah very much, but it's been three years. Grieving is comforting. Because it keeps you safe." It is the exact same revelation I had. I'm glad he's had it too. "If I let it go, if I accept what happened, then I have to . . . open myself up again, and that's terrifying."

"Yes. Hope is terrifying. What else do we have? You said it yourself, when you were talking to Albert about romance novels. The work that goes into a happy ending is the hardest work. The world doesn't value it. The work to be in love, the work to be happy. It's the hardest work, but I'm willing to do it. I have never felt this way before."

"Neither have I. I'm going to try to explain it in a way that makes sense because I know . . . She was the love of my life. *That* life. Not this one. This one—the one where I'm a difficult, closed-off, hopeful, wounded man—in this one, it's you. It could only *ever* be you." He tilts my chin upward, and my gaze meets his. "You are the only woman for the man I am now." He pauses. "That day you read the memoir . . . You understand me, Amelia. You don't just accept me. No matter which world, which life we're talking about, I've never experienced that before."

I'm warmed by this, all the way through. It's true for me too, I realize. It's not just acceptance, but a deep understanding and appreciation. We've both lost. We both used creativity to get us through. We both need creativity.

"You are not second in any way," he says. "I was dying. Slowly but surely. Everything that was good about life was gone for me. My only purpose was writing that damn book for her, and you . . . We can get married. We can write books together. We can . . . we can try to have kids. If you want."

"I want everything. I want to hope for everything, and I will love you no matter what."

I realize that there are logistics. That he has a house in Washington. I live here and . . .

"We'll have to hire someone to work here," he says. "Because I'm selfish and I'm going to want to bring you back to Bainbridge Island sometimes, but I want to live here with you. Most of the life I have left there hasn't been great. Though I would love to bring you there. Show it to you. I would love for there to be something happier there for me."

"It's a deal."

Here was a man who had been so badly hurt, willing to give up everything for me. I can hardly believe it.

I wanted to believe happy endings were real. I needed to. I wrote about them even when everything seemed lost. When my whole life was a dark moment I couldn't see the end of.

I kept dreaming.

It's finally my turn to have it. All because of the man in room 32.

All because he was brave enough to push through to the happily ever after.

Some people say happy endings are the easy way out. That they're trite or cliché. That tragedy is what adds value to film or literature. Nathan and I know how wrong that is.

We choose joy. We choose each other. We choose to live.

That's what a happy ending is.

EPILOGUE

The Happily Ever After (HEA)—a core tenet of the romance genre. The reader can be assured that no matter how difficult the journey is, the protagonists end up together.

Everything is pink.

The balloons that are fashioned in an arc over the pool, the wild, flowery scene projected onto the dive-in movie screen, the plastic flamingos placed around the lawn, and my dress.

When Nathan and I decided to get married, we knew it had to be here.

When, after reading his very first romance novel (not mine) and weeping like a child, Albert offered to marry us, I knew it had to be him.

Though, when he'd told us he was an officiant, I'd said, "You're never beating those on-the-run-from-the-law allegations, Albert."

Everything is pink, and more importantly, everyone is here.

Rancho Encanto is blooming. The apartments have been rebuilt, better than they were before. Businesses have been reconstructed, and the new elementary school, with its glorious library donated by Nathan's publisher, is amazing.

My town has healed, and I'm in love.

Elise is my maid of honor, her own engagement ring sparkling on her finger.

An old friend of Nathan's came from Washington. His agent is here, which is hilarious. He's very New York in this overly bright setting.

I like him, but I'm happy with the woman I found to represent me, and even happier with the book deal she got me. If the book, about a woman starting over and finding everything she ever needed, is a little autobiographical, I'm not sorry.

Emma is my flower girl, and as pink as everything else.

Then there are my ladies. Gladys, Ruth, Lydia, Wilma, and my dear Alice. All in frothy pink dresses, with electric-pink lipstick.

"Amelia, if you need to talk before your wedding night, we're here for you," Wilma says, rubbing my hand.

I look up at Alice, too stunned to speak.

Alice laughs. "Haven't you read her books yet, Wilma? I think she could teach you a few new tricks."

"Oh, darlin', I invented most of those tricks," Wilma says, winking.

When it's time for me to walk down the aisle, Wilma, Lydia, and Ruth take the train of my dress, and Gladys takes one arm, while Alice takes the other.

They walk me down the aisle toward Nathan, into the very brightest world.

We say our vows. I know he's done this before, but he told me last night it feels like he hasn't. Because these are new promises, from him to me. That means they're brand new.

We promise each other our lives, our hopes. Our dreams.

When we kiss, a raucous cheer, led by Alice, goes up from the crowd.

Then we move all the chairs so we can dance.

As Nathan leads me to the dance floor, Gladys, Lydia, Wilma, Ruth, and Alice stop us. They're all beaming.

"Beautiful," Lydia says.

Gladys touches Nathan's arm. His biceps, I'm pretty sure. "It's a very nice suit," she says. "Men should wear tuxedos more."

"I think they're pretty firmly for special occasions," I say.

"If they wanted an occasion to delight me, I'd find that special," she says.

Nathan looks at me, and I smile and nod just slightly.

"Do you want to dance, Gladys?" he asks.

"Oh, no! Your first dance has to be with your wife." She's so happy she's glowing, though. "After that, come find me on the dance floor."

Nathan takes me to the middle of the grass and spins me around, drawing me in close.

"Did you want a kiss? Or were you just looking for a power strip?"

"Definitely the power strip," he says.

But he kisses me until I'm dizzy.

When we part, I realize all my ladies, and everyone else, have joined us on the grass, dancing right along with us.

I wrap my arms around Nathan's neck and sway in time to the music.

"I know how I would write this," I whisper against his mouth.

"How?"

"Just like this."

ACKNOWLEDGMENTS

It takes a village to make a book the best it can be. I want to thank my editors Selena James and Sasha Knight for their insights, which went a long way in taking this story and making it the best it could be.

As always, I owe thanks to my first readers and best friends—Jackie Ashenden, Nicole Helm, and Megan Crane.

A special thanks to Joshua Tree National Park, where my family went for spring break that first year after we lost my mom. There was magic there, and rainbows in the desert, and I knew I wanted to write a book set there about loss and grief and hope and love. Because the greatest is always love, no matter what.

ABOUT THE AUTHOR

Photo © 2023 Kerry Shroy

Maisey Yates is a *New York Times* bestselling author of more than one hundred romance novels. Whether she's writing strong, hardworking cowboys, dissolute princes, or multigenerational family stories, she loves getting lost in fictional worlds. An avid knitter with a dangerous yarn addiction and an aversion to housework, Maisey lives with her husband and three kids in rural Oregon. For more information, visit www.maiseyyates.com.